Caleb shifted again as he reached over and took another sip of tea. "I've been giving that some thought. Do you remember what you said to me your second day here?" He shook his head. "Probably not, you were stoned. Anyway, you said you needed to pretend to fit in so no one would know you planned to escape."

I remembered making that plan with Jake, I didn't remember spilling that to the chief.

He continued, "I think we should pretend to get along. Build trust. Act as though we are trying to make our marriage work."

I swallowed, but had no saliva left. I grabbed my tea and gulped down the now tepid, bitter liquid. "How far are you thinking of taking the farce?"

"Don't go down that road, Grace," he said softly. "You know I won't disrespect you."

Captive Hearts

by

Gina Leuci

A Well of Lies, Book Two

This is a work of fiction. Names, characters, places, and incidents are either the product of the author's imagination or are used fictitiously, and any resemblance to actual persons living or dead, business establishments, events, or locales, is entirely coincidental.

Captive Hearts

COPYRIGHT © 2018 by Gina Leuci

Cover Art by *Diana Carlile*

The Wild Rose Press, Inc.
PO Box 708
Adams Basin, NY 14410-0708
Visit us at www.thewildrosepress.com

Publishing History
First Crimson Rose Edition, 2018
Print ISBN 978-1-5092-2347-3
Digital ISBN 978-1-5092-2348-0

A Well of Lies, Book Two
Published in the United States of America

Dedication

To my son, Connor.
You make this mum very proud.

Acknowledgments

Caged Souls and *Captive Hearts* would not exist without the help and support of others. So a quick thank you to Melissa for answering random texts on medical questions; Sheila for talking all things PA—I still need to try your pot pie! Emily for being another set of editing eyes. The amazing writers of NHRWA. My family for understanding when I head off to my writing cave. Most of all, a shout out to my amazing editor at The Wild Rose Press: Kaycee John. Thanks for loving this story as much as I do, and for making me a better writer.

Chapter One

"Wake up, Grace."

I heard the voice, but I resisted. Mornings aren't my best time. "Five minutes," I mumbled.

"Now."

It was a male voice. That was the first thing to register. Second was the sound came from beneath me. I realized then that I was practically wrapped around a very warm, very hard, masculine man. I opened my eyes and met the steely blue ones belonging to Caleb Wellington.

Memories of a storm the day before and the two of us seeking shelter under an overhang of rocks invaded my moment of lucidity. We'd fallen asleep with him spooned against me under the rocks, behind the curtain of branches he'd used to protect us from the driving rain. At some time during the night, I not only turned around, I'd crawled up onto him, more than likely trying to find comfort on something other than the uneven surface under my body.

I barely had a moment to catch up with my brain before another voice, one that sent immediate shivers down my spine, let me know we were no longer alone. "You really screwed the pooch this time."

Damn. Roger Wellington, the town manager of Wellington, Pennsylvania—and my current arch nemesis—was here. I had only seconds before I recognized the branches we used last night to shelter us within our rock hideaway were no longer in place. Instead, there were several denim-clad legs and boots blocking the morning sun.

"Get them out of there," Roger ordered.

Before my morning brain had time to function, two sets of legs knelt on the ground and hands were on my arms and legs, pulling me away from the warm body I'd lain on all night.

"What the…" I sputtered as I slid across the dirt, face down.

"No need to be so rough." My human pillow's deep timbre was muffled as he rolled out into the open before he, too, was manhandled and lifted to his feet.

Officers Tom and Brent reached out to hold Caleb by his arms, as though he had done something wrong. Mine were still held by Officer Greg on one side and the town's computer and security expert, Randy, on the other.

Why did it suddenly feel like this was not a rescue mission for two people who'd been trapped in a storm? I looked at the man who'd protected me in more ways than one the day before. Caleb's gaze looked hooded and closed off as he faced his boss, while the town's top elected official wore a smug expression.

"Don't say a word," the older man warned. "I have four witnesses to how the two of you were wrapped around each other." He turned to me, his gaze moving up and down my body, taking in my clothes that had seen better days before shaking his head and giving me a dismissive snort.

My foggy morning brain finally woke. This wasn't a rescue. This was about my rejection of Roger's precious son. I shuddered at just the thought of Leland. Yesterday he'd informed me that the story about my summer internship had all been a lie. Nine of us had been lured to Wellington, not to spend the summer out in the country, free of computers and phones like we'd believed, but to be forced into marriage with one of the Wellingtons. Leland had chosen me, and when he'd tried to take things too far, I fought him off. The arrival of Caleb, the town's police chief, had not been as fortunate in Lee's mind, and a bad situation turned even worse.

Now, neither the chief nor I are Roger's favorite people. Understandable, under the circumstances, but that didn't explain why he rallied the entire police force to escort us back to town as if we were prisoners.

It was a long walk on a rocky path, and I had no shoes. Yesterday, while I ran through the woods like there was no tomorrow, the rain and wind hadn't bothered me. The rush of adrenaline kept me going and prevented me from feeling a single stone. Now, my bruised feet connected with every broken acorn, every pebble, every tree root, and slowed our pace.

When I stumbled, only one person moved to my side, pushing past the officers who should have helped me. Caleb's voice was calm and steady as he pulled me to my feet. "Are you okay?"

I looked up into his blue eyes and saw concern. Last night, we'd forged an odd sort of truce after a tumultuous start to my summer in his town. He'd saved me from an attack, which some might say he'd done as part of his duties as Super Cop. Then he'd protected me from the ravages of the high winds and falling tree limbs. I could write that off as duty to protect.

But he'd also kissed me. That wasn't part of his job description. Neither was his promise to get me back to my home in Vermont.

Caleb, the police chief who'd sworn to tend to my safety during my stay in Wellington, had become my protector here in this backwoods town. Despite the past twenty-four hours, I had an ally.

"I'm fine," I finally answered.

Snarling with impatience, Roger pushed past the officers who encircled us. "What's the hold up?"

The older man held the highest position of authority in the town; today he was on the warpath and we were his target. I'd rebuked his son's advances, and I had the feeling Daddy Big Wig wasn't too thrilled that his best-laid plans for his offspring had gone awry.

Caleb gave no one time to speak. "Grace has no shoes. Let me carry her." Before anyone could protest, myself included, he continued, "We'll be able to move faster." At the older man's nod, he knelt in front of me. "Piggy back."

My face flamed. I looked to the men surrounding us, waiting impatiently for us to move. "Ah, that's not necessary, I can walk."

"Your feet will be cut to ribbons out here, if they aren't already."

He had a point. I relented and clasped my arms at his neck. He stood, taking my legs in his hands to wrap around his waist. "This is so embarrassing," I muttered. "Let me know when I get heavy, and I'll walk again."

He made a sound, like a snort, but continued his easy pace, not slowing once. While it was humiliating to be carried, my feet did appreciate the break. Besides, the sooner we were back in town, the sooner I could find out why we were being treated like major felons.

"What's their beef?" I spoke softly. "They're taking a simple rescue mission a bit serious, don't you think?"

Caleb shook his head. "I'm sorry about this."

My fingers clasped a bit tighter on his shoulders. Something was up. Something big. I looked at the somber expressions on the men escorting us out of the woods. The sense of hope I went to sleep with last night disappeared. Anxiety began to build. I remained silent as the search and rescue party moved through the woods. Tree limbs, broken during the previous night's storm, littered the trail, a testament to the severity of the weather Caleb and I had sheltered from. Despite the return of the sun, I had a feeling there was a new storm on the horizon.

Once we reached the end of the path, we boarded a shuttle bus under the steely watch of the town's elected leader. I still didn't understand what the big deal was and when the bus stopped in front of the church, I became even more stumped.

"Don't tell me they're making us go to the service?" I whispered. "I know it's Sunday and all, but look at me. I need a shower." I took in Caleb's wrinkled shirt and mud-caked jeans. "So do you."

"Grace, about that—"

Roger turned on us and barked, "No talking."

I threw up both hands. "What is your problem? I know you don't like me, but no talking? Seriously?"

My one ally on this return home tapped my leg, indicating I should keep quiet. Then he mouthed the words 'I'm sorry' again.

What the hell wasn't he saying? The last thing I

needed were more secrets. I'd already figured out we were being treated like prisoners because *we were* prisoners, which made no sense.

I had been the victim yesterday. Leland wanted to have sex with me. He'd made it clear he'd chosen me to become his wife and not to argue the inevitable. Caleb arrived while I was fighting off the young Lothario's advances.

What happened next wasn't my fault. Leland pitched a temper tantrum and began ranting at the top of his lungs about Caleb ruining his chance to marry me. Then, in the midst of his rant, he kicked me in the ribs. Again, I was the victim.

Okay, so maybe—just maybe—Caleb reacted a bit harshly and ended up breaking the ass hat's arm. In my estimation, he deserved everything he got.

Taking Caleb to task for police brutality was one thing. But it certainly didn't explain why we were escorted into the crowded church moments before the Sunday morning service was slated to begin.

I felt every eye in the room staring at us. My tee-shirt was caked with mud. My jeans, having been soaked by the rain, had air dried into stiff denim. Seeing the dirt smearing Caleb's face, I was sure mine wasn't any cleaner. I'd taken my wet, matted hair out of its ponytail during the night, so now it hung in a knotted mess around my face. Not my Sunday best.

After Pastor Rick walked to the front of the altar, we were jostled forward. "Oh, good," he said, "you located them."

If my mood was better, I might have found the comment funny. Why did they pretend a person could actually go missing in a place where everybody was forced to wear a tracking bracelet?

"I demand a town meeting," Roger bellowed. "We found these two cavorting in the woods.

Cavorting?

"We weren't—" Caleb tried to speak, but a motion from the older man silenced him.

"You keep quiet." Roger turned and stormed down the aisle until he reached Jake Collings, my best friend who'd come with me from Vermont to Wellington, on what we'd believed would be a fun-filled summer, working in the country fresh air. Little did we know the town had other plans.

Roger grabbed Jake's arm and, while dragging him to the front of the church, called out, "Hope, get up here, now."

"Yes, Daddy." His daughter responded quickly, jumping up from the pew and rushing to do his bidding.

"Last night, this man—" Roger nudged Jake forward "—had sex with my daughter. I caught them in the act. Then today, we found these two." He sneered the words as he nodded at me and Caleb. "Wrapped around each other in a dark cave. The four of them have dishonored our belief system."

"I see." Pastor Rick shook his head. "Then there is only one thing we can do to rectify the situation. Does council agree this is the best course of action?"

"What course of action?" I asked, looking around. No one answered.

"Wait just a minute," the bedraggled chief of police protested. "You all are overstepping here. Nothing happened last night. Those were near hurricane force winds with tree branches crashing all around us. The safest course was to seek shelter."

Pastor Rick tsked. "You know unmarried men and woman are forbidden to spend a night alone together."

"But there was a storm," I sputtered. "We couldn't get back to town."

Pulling the ace from his deck, Roger launched Jake forward. "What if this one got my daughter pregnant?"

I looked over at Jake, someone I'd known most of my life. His face was covered with red splotches. "Did you have sex?" I hissed.

He grimaced. "He caught us bare-assed."

I groaned. Jake and Hope. Caught doing the deed. Probably just what the blonde seductress had planned. Given a few more minutes, Leland, Hope's twin and partner in coercion, would have made sure he and I were caught in a similar position.

Except for one thing: I wasn't willing and managed to fight him off until my Good Samaritan arrived and brought things to a stop.

"The decision has been made," Pastor Rick announced. "They shall be married at once."

"*Married?*" I whipped around, looking at the residents of town in attendance for the church service. "What does he mean, married?"

Caleb didn't look at me. Instead, he faced front. "Pastor Rick, Grace is innocent in this. I made the decision to seek shelter instead of trying to make it back to Jefferson's farm."

Hands fisted, Roger intruded into the conversation. "Then you will face the consequences of your actions, Caleb. You know the rules. Your father—"

The chief's jaw tightened as he spoke through clenched teeth. "Don't bring my father into this."

Instead, Roger's voice raised high enough to echo

off the church rafters. "Your father disgraced this town when he couldn't keep it in his pants."

Gasps and murmurs filled the air. I spotted several mothers place their hands over their children's ears. My head swiveled back and forth, taking in the scene around me in stunned disbelief.

The older man waved a finger under Caleb's nose. "You seem to be following in his footsteps, young man. If you don't watch it, you'll be banished from town like him." Then he added—and seemed to enjoy it—"Like your father, you'll be forbidden to see your children."

Caleb's daughter, Elena, cried out, "Daddy?"

My heart broke for the eight-year old. I hadn't thought about his children being in the room while all the dirty laundry was aired for the entire congregation to hear. I turned to Roger. "You're only doing this because of what happened yesterday."

"Shut up before you disgrace yourself further. You were ready to have sex with my son before you were interrupted. Then, only hours later you spent the night with another man. You're nothing more than a whore."

"You son of a bitch."

For the second time in two days, the usually calm and unflappable police chief lost his cool. His fist went up, but two officers still by our sides caught him mid-swing and pulled him back. More gasps and louder whispers added to the chaos.

"Gentlemen," Pastor Rick intervened. "You are in the house of God. Control yourselves. The decision has been made. Jake and Hope, Caleb and Grace, please turn to each other and take hands."

Someone took my shoulders, I wasn't sure who, and turned me to face Caleb who looked almost as stunned as I. Our hands were forcibly joined. I stared up at him. He didn't look at me but instead fixed his gaze at a spot over my head. How he could shut down his emotions like that I didn't understand.

"With the joining of hands," Pastor Rick intoned, "we honor God, our heavenly Father, in joining these two couples in the bonds of holy matrimony. We pray to You, oh God, to forgive them for their indiscretions and help them to move forward as one unity, to praise and bless You with their love for each other."

I tuned out the words. A week ago, I'd stood in this room watching the wedding of my college roommate to a man she loved. The ceremony had been simple and beautiful as Caroline and Aaron stood with their hands together, gazing lovingly into each other's eyes. The church had been decorated with fresh cut flowers. The members of the church had been there to celebrate a joyous occasion. While I'd told my friend she was rushing into the relationship, I'd still been happy she'd found the man of her dreams.

Now the same words that had been spoken a week before were repeated. I stood where my friend had, except I was covered in mud, my hair tangled, and the man whose hands were holding mine was in as much disrepair as me.

I looked out to the crowd of Wellington townsfolk and spotted Leland, his arm in a sling, anger emanating from every pore. This was payback because I'd continually said no to his advances. Jackie, my former boss at the school cafeteria, wore a bigger scowl than usual on her pinched and homely face.

My summer house parents, Kurt and Amy, looked calm and peaceful, as though shotgun weddings were a normal occurrence.

Perhaps for Wellington, they were.

I looked over at Jake, wearing his usual Sunday attire of khakis and golf shirt. While he was dressed a hell of a lot better than I, his wide-eyed gaze showed his shock at the unexpected nuptials. His bride, on the other hand, had decked herself out in a floral sundress. Her makeup was flawless; diamond earrings sparkled below her up swept blonde hair. If her blue eyes, twinkling with a spark of glee, were any indication, I'd guess she'd been forewarned of this *impromptu* ceremony.

I'd warned Jake, my friend since elementary school, to not hook up with the Wonder Twin, but the girl had played him like a guitar, strumming his strings until he'd snapped. This whole thing had all been planned. Probably right down to Daddy catching them in the act. While her sibling wasn't getting where he wanted with me, another few minutes and Leland may have made it look close enough to have had the double wedding he'd wanted with his twin.

The next thing I heard was the pastor saying, "I now pronounce you husband and wife."

"Wait. What?" I gasped. I hadn't exchanged any vows. I'd just stood there, not listening to half of what had been said. No words, no rings.

"As you take on the Wellington name, you will be expected to learn and accept the rules and moral code we expect of all of our family," Pastor Rick instructed before he looked past us, focusing his attention on the congregation. "There are details which need to be made immediately. While I know many of you will be out assessing the properties for damage, I would like to ask if there are any volunteers to prepare apartments for the new couples?"

Apartments? This couldn't be happening. I looked down at my hands, still clasped within much larger ones as arrangements were made.

"What about my children?" Caleb's words, while non-confrontational, were controlled. I knew he was as unhappy about our new-found situation as I was.

The room seemed to close in. I heard conversations around me, yet it was as though I was just an observer watching someone else's life being shanghaied.

Pastor Rick responded, "I'm sure they can continue to stay with your mother until a house becomes available for you later. Tomorrow, you will meet with the jeweler to order rings and then with Dr. Todd. As is custom, you will be relieved of your work duties for the next two weeks. In the meantime, have a seat, we will proceed with the service."

With a slight tug on my arm, I was led to the pew where Caleb's mother, stepfather, and three children sat. They scooted over to make room. I sat in stunned silence as the youngest, Shawna, crawled into her father's arms.

I was married.

I wasn't going home.

I felt my breath hitch. *Don't cry. Don't cry.*

The man beside me, my hus—Nope, not going there—leaned down to whisper in my ear. "Don't worry. I'll fix this. Somehow."

Chapter Two

Married.

I stared into the mirror in the restroom of the fellowship hall at the stranger before me. I wasn't surprised to see the wrinkled shirt or the denim jeans that had been soaked in the rain, then dried into stiff, uncomfortable cardboard. My hair was flat in some places and stuck out in strange angles in others.

It was the pale face and vacant eyes I didn't recognize.

My brain tried to process the past twenty-four hours. When I'd rejected Leland, after weeks of telling him I didn't want a summer romance, he'd blurted the truth about why the interns had been brought to this secluded town. The residents needed spouses, and the son of the town administrator was laying his claim on me. I gripped the counter top as the memories flooded. The police chief had arrived in time to stop things from going to the next level.

I lifted the corner of my shirt to examine the black and blue bruise forming on my ribs where Leland had landed his vicious kick. The attack had been unexpected, but watching Caleb respond by grabbing him and snapping his arm in retaliation had been more shocking. It was at that moment Roger had arrived, screaming about Jake and Hope's infidelities, and in the ensuing chaos, I fled the scene.

I released my shirt and turned from the mirror, leaning against the Formica counter. Running had seemed the best option at the time, despite the incoming storm. The town's top cop had followed.

He'd found me, of course. The tracking device encased in the electronic bracelets everyone wore ensured no one ever got lost in this gated Pennsylvania town. Or escaped. But by the time Caleb caught up to me at the lake, the storm hit, and there was no time to head back to town, especially as I'd kicked off the borrowed over-sized boots.

Roger insisted that I'd been compromised. Ha. What an archaic term. Not for Wellington. No siree. Here they took nonsense like that seriously. Yes, we'd spent the night together. On the ground, under a rock, for God's sake. Clothes on.

Sure, when the search party found us, I may have been nestled or possibly sprawled over said male body, but that had only been because there wasn't a lot of room in our make-shift shelter. And he'd been warm, and large and protective as the wind howled throughout the night.

Well, there was that kiss. No, even that had been a farce. An interesting and appealing distraction, but a farce, none the less, as my rescuer had used that moment to check my ribs after the brutal kick. He'd known it would be the only way he could ensure I'd not been hurt more than I'd admit to. He'd won that round. Not that I'd really minded in the end.

That didn't seem to matter to the pastor or anyone else in town. As far as they were concerned, we'd slept together.

As for Jake and Hope? I could only shake my head

at those two fools. I'd known all along that the goddess had her sights on my best friend, but I hadn't suspected she'd set such an elaborate trap where she'd make sure her own father caught her fornicating with the summer intern. Sex in this moralistic town meant automatic marriage. The blonde diva got exactly what she wanted.

The bathroom door swung open, and one of the students from the elementary school came in and smiled at me. I forced my lips up in response to the child and pushed myself away from the counter. I couldn't hide in here all day.

Sundays meant the entire town joined together for a pot-luck fellowship meal after church. I'd taken enough time in the restroom that the food line was empty. I took a paper plate and slopped something onto it, not really looking. Not really caring. Unlike the wedding last week, *The Hall* as they referred to the large, barn-like building they gathered in, was bare. No music, no streamers, no decorations of any kind.

With food on my plate, I turned to look at the rows of tables filled with people. I didn't know where to sit. Caroline and Aaron were away, allowed to leave for their honeymoon to visit her family in Vermont. I had no intention on sitting with Leland and the bully brothers: A.J. and Phillip.

Jake—oh, dear, wonderful friend of mine, sat beside the object of his indiscretion at a table in the center of the room. Hope's parents remained within reach, in case the new son-in-law decided to jump ship. I caught his gaze and recognized the lost and confused stare I'd witnessed in the mirror a moment ago, but there was nothing I could do for him.

I moved to the doorway leading to the covered

courtyard area connecting both The Hall and church, where more residents sat at picnic tables, enjoying their weekly Sunday meal. I spotted Caleb and his family at their usual table by the open glass door, leading to the playground outside.

Normalcy ensued. Rita, his mom, talked with her husband, Conrad, while cutting up food on a plate for the three-year old, Shawna. Five-year old Justin shoved strips of bacon into his mouth. Eliza, the oldest at eight, stood beside her father, her hands going a mile a minute as she spoke. Her expression was not one of happiness.

His family. His children. I felt a tremble begin in my knees. I can't be married. Not to him. Not to a man I'd met seven weeks ago. Not to a man with children. Not to a man, who by the very definition of his job title, was the reason I was still in this God-forsaken, backwoods town.

His gaze lifted to meet mine across the crowded room, and maybe he recognized my lost stare. He motioned for his daughter to sit before he wove around the tables in long strides and reached me in the blink of an eye.

"I'll take this for you." His voice was smooth and calm which I couldn't understand, because my insides were twisted into knots.

"How can you be calm?" I didn't even recognize my voice. It sounded hollow.

Then I saw the darkness flash in his eyes, and I knew. It was all a façade. "We'll talk later. For now, let's get through dinner."

The thought of making polite with the new in-laws was daunting. "I'm not hungry."

He frowned as he took in the plate that had one

handful of fresh cut vegetables and a single plop of some kind of casserole. "You didn't have supper last night, and it's almost noon. When did you last eat?"

"I don't know." The past day was a bit hazy now. My brain wasn't working. When had I eaten? "I think I had an apple yesterday when helping out with the horses."

He turned on his heel and headed back into The Hall. I silently followed him as he returned to the food tables to add several more items to my plate then motioned me to follow. "I'm not one of your children. You can't tell me what to eat." The words were harsh. Sarcastic. But there was no heat behind it.

When he stopped suddenly, I almost crashed into him. "I understand you are stressed and confused and the last place you want to be is with anyone in this town, especially me. But don't starve yourself. You need to eat something. Please."

It was the *please* which did it. I backed off my attitude and found a place across from him at the table. His parents sent me warm smiles that I didn't know how to respond to.

Still too numb to taste anything, I ate, not because I was hungry, but it kept my hands busy. People seemed to crowd around, making me feel claustrophobic. The residents of Wellington carried on with their Sunday routine as though nothing had changed. As though they hadn't just witnessed two near strangers being forced to marry into their community.

I pushed food around on my plate. Why would they? Was this normal for them? Bring strangers into town and marry them off so they can never leave?

Rita seemed to take the wedding of her son in

stride. "There won't be any food at the apartment tonight, so why don't you two plan on eating at our house."

"Yes, thank you, Mama," Caleb said. "We will."

I shoved a forkful of lettuce in my mouth. Like hell we will. How dare he make decisions for me? Damn him. Still arrogant and overbearing as ever.

"I want to spend as much time with the kids as possible," he continued. "This transition isn't going to be easy."

I nearly choked on my salad. Well, shit, wasn't I the selfish one? Good thing I'd kept my mouth shut. I hadn't thought what this was going to mean with regard to the children. Holy Mother Mary. Kids. If we were married, then that meant I was now a—Nope. Not going there either.

Connie, the phone operator, stopped by the table. "Hiya, newlyweds." Her super-friendly voice grated on my nerves, and I shoved another forkful of food in my mouth to keep from snarling.

"I want you to know I will be helping with setting up your new place," she announced. "Why don't you bring your belongings over to the apartments on West Eighth Street at four, and we'll show you which unit is yours."

"Thank you, Connie," Caleb said, "for giving up your Sunday with family to do this. It's very kind."

I stared, again shocked at the cordial demeanor. This was a new side to Caleb I hadn't seen before.

"Aww, sweetie. We're all family. I'm happy to do this for you."

When the chatty woman finally moved on, I observed the man I'd been forced to join hands with earlier. I'd never seen him rattled before, or at least, I'd never noticed the signs. On the outside, he was being super polite and gracious, but looking close, I saw the tense jaw, the shoulders pulled back, and the closed off stare. He had all of his emotions under check. Total control.

Me? I wanted to scream. I wanted to throw things. But I was surrounded by the people who'd forced a marriage down my throat, and throwing a tantrum would probably not do a lick of good. So I took my cues from him and finished my meal without telling any of the well-wishers who stopped to add their congratulations, where to shove it.

****

I took the longest, hottest shower when I finally did make it back to my temporary summer home that I'd resided in for the past seven weeks. While I was clean, it didn't help clear my mind.

I packed my few belongings into my suitcase and looked around my tiny pink room and realized I would miss it. I went upstairs to say goodbye to my host family.

"Thank you for all your wonderful hospitality," I said as Amy wrapped her arms around me in a huge hug.

"It was our pleasure, dear."

Kurt moved to plant a kiss on my forehead. "Caleb is a good man. He'll treat you right." I didn't know how to answer, so I nodded.

"Yes," the gray-haired grandmother continued. "God speaks in mysterious ways."

"I don't see how God has anything to do with this," I mumbled.

"Oh, my sweet girl, of course He does." She grasped my hands. "Why, the storm coming through, trapping you two together? That was God's doing. It's part of His master plan."

I snorted. "No, the storm was just a storm. The marriage was Roger retaliating for his son's bad decisions."

She patted my hands. "I know believing in God is new for you. In time, you will learn and trust in his ways."

Kurt stepped forward. "There isn't another shuttle before four. Do you want me to come with you and carry your suitcase?"

I smiled up at him. He was a kind man. "No. I've got it. The walk will do me good."

I left my host family home, cursing the sun and its bright day. My mood was more suited to the storms from yesterday. I kept my pace slow, in no rush to get to my new destination. The house I'd stayed in the past several weeks since my arrival was already on the west side of town, so I didn't have too far to go. A few blocks up, a couple blocks over.

The apartment complex was the only four-story building on the street, so I knew where I needed to go. The police cruiser parked out front gave added confirmation.

Seeing the chief waiting for me outside gave me mixed emotions. The kisses we'd shared the night before had been hot, and at the time I'd enjoyed them way too much. But with the turn of events this morning, I didn't want to have anything to do with any Wellington, not even this one.

I'm sure he wasn't thrilled with the cards he had

been dealt. He was forced to leave his children in the care of his mother. Over the weeks, I'd seen how he doted on them. While his mother was a constant in their lives, Caleb was a single parent, doing everything he could to fulfill the role vacated by his deceased wife.

He pushed from his stance against the wall of the building and walked down the street to meet me. "I'll take that for you."

I handed over my rolling luggage and watched as he lowered the top handle and lifted it by the one on the side. He motioned me to enter the building. "We're on the third floor. There are no elevators."

At least there was air conditioning, which I was thankful for as I climbed the stairs of the building which looked to have been built early in the town's history. The stairwell had been painted fairly recently, but nothing could detract from the age of the building itself.

We entered a hallway and went right, stopping at an open door at unit 309. "This is it. I sent Connie home."

Thank God for small miracles. There was no way I could handle her chattiness. I didn't think I could handle any of this right now.

I walked in and stopped. It wasn't very big. The kitchen and living room were one large room, separated by a small table with four chairs around it. The furniture consisted of a single chair and a loveseat. No long couch. A bookshelf, void of books, but there was a radio. One end table held the single lamp in the room. The only other lighting was a three-bulb fixture over the table.

I moved to the kitchen and opened the fridge,

which held a few casserole dishes, leftovers from the fellowship meal, I assume. I opened cabinets and found a few pots and pans. Enough to get a couple started.

There were three closed doors along the side wall of the living room, and I strode over as he continued to stand by, watching as I explored. The first one was the bedroom. A king-sized bed filled the confines of the room, leaving little space for the end tables and bureaus. Lamps and alarm clocks were the only adornments. The hand-made quilt with purples and greens was the only splash of color in the white-walled room.

I didn't want to think about the bed, or the size of it, or what it meant for sleeping arrangements tonight, so I opened door two. The bathroom. The chocolate brown tub, toilet, and sink screamed it hadn't been updated since before I was born, but it was clean. I moved on to the third door, praying for a guest bedroom.

"Oh, dear God." I gripped the door frame. "They don't waste time."

I closed the door and tried to close my mind from the implications of what the crib and rocking chair implied. I moved on auto-pilot to sit on the loveseat. The furniture was built from wood with large cushions, giving it a block look. The sheer size—or lack thereof—and style was designed to ensure very little comfort involved, and definitely ensuring no room to sleep on the tiny furniture. That left the one bed for the two of us to sleep on. Together.

I stared in numb silence as Caleb took a seat in the chair, waiting for me to talk. I crossed my arms to stare back at him.

"Last night you said you were going to get me out of this place and today—" I stopped. I couldn't say the word that had been echoing in my head for a couple hours now, but for the first time today I felt anger. My voice cracked as I faced him. "Was this all part of the plan? Find some way to put us in compromising positions, it doesn't matter with who?"

He leaned forward, balancing his forearms on his thighs. "No. Grace—"

I raised one hand. "Stop right there. I don't want to hear anything right now. I have no reason to believe anything you say." I stood and put the furniture between us. "Words don't mean anything. If you're not part of this, then you sure as hell better figure out how to be the damn solution."

Chapter Three

I skipped dinner. The last thing I wanted was to acknowledge this farce of a marriage by sitting down for a meal with the in-laws. At the moment, there was no concrete plan on how to precipitate an annulment, as never in the history of Wellington had there been a request for one. I know, because I asked.

One thing I was sure of, I had no intention of consummating this…this…*thing.* When Caleb returned from his parents, I was behind closed doors of the bedroom. I'd left a blanket and pillow on the floor in the living room. My point was made.

Monday morning brought on new challenges. We were polite to each other as we moved from bedroom to bathroom, to kitchen. I'm not sure how to explain how I felt, except that numb might be the closest. Nothing seemed real. The events of the previous two days remained more of a haze of a dream.

Except I was still in Wellington, and there was a man in my bedroom.

I pretended not to look as Caleb pulled a t-shirt on as I walked in, but how could I not stare at the massive six-pack he sported? I felt a quickening of my pulse and immediately turned and walked back to the living room area. I had to allow him time to change and give me time to push away whatever attraction I thought I'd had for this man over the past weeks.

"I got a call when you were in the shower," he called out. "Our first appointment is at the jewelers at nine-thirty. At ten-thirty we need to be at the clinic."

I wandered back to the doorway. He wore his usual blue jeans and tee. I'd seen him dressed that way several times over the past two months, and normally I would drool. Today felt more clinical. I noticed how the blue fabric conformed to the muscles on his chest and how his biceps bulged beneath the short sleeves. There is no denying the man was attractive. I felt a pull of something magnetic between us.

I'd fought this attraction for Caleb for weeks. I'd shared a couple kisses with the man. Hot, mind-boggling kisses. Any woman with a pulse had to admit he was sexy. Right now, I pushed that all aside. I'd been forced into an unimaginable situation and had no intentions on acting on a moment of lust.

I needed to find my anger, or sarcasm. Or some kind of emotion other than this feeling of watching my life unfold before me as though I was outside looking in. "Can't we skip it? Pretend none of this happened?"

He grabbed socks from the top drawer of the dresser. He must have unpacked before I'd arrived yesterday. My clothes still lay in my open suitcase on the floor. "Ignoring it won't make it any less legal or binding."

"How can it be binding? We never actually exchanged vows. Now that I think about it, did Caroline even say *I do*? I don't remember that part." I paced the tiny confines of the room, nearly tripping over Caleb as he now sat on the edge of the bed "This whole thing is bogus. You need to make it go away."

"I'll go to the council meeting this week and plead

our case. Due to the Fourth of July falling tomorrow, it won't happen until Wednesday."

I snorted, watching as he put on his boots, talking as though today was like any other day. "Like any of them will even listen. Roger has had it out for me since day one. I'm surprised he allowed his precious son to come anywhere near me this summer."

He gave me one of his soulful looks that screamed a maturity far beyond his years, or at least far beyond mine. "Let's just get through today, Grace. There's not much in the way of food here, so how about we go to the diner for breakfast. We can hit the store this afternoon and pick up some essentials."

"Like what?" I huffed, his calm reasoning in direct opposition to my growing agitated state. "A situation like this deserves copious amounts of alcohol, and we're not going to find any of that in this wholesome, dry town."

He shook his head. "Not even old enough to drink, and you think alcohol is the solution? I thought you avoided the party scene."

With hands on my hips, I whipped to face him, pouncing on his rebuke. "You know nothing about me. Just because I told you what happened to me during my freshman year at college, doesn't mean I never drink."

Other than a few glasses of wine, I hadn't been drunk since the night I'd been roofied. And of course my first weekend here when I'd been invited to a private party in the woods, sponsored by some of the Wellington rules-breakers. I wasn't about to let him know that, so I continued my attack as I followed him out of the bedroom into the living/kitchen area. "Don't tell me that when you were twenty and in the Marines, you didn't drink. I won't believe it."

Caleb gave a slight shrug. "I'll admit I did have the occasional beer, but not once did I ever drink to become drunk."

"Fine. You're the epitome of a saint. You don't drink. You don't smoke. You…"

"Do you smoke?" he interrupted.

"Well, no."

"Good. Nasty habit." He gave a pointed look to my bare feet. "Are you hungry? We should get going if you want time to eat before our first appointment."

I slipped on my sandals and moved out of the apartment as he held the door open. He'd effectively ended the conversation by distracting me. It didn't go unnoticed, and I continued to fume silently.

We didn't speak much during breakfast. At least not to each other. He was a popular man. Every person who entered or exited the diner said hello. And no one, *not one*, mentioned yesterday's joyous occasion.

The trip to the jewelry counter, located inside the big outlet store, was quick, but painful. Frank, who was the manager of the store, also ran the jewelry counter.

He was a tiny man, shorter than my own five foot seven, and I think he had a running board behind the glass counter to lift him high enough to see over. With his graying hair and white beard, he reminded me of a garden gnome. Except gnomes don't talk, and this little goblin was talking a mile a minute.

"We have a selection of matching bands to choose from. Why don't you take a look-see and decide? In the meantime, I need to measure your fingers for size." He took my hand and slipped a band over my finger until he had the right size, then repeated the procedure on

Caleb, writing down the measurements then turned back to us. "See any you like?"

The display he'd pulled out of the cabinet had six different designs, from completely plain, to almost ornately intricate. I shuddered. No matter which one I picked, it would make this farce of a situation all the more real.

My body vibrated with an emotion I couldn't explain. I turned away from the store manager to whisper to Caleb. "I don't think I can do this. Can I talk to you?" I pulled him away from Frank and any other curious ears, stepping down an aisle full of handbags "We can't order rings. We're not married. Or at least, we won't be as soon as you talk to council."

I wondered if he'd give me some kind of excuse and say there was nothing he could do. I expected it. Instead, he took my hand and gave it a squeeze. "Okay. I'll handle it." He walked back over to the jeweler, and I trailed behind, shoving my hands in my pockets as I listened in. "This is an important decision. We want to make the right one. How about we come back in a couple days to look again. Give us time to think on it."

Frank hesitated, as though he was going to argue, but then pasted on a thin smile, almost hidden by the beard. "Of course. After all, if you are going to wear this the rest of your life, you want to choose the best one for you." In a matter of moments, we'd escaped the store manager and exited the large store.

"Thank you," I said as I gulped in the fresh air filled with the smell of fresh mowed grass. "That ring... That symbol..." I shivered.

Caleb looked beyond me, his stare the closed-off one I had gotten used to seeing at the beginning of the summer. I bit my lip. "This can't be easy for you, either." I muttered, trying not to be completely selfish.

He refocused, his blue eyes held a hint of sadness. "No. I wasn't exactly looking to remarry yet. It's too soon for my kids."

I wrapped my arms around my waist. I didn't know what to say. I wasn't about to apologize for running away from the fracas at the farm on Saturday. And it's not like I knew getting stranded alone in the woods was another freaking taboo.

He sighed and motioned for me to start walking. "Come, we have another appointment to get through."

I dragged my feet. "Of all people, why do we have to meet with Dr. Todd?"

There was an almost unnoticeable hiccup in his pace, and if I weren't already a jumble of nerves about meeting with the hated doctor, I may not have noticed it. But his slight hesitation had my stomach doing flip flops. My experiences at the hospital were limited, but had been enough to know I hated that particular doctor to the core. The last thing I wanted was to have a doctor-patient visit with the loathsome man and Caleb damn well knew it—and why.

"His job is to counsel all newlyweds on the joys of parenthood."

I froze. Caleb took two long strides before he realized I hadn't moved. He wore a pained expression when he turned back to get me. "I'm sorry, Grace. This is one appointment I can't get us out of."

"It's easy," I said, stomping one foot. "We. Just. Don't. Go."

Caleb waved a hand around, motioning down the street. "It's not that easy. You've been here long enough to know if you don't show up, the police are sent to escort you."

I threw my hands up with frustration. "You are the freaking police chief. Order your officers to back down if they arrive."

He gave a long-suffering sigh. "Technically, during the next two weeks, I'm off-duty, which means I'm a regular citizen. I have no say."

I cocked my head. "The longer I am in this place, the more I don't understand it. The rules are bizarre. Antiquated. It's like they were formed in 1900 and haven't updated with the times at all."

"That's basically true." He motioned for me to walk again. The streets were practically empty. Most of the townsfolk were at their respective jobs, and Caleb led me down side streets away from the downtown area, as we walked the few blocks toward the clinic "Let's get through this next appointment together. To tell you the truth, it's new for me. I didn't live here during my first marriage."

"What? Are you curious? Or too much of a rules follower." I taunted him. "I don't want to be anywhere near that man. I don't trust him. He'll probably find another reason to drug me, and you, and perform some kind of twisted experiment on us."

Caleb grunted. "It won't be like that. I promise."

"Huh." I stood my ground. "You can't promise anything. You admitted you have no idea how this meeting will go because you've never attended one. Besides, you *promised* to get me home and less than twelve hours later we were married." It was petulant and cruel, but it hit its mark.

He blew out a deep breath, running a hand over his

head. Yep, he was frustrated. With the situation? Possibly. With me? More than likely. I didn't really care, though.

"I know. I'm sorry, Grace. I didn't say getting you out of here would be easy, and I certainly didn't consider how the town would react to our being out all night." He moved closer, blocking out the morning sun as he put his hands on my shoulders. "I might not know what the doctor is going to talk about exactly, but I do promise I will not allow any harm to come to you."

Maybe it was his hands, secure on my shoulders, maybe it was his firm tone, or maybe it was because I'd seen over the past seven weeks that he was actually a pretty fair guy, but I believed him.

I gave up. "Fine, but know that I am not happy about this at all. And if he does anything to me, *anything...*"

"He won't. Trust me, Grace."

Huh. I don't think I can trust anyone here, not anymore, but when Caleb reached down for my hand, I took it. We were going to meet with Dr. Todd, and I had a very bad feeling about it.

****

"The key to a healthy marriage is a healthy sex life," the doctor stated as he sat across from us in his high-backed rolling chair behind his desk. "We pride ourselves on how prolific our townsfolk are and believe it is because we are educated on carefully tracking menses, as well as when and how often we have sex."

I gripped the arms of the chair so tight my knuckles were white. I had to be trapped in a horror movie, it's the only explanation.

"The most fertile time to become pregnant is

during the five days before your menstrual cycle." He gave me an inquisitive stare. "Do you know the date of your last period?"

Not only were my knuckles white, but my legs began to shake. I wanted, no needed, to bolt. "What? No."

"Hmm, okay." The man typed into the computer on his desk then flipped open a small pocket calendar, making a notation on one of the pages. "Based on your last purchase of tampons, I have marked in here the projected start for your next period."

He handed over the pocket-sized calendar. When I didn't take it, he placed it on the edge of the desk in front of me. "From now on, you'll be tracking your cycle on this calendar along with each time you have sex. A minimum of two to three times a week is recommended."

I strangled on a cry.

Caleb placed a large hand over mine and gave a reassuring squeeze. "Todd, you know the situation between us is a bit unusual. The wedding was not exactly planned. Having children is not exactly a topic we've discussed. We have a lot more on our plates at the moment."

The man in the white coat waved his hand as though such thoughts were inconsequential. "If you're talking love, that's only a small part of marriage. Family is the glue. The rest comes as you build on that foundation."

"You're shitting me, right?" I finally found my voice. "What kind of town is this?"

He settled his glasses more firmly on his long, pointed nose. "There's no need for vulgarity,"

That did it. For the first time in two days I finally felt my first real emotion.

"*Vulgarity?* I'll give you vulgarity." I leaped up, leaned over the desk, and got in his face. Close enough to see the blackheads at the corners of his nose. "You want to talk sex? Fine. Go fuck yourself."

I grabbed the calendar and threw it, hitting him in the face, knocking his specs to the desk. "And when you do, don't forget to track it. I'll see you in hell before I give you any information on my life."

For a large man, Caleb reacted quickly and positioned himself between me and the desk, pushing me backward until there was as much distance as could be in the cramped office.

"Let me go. I'm just getting started."

"That's what I'm afraid of." He used his police chief voice, soft but steely firm, while maintaining a secure grip on my upper arms. "I get where you are coming from. I understand your frustration, but don't let it get physical. Any type of altercation means jail time."

"But…"

Doctor Depraved stood behind his desk, his fingertips tapping on the wooden surface. "When you have your *wife* under control, Caleb," he sneered, "there is another piece of business to attend to."

If I hadn't been eye level with the wide chest, I may not have noticed the ever so slight intake of breath before he turned back to the man behind the desk. "Now what?"

"A small video. Bridget has it set up in conference room two."

Forty-five minutes later, we exited the clinic, and I

moved almost on auto-pilot as we moved from the cool interior into the bright, cloudless day. "I cannot un-see that." I pressed the back of my hands to my flaming face. "You could have warned me."

Caleb was quiet, perhaps just as stunned as me? "I've never seen it before."

I scoffed. "But you had to know what they show."

We walked down the sidewalk; I was too much in shock to care which way we headed. "No one discusses the details," he explained. "All I've ever heard is they showed a sex education movie."

I grabbed his arm, turning him to face me. "That was *not* a sex-ed video," I huffed. "*That* was a porn flick with a voice over." I spotted the twist in his mouth before he turned his face away. "It's not funny, Caleb." I threw my hands up in disgust and walked ahead. "Gahd, you are such a guy."

The video itself had been bad enough, but watching it beside this hulk of a man while the narrator described the mechanics of sex, then oral sex, in excruciating detail, made it worse. I'd wanted to crawl under a table.

Caleb's longer stride had him keeping pace with me as we headed toward the center of town. "You're right. The video isn't funny, but your reaction, well…?" He gave a slight shrug earning him a jab in the arm.

I could hear the distant sound of tractors and wondered if Kevin, another of the so-called summer interns, was mowing the lawns in the downtown area again. It was almost lunchtime now. The streets were busy as people headed out to do errands or hit the diner for lunch. At the moment, I hated each and every one of the townsfolk of Wellington. How could they allow two couples to be forced to marry against their will? How could they be so accepting of a 'law' that had to date back to the founding of the town? Laws that us newcomers were completely unaware of.

"Please tell me there are no more surprises I need to know about." I asked the question hoping for reassurances, but when Caleb didn't answer immediately I felt my chest tightening.

His words, when he finally spoke, did nothing to alleviate my fear. "As far as I know, there are no more videos until a couple is expecting."

I felt another rush of heat engulf my face. I spun around to face him halting him in the middle of the sidewalk. I finger jabbed him in the chest. "Let's get something clear, here and now. You. Me. We are not married. I don't care what the pastor guy claims. And what we saw back there?" I shuddered. "Not happening. So there will be no more explicit movies."

Caleb put his hands up in surrender. "Whoa, Grace, we're in this together. I think you know I have no intentions to rush anything."

"*Rush?* There's nothing to rush. I'm out of here at the end of the summer, if not sooner. End of story. End of whatever the hell this is." I turned and stormed away, but not before I noticed my outburst hadn't gone unnoticed by an older couple walking hand in hand across the street. Good. Let them see how pissed I was. Surely someone in this messed up Jonesville-wanna-be town would start to question the town elders.

Caleb caught up and his tone was low, for my ears only. "I told you, I will go to the council meeting on Wednesday." A random thought crossed my mind, and I slowed my pace again. "Now what?" he asked.

"What if..." I tried to formulate my thought into a

coherent, reasonable request. "Caroline and Aaron got married and got to go home to visit her family, right?"

He caught on. "You want to know if you get to go home as well."

A slight glimmer of hope invaded my overwhelmed thoughts. "Makes sense. The precedent was set." It would get me out of this gated hell-hole, and once I was out, I would never return.

"I'll see what I can do. As a matter of fact," he nodded toward the building housing the town offices. "Want me to go speak with our illustrious manager now?"

I nodded.

"Fine. Why don't you wait for me over at the park?"

I watched until he entered Town Hall, but I didn't cross the street to the playground filled with kids. I wanted to hear what was said. I followed and entered the building. I asked the first person I spotted to direct me to the town manager's office then walked down narrow hallway. The door was open just enough to hear inside, and I heard Caleb's deep tone.

"Don't you think this has gone far enough?"

Roger's snarky voice echoed out into the hallway. "You knew the plan from the beginning, but you interfered."

"When you said you wanted to recruit from colleges, I was against it," Caleb retorted. "This town has always searched out those looking for a safe sanctuary, not us picking and choosing and holding people here against their will."

"They all came willingly. They all signed a contract."

"They all came here with the understanding they would be returning home." Caleb's voice was terse but controlled.

I pressed against the wall, trying to peek around the door, but I couldn't see either man as Roger continued to speak. "And all but two decided to stay on of their own accord."

"Do you hear yourself? The two who want to go home were coerced into a compromising situation to benefit *your* children. How convenient."

There was a loud bang, causing me to jump. Roger's voice turned from ice to anger. "Why did you have to interfere? Five more minutes and both of my children would be happily married right now."

I strained to hear Caleb's response. "Are you condoning rape to get what you want?"

"Of course not. The mere appearance of a sexual interlude would have provided the opportunity for them to be married. Instead, you intervened, broke my son's arm, and then spent the night with the girl yourself."

"The only thing I did was stop Leland from ending up with a prison record, because from what I witnessed, Grace wanted nothing to do with him. As for the rest, the storm hit, and we couldn't safely make it back. We found shelter and fell asleep."

"From the way you two were tangled together, you can't tell me nothing happened. You're just like your father, ruining the reputation of young girls. You're lucky you're not in a cell for what you did to my son."

Roger was back to his snide self, and I half wanted to run in and punch his smug face. The other half of me wanted to know how Caleb would react. I gripped the door jamb as I held my breath, needing to hear the rest.

"By the way," the owner of the deeper voice said, "I am attending the council meeting on Wednesday. I will be putting in a request to take Grace to Vermont so I can meet my new in-laws, like Aaron did with Caroline."

"Have you consummated the marriage?" From his tone, Roger knew we hadn't.

"Excuse me?"

I pressed a hand to my mouth to muffle my gasp of shock. I didn't want Roger to know I was there.

Roger continued in a confident tone, "It's my understanding you haven't even ordered your wedding rings. Until I know you are both taking the marriage seriously, that girl is still under her contract. No phone. No internet. No contact with her family."

Caleb began to pace, and I pressed against the wall so he wouldn't see me. "Jesus. Why did I ever come back to this place?"

"Don't you take the Lord's name in vain, young man." The town manager was going full steam. "You want to go visit her parents, then you get her pregnant. Give her incentive to stay. She won't leave her child behind, and we won't allow a Wellington to be raised out in that dangerous civilization."

"You're being unreasonable. This marriage is a farce, and you know it." Caleb's voice, while still low, maintained his steely control. "I've decided to send Grace home to Vermont." Tears of relief sprung to my eyes at Caleb's declaration.

"Not happening." Roger's nonchalant tone had me peeking through the open doorway again, this time not caring if I was noticed. "We have high moral standards that includes no divorce. Unless you plan on leaving

Wellington with her, she stays."

"I never signed on for this, Roger. We brought everyone here under false pretenses, and your children happened to choose the two people who want to go home." I heard Caleb's boots hit the floor while he paced the office, his voice rising as he spoke. "Up until now, I've gone along with keeping them here because they signed a contract, but I re-read the wording the other day, and everything about this is off."

My fingers were white-knuckled on the door jamb. It took everything in my power not to burst inside the office, but I had to hear what Caleb said, and I didn't want to interrupt as things were just getting good. Caleb was standing up to Roger. He was keeping his promise.

"What they signed, the so-called contract you had drawn up, never says they are leaving at the end of the summer," Caleb revealed.

I stepped back from the door in shock. Holy shit. He was right. The wording had said: *For the duration of your stay.*

Roger wasn't surprised. "What's your point?"

"You never intended for them to leave when you sent me on that recruitment mission, did you?" I didn't hear a response before Caleb continued. "I'm an officer of the law. I refuse to be a part of holding someone here against their will."

"Like I said," Roger stated, "If you help her out, you go, too."

There was only a slight hesitation, before I heard a response. "Fine."

"If that's your decision," the town manager's voice was almost too casual and I once again moved toward the door. "It's a shame, though, that your children

39

won't have their father around. You brought them home to raise them under the safety and security we offer here in Wellington. They are one of us. They stay."

Even through the door, I felt the air go icy cold. "Those are my children, Roger."

"They are Wellingtons. No child under the age of eighteen leaves these gates. That is our law. You knew that when you moved back."

Roger's voice faded a bit, maybe he moved further into the room, I'm not sure, but I had to press against the door again to hear him. "The choice is yours. You can stay and make the best of your new marriage, have a few more kids, and enjoy the freedoms of what our life here offers. Or you can cause another scandal by helping Grace leave these gates. If you do, you'll be banished from town, like your father, and lose custody of your children, like your father. I think you know what you need to do. You can go now. Don't bother coming to the meeting. The rest of council will already be briefed."

As Caleb exited the room, he nearly tripped over me. "Grace." His arm snaked behind my back, and he led me quickly out of the building and away until he sat me at an empty bench just outside the entrance.

He squatted in front of me, eye level. "How much did you hear?"

"All of it." My stomach cramped. My eyes hurt from holding in tears. "I'm not going home, am I?"

"Never say never."

I held out my arm with the bracelet. "Take it off, I know you can, and let me leave."

He traced the skin around the bracelet and sighed. "Unfortunately, I'm not the only cop in town. If the bracelet is disengaged or shut off, an alarm goes off at the station. The entire town will be shut down before you reach the gates."

I saw the shadows in his eyes. "And if you help me, your kids will be taken from you. This town is a prison, don't you see that?"

He took a seat beside me and placed my hand between his two. "Maybe I've known all along, but a part of me wanted to believe it was a place of security for my children who'd lost their mother to violence. I needed to come home. I needed to belong. I saw what I wanted to see."

"What do we do now?" While I asked, I knew this man didn't have the answers. And even if his eyes were opening to the true nature of what was in front of him, I couldn't be quite sure I had a true ally. While he'd promised to get me home, I couldn't ask him to sacrifice his children for me.

As of this moment, going home to my family was not happening, and it scared the hell out of me.

Chapter Four

It's very easy to crawl inside oneself and not want to come out. I went back to the apartment, got into bed, hid under the covers, and stayed there. I didn't cry. The pain in my chest was too much for any type of emotional outpouring.

I wanted my parents. I wanted to talk to my dad, who always knows the right thing to say no matter how crazy the situation. I wanted my mom, who despite her preoccupation with the restaurant, always takes time to hug and check in with me and my sister. And Sarah. More than anything, I wanted to see her kooky, smiley face and hear her loud, obnoxious laughter.

But Roger had made it clear I was never going back home to Vermont.

Unless I was pregnant.

The fetal position wasn't small enough for the way I felt. I should never have come here this summer. Hah! Like I could have ever predicted the complete insanity of this tucked-away town.

I would wager a bet, if I ventured to the nearest town outside of Wellington and asked what they thought about the people here, they'd have nothing but good things to say. Sure, they lived behind a gate, but the residents appeared to move freely in and out, going to jobs, to college, and all are super polite.

The façade of this place was amazing. I've had my

ups and downs, but I can't deny how, with a few exceptions, most of the people I've met here are friendly and welcoming. I never thought I'd stay once the summer intern program was over.

Caleb checked on me before heading to his parents for dinner and to tuck his kids in. He checked on me again when he got home, before heading into the other bedroom to sleep on the floor.

In the morning, he made me tea and eggs and put them on the nightstand. "Grace, today is Independence Day. There are lots of activities going on throughout town. A parade this afternoon. Fireworks later. Do you feel up to it?"

I ignored him and the food. I know he left the apartment at one point, but other than going to the bathroom, the bed was my new haven.

I pretended to be asleep when I heard him return. I had no concept of time so I was surprised to hear a knock on the apartment door a while later. I rolled over, uncovering my head from under the pillow so I could hear who the visitor was.

"Hi, Mom."

Rita. Oh, sure. Caleb had his mom around to see and talk to. I can't even call mine.

"Is she still in the room?" I heard the woman ask. If he answered, I didn't hear the response. Maybe he nodded, but his mom continued. "Is there anything I can do?"

"I don't think so. Can I ask a question, though?"

By the fluctuating tone, I could tell they'd moved from the door toward the couch. "When you married Dad, did you have a hard time adjusting here?"

His mother seemed unfazed by the sudden

question. "Sure I did. I was seventeen, almost eighteen. I wasn't able to finish high school and moving away from my family was difficult."

"Strange, but I never heard how you met. I guess, when I was old enough, you and Dad were in the midst of the divorce, and Dad was, well…"

"Yes, I suppose at that time I wouldn't have been receptive."

When the air conditioner cycled on, I shifted on the bed, rolling so my head was at the bottom, closer to the closed bedroom door so I could listen to their conversation.

"Your father was a real charmer back then. He was fresh out of the police academy and looking to get experience, so he'd do whatever grunt work he could get at the police station in town which was located only a block from my high school."

The older woman gave a little chuckle. "He always managed to finish his shift in time to walk me home. Then it led to going for a soda. We'd only known each other three months before we had sex, and before long I was pregnant with your sister.

"Bruce immediately stepped up to do the right thing. He said there was no other option but to get married, and he swooped me up and brought me here to Wellington."

Caleb continued to question his mom. "But you got to go home to see your parents, right?"

"Oh, goodness, no, I never went back," she said. "They disowned me when I got pregnant so young."

I sat on the edge of the bed, needing to hear every word. It was as though Rita didn't realize she was confirming my every suspicion about this town. And from Caleb's questions, her revelations were equally eye-opening for him.

"You never tried to reach out? Or they, you?"

"Your father said there was no need. If my parents didn't accept the situation when it happened, then they weren't good parents and didn't deserve my time."

Was Caleb thinking the same thing I was? Bruce had used a ruse to keep Rita here? "What about when you divorced? Did you think about going home?"

"Oh, heavens, no, not with you children to think about. Besides, there were too much drugs and violence outside of our gates. No, no. This was a much better place to raise you. You should understand. It's why you came back here to raise your children."

I heard rustling and knew his mom was getting ready to leave. "Give her time. It's a shock right now, but she's been here a couple months now. Surely she has seen what our wonderful town can provide for her."

"Yes, I'm sure she has."

They'd moved closer to the door. "We'll be heading down to The Square for the festivities. Are you coming?"

"No. I'll stay here. Can you give the kiddos a hug from me?"

"You know I will. I love you, son."

I sank back onto the bed. This farce of bringing people here to marry had been going on for quite a while, but under a more subtle façade. From what I heard, I don't think Caleb's mother even grasped the enormity of her captivity over the years.

If this behavior had been going on for years, no wonder no one had intervened on my behalf at the church. I crawled back under the covers and wished for sleep. Wished for anything but the dreaded sense of hopelessness filling my soul.

Not much later, I heard another knock on the apartment door and groaned. Why couldn't people leave us alone?

"Is Grace here?"

I recognized Jake's voice immediately. I should talk to him, but getting out of bed would take too much effort. He was trapped as much as I was in a forced marriage, but in a way he'd brought his on himself. I'd told him not to sleep with Hope the Siren.

Caleb answered, "Let me check." The door swung open, but I already had the pillow over my head again. "You have a visitor."

I grunted back. "Not now."

He stood at the bedroom door for a few moments. Not moving. Staring at me. I could feel the intensity but I refused to budge and he caved first, closing the door once again.

"Sorry, Jake. She isn't feeling well today."

"Oh, okay." My heart bled a little at my friend's dejected tone before I heard him leave.

The door swung open again. "Grace, it's time to get up. Get moving."

"No." I was being stubborn. I wanted to go home, and this place was not my home. "Leave me be."

I heard him walk away and when I peeked out, I realized he'd left the bedroom door open. Ugh. I still refused to get up. I moved my head to the top of the pillow but covered it with the sheet and blanket.

The pipes rumbled a bit a second before the water turned on in the shower, and I prayed to be asleep by the time he finished. Caleb had other plans. He returned to the room, and before I realized what he was doing, he pulled the blankets off me.

"What the hell?" I tried grabbing the corner, but he made sure they reached the floor. Then he reached down and picked me up off the bed.

"Put me down." I struggled, but to no avail. In a few large strides, he exited the bedroom and had me in the bathroom. "What do you think you are doing? Stop."

While I kicked and punched, he stepped into the tub, me still in his arms, both of us still fully clothed— well, I wore only a shirt and panties, but he had on jeans and a tee shirt. He then put me down under the spray.

"Oh, my freaking word!" I screeched. "It's bloody cold. You son of a bitch." I lunged at him, my arms swinging, but he held me at arm's length under the frigid water. "I hate you." I swung. And missed. "I hate you and this horrible place."

"Thatta girl." His voice was tight while I nearly choked on my own emotions. "Fight me. Yell at me."

I stopped to stare at him. What the hell was he up to? The tightness in my chest constricted more, and I gasped for breath.

"Come on. Let the emotions out, Grace," he ordered. "You're a fighter, and I won't allow you to lie down and die at a little set back."

My clothes plastered to my skin. The water felt like shards of ice, and my teeth were almost at the point of chattering. I wanted to give up. I wanted to disappear, but Caleb was a force to be reckoned with. All I had to do was look into his blue eyes to see the steel determination.

"I hate you." But this time it came out as a whisper a second before the tears came. Tears I'd been unable to cry since Pastor Rick had declared me a married woman.

When the tears fell, my knees buckled. Caleb stepped forward, wrapping his arms around me, pulling me to his chest. With one hand he turned the knob to hot and in moments I warmed up, both from the water and from his strength.

"That's it, let it all go," he murmured.

I did, sobbing into his shirt while the tiny bathroom filled with steam, until the tears stopped and the hiccuping began.

"Feel better?" His deep voice was a timbre beneath my ear at his chest.

"No. I feel wrung out."

He brushed a soothing hand down my wet hair. "I'm sure. Do you think you can stand on your own?"

I had to think about it. Caleb pretty much supported my weight at the moment. One arm wrapped securely around my waist while the other continued the strokes down my head. I might be able to stand, but I kind of liked where I was at the moment. I might not like this man at the moment, but I needed him. I needed his strength. I needed his courage.

This summer had been a roller coaster ride of emotions, and I didn't know if I had it in me to keep going. I was tired of being strong. Part of me wanted to crawl back into the bed and sleep. Maybe when I woke I'd discover this was all a dream.

"Can you stand on your own?"

He wanted an answer, so I gathered the strength to give him the one I figured he wanted to hear. "Yes."

Caleb moved back far enough to lift my chin, seeking out the truth in my eyes. He nodded. "I'm going to step out of the shower and give you privacy to clean up. If you hand me your wet clothes, I'll take them down to the laundry room."

I was glad for the instruction as my own thought process was moving slow. When he closed the curtain between us, I felt bereft and alone. And colder. I stripped and then stared at the shadow on the other side of the curtain.

"Umm, are you decent?" I called out.

"If you mean am I covered, the answer is yes."

I grabbed the shower curtain to hold in place as I peeked around and held out my sopping clothes. Caleb was covered. In just a towel around his waist. I squeezed my eyes shut and held out my handful of sodden clothes. "Here."

He took my clothes, and I opened one eye for a quick second before shoving the curtain back in place between us. I'd seen him without a shirt before, down at the lake and again when playing baseball, but I hadn't been naked and wet only a foot away. Holy Sculpted Adonis. No man should look that good. There was a new wave of heat that washed over me that had nothing to do with the shower. Maybe I should turn the water back to cold? Does that help women? At least I know the shock of the past couple days hadn't completely shut off all my emotions.

I needed a distraction so I talked. "Caleb? Where is the laundry? I don't remember seeing it."

The shower curtain was dark enough to keep us from seeing details, but I could still see his shadow as he bent down to gather all the wet items. If I could see him, he could see me. I turned to the wall, reaching for the shampoo as an excuse to turn away, suddenly insecure.

He didn't seem to notice as he moved around in the small room. "There's a shared laundry room on every floor of the apartment building. It's located next to the stairwell. Are you good if I go take care of these?"

"Yes." I was, too. I took a few more minutes to wash my hair and stand under the now tepid stream, but for the first time in two days, I felt more normal. Maybe it was the crying. I'd needed that. Or the hot water washing away the stress. Or maybe it was the jolt of something a little hotter that had flooded my body as I'd peeked out at the man who'd forced me to get out of my head and get moving again.

I brushed my teeth, which felt damn good, ran a comb through my hair, and wrapped myself in a towel to go to the bedroom to get dressed. Caleb had stripped the bedsheets and must have taken those to the laundry as well. I walked over to my suitcase, which I still hadn't unpacked, and grabbed shorts and a shirt sporting a Down Syndrome Awareness ribbon and dressed quickly, not wanting to be naked when my new roommate returned.

I went to the window, opened it to the screen, and stared out. The streets were empty, but I heard band music in the distance and children's laughter. The July Fourth celebrations were in full swing.

When Caleb returned, I suddenly felt shy and maybe a bit embarrassed, but he didn't notice. Or at least he didn't mention it. "Are you hungry?"

My stomach growled at the mere mention. "Famished."

With a nod of his head, he motioned me toward the kitchen. He'd gone shopping. The fridge and cabinets had more to choose from. Working side by side, we got macaroni boiling and made a quick Alfredo sauce. Only after we'd eaten did we begin to talk.

I wiped my mouth on a napkin and looked up from my empty plate. I was clean, had a full belly, and had the man eating across from me to thank for it, but I was still embarrassed by my behavior. "Thank you for earlier."

"No problem." He stood to gather the dishes. When I went to stand he shook his head. "I've got it."

I watched as he got the dish tub filled with soap. I couldn't sit, though, after spending so much time hiding. "What do we have to drink?"

"Not much. I didn't know what you like. I did buy an assortment of teas to choose from, though."

I silently scoffed at the wording. No one actually bought anything here. Or at least there was no exchange of money. The bracelets everyone was forced to wear contained our personal information and all we had to do was swipe it against the register and voila, it was yours. Maybe it could be considered a personal credit card, if you will, but since no one actually got a paycheck for their work, it was almost like a formality.

I grabbed the tea kettle and Caleb, still at the sink, filled it. Once it was set to heat, I stared at the selection of herbals. "What kind do you want?"

"Whatever you like." He wiped the last dish and put it away.

Like? I had no idea. "I, ah, don't drink tea. I've always had coffee."

His slow smile was warm and non-judgmental.

"Grab some cups, I'll choose."

A few minutes later, we moved to the living room, steaming mugs in hand. "I overheard your conversation with your mom earlier." I nibbled on my lip as I waited for his reaction.

"I'm glad."

His quick response wasn't what I'd expected to hear.

"Did you draw the same conclusion I did?" I asked. I know what I thought, but I didn't want to be rude and say something about his family he would be mad at me for, not after he'd just been so nice to me.

He took pity on me. "I think my father deliberately got my mother pregnant so he could marry her and bring her here to live."

I took a sip of the liquid and made a face. Ugh. It needed sugar. I set it on the end table. "And maybe lied to her about her parents not wanting to see her again?" I asked.

Caleb put his tea on the table and leaned over to take my hands in his. "I owe you a huge apology, Grace. I should never have brought you, any of you, here."

"Why did you?" I wasn't mad. I didn't yell. It was a question to appease my curiosity about this man who seemed almost as lost as I felt at the moment.

He took a moment before speaking, as though he wasn't quite sure how to explain himself. "Growing up here, everything we do, all the rules and laws, it's all normal, or at least it's normal for us." He struggled with the words—a rarity in itself, so I kept quiet and let him talk. "I left, not because I disagreed with our life, but because even though it had been eight years since the

52

scandal of my parents' divorce, I still felt I lived in the shadow of my father's mistakes. Leaving the way I did, though, was akin to disavowing my allegiance to Wellington. In a way, I disgraced my family a second time.

"When I joined the Marines, it was like a whole new world opened up to me. I'd found a new home, a new family. I met Jill and everything was perfect. Until her death."

"How did she die?" I'd been curious for so long, I finally had to know. Caleb sat back, his hands finally releasing me, and I saw the weight of the world in his expression.

"It happened on base." He shook his head. "The one place other than here I thought for sure would be a safe place. Anyway, a fellow marine had a falling out with his wife. He believed she was having an affair and decided to confront her at the playground. He pulled out a gun and opened fire. Someone decided to tackle him and when he did, the next bullet went astray." His hesitation said it all, and I reached over to put my hand on top of his. He turned his palm up and clasped mine.

"The bullet caught Jill dead center in the head. Eliza was in school. The baby was in the stroller, too young to know anything, but Justin witnessed it."

"Oh, dear God."

His fingers squeezed mine. At my reaction? Or to punctuate his reasoning, I wasn't sure, but Caleb continued. "My priority became protecting my children at all costs. Home was the first place I thought of."

I gulped. "Sure. It makes sense."

"Coming back, though, not all of the townspeople welcomed me. Most did, but to the council, I needed to prove myself. Prove my loyalty to Wellington. Ironically, my father's old job as police chief was open, and I was the most qualified.

"Randy came with me. He's Jill's brother. He and his sister were close, and he wanted to be a part of her children's lives. Anyway, he brought with him a certain skill set which helped boost the security in the town, something we were both thrilled to do under the circumstances."

Caleb's thumbs rubbed the back of my hands as he spoke. I'm not sure if he realized what he was doing. My guess, for him it was an unconscious motion, but I was aware of each and every swirl they made. I forced myself to look at him as he spoke, trying to dismiss what his touch was doing, and how the motion of his thumbs sent an echoing electric pulse in my stomach.

"When we were told this year that rather than scouting the surrounding cities and towns for runaways that we were going on an extended mission to bring in a more educated, more worthy group of individuals, I protested."

His eyes begged me to believe him.

"I'm sure you did," I said.

"But the council has a way of making me feel unworthy, and I still felt a need to prove my loyalty, so I did everything they asked of me. I swear, though, Grace," he clenched my hand in both of his, "I never, not once when I set out on that mission, thought if someone wanted to go home at the end of the summer, that the council would find a way to force them to stay."

"I think Roger is the driving force," I muttered, "but the others don't argue with him. How do I leave?"

His breath came out on a huff. "It won't be easy. The security system here was quite unique even before I came back. With Randy's help, we brought it up to a near fortress. The tracking devices are state of the art."

I curled my lip up, "Much like an ankle bracelet for those under house arrest."

Caleb closed his eyes briefly as he nodded his agreement. "Similar, but sleeker and more advanced. If and when they are disengaged for any reason, an alarm goes off at the precinct and on every officer's phone."

"I know the hospital is able to remove the bracelets for certain procedures."

"Yes, but before they do, the patient's name is logged into the computer and the reason, such as having an x-ray. As soon as the patient leaves the room, the bracelet is immediately put back on."

Now that we were talking and Caleb was forthcoming, I had more questions. I shifted on the uncomfortable, block-style furniture, attempting to get more comfortable as we spoke. "What happens for all the people who go to work outside of the gates?"

Caleb, too, shifted, sitting back with his arm stretched along the back of the couch, his arm now almost touching my neck. Part of me—the part that had fallen asleep in his arms under a rock shelter—wanted to lean my head back and get back to the truce of Saturday night. The other part, my less trusting side, had me sitting straight, avoiding any contact.

"Their GPS security is set for access to leave town. It also has a special button on it for them to press every hour, confirming they are safe. If they don't respond when it vibrates, then a search party is immediately dispatched."

"I had no idea how far-reaching and invasive the system is." I looked down at the bracelet and knew it was the key to leaving. "Would Randy change the security if you asked him?"

Caleb shook his head. "No. He came to me last night and said he'd been ordered to enhance the security on both of us so the council members would be alerted if either of us went even beyond the general town area. Going out to Jefferson's Farm and the lake will even alert them, and an officer will be sent out to ensure it is as far as we attempt to go."

I felt the tightness returning to my chest. Roger meant business in keeping us trapped here. "And if they suspect you help me, in any way, they'll take your kids from you. So what do we do?"

Caleb shifted again as he reached over and took another sip of tea. "I've been giving that some thought. Do you remember what you said to me your second day here?" He shook his head. "Probably not, you were stoned. Anyway, you said you needed to pretend to fit in so no one would know you planned to escape."

I remembered making that plan with Jake. I didn't remember spilling that to the chief.

He continued, "I think we should pretend to get along. Build trust. Act as though we are trying to make our marriage work."

I swallowed, but had no saliva left. I grabbed my tea and gulped down the now tepid, bitter liquid. "How far are you thinking of taking the farce?"

"Don't go down that road, Grace," he said softly. "You know I won't disrespect you."

I guess I did. He was a gentleman. He'd broken Leland's arm in the process of protecting me. I slowly nodded my agreement. "What do you have in mind?"

"If people see us together, holding hands, getting along, maybe by the time summer ends, we'll have earned the right to have the security lowered, and we can strike the advantage."

That might work. "If I'm not home by the time I'm supposed to go back to school in August, my parents will come looking for me. What will Roger do then?"

"I honestly don't think he's planned that far ahead. I believe he counted on everyone falling in love with our little town. Falling in love, period. He expected everyone to contact their families and say they were staying and it being of their own free will, much like Caroline."

"That's stupid. We're not runaways. We have families who love us." I shook my head in disgust. "I'm with you. I like having a plan. Thank you."

He looked at the clock on the kitchen stove. "It's almost seven-thirty. Are you up for the fireworks? The whole town will see our solidarity."

The whole town? The town who'd encouraged the marriage between us because of the mere possibility of impropriety?

I closed my eyes as I called for inner strength. "We're in this together, right?"

"Together."

Chapter Five

I heard the noise of the crowd the moment we stepped out of the apartment building. All four hundred or so residents of Wellington had converged on the streets on the edge of The Square. When they all came together on Sunday for mass and a fellowship meal, that was a time for reverence.

Today, they partied.

As we walked the few blocks, the sound of the school band playing "God Bless America" echoed down the streets. Fourth of July. Independence Day. In a town holding its residence hostage. My pace slowed.

Caleb looked down at me. "Okay?"

No. I wanted to scream the word. I wanted to turn tail and run. "I feel hypocritical, celebrating a day of independence with a town that has taken away my rights."

The distant look he gave wasn't him closing off this time. No, I spotted the hint of pain in the blue flecks before his shoulders squared. "Think of it more of you taking the first step to secure your freedom again."

I rubbed my clammy palms against my shorts. "Do you think it will work? Do you think we can fool them?"

His answer was to hold his hand out. "If we show a united front, yes."

I took it. Not for the first time, I noticed the difference in size as his fingers folded between mine. Today, at this moment, our age difference seemed massive, but part of me knew it was due to his confidence. My own fears of my future had me wishing to be a little girl back in the safety of my parents' home.

I needed to stop my self-pity. I was twenty, not a child. It was time to put on my big girl panties and show the world I'm a fighter. I squeezed his hand. "Let's do this."

Then we turned the corner and came face to face with Leland, A.J., Tim, and Phillip. My new-found determination came to a screeching halt.

"Gentlemen." Caleb nodded, continuing to move forward taking me along with him. The current Hate Grace Club spread out, blocking our path on the sidewalk. "Is there a problem?" he drawled.

"Yeah, we're walking here," A.J. taunted. "Move to the other side of the street."

"Now is that any way to treat your brother?" Caleb drawled, and my skin pebbled at the underlying warning, which didn't look as though it would be heeded.

I looked at the row of Caleb's younger half-siblings, plus Leland, and saw them move into a stance preparing to fight, yet the man beside me remained amazingly calm.

"You owe Lee an apology," Phillip insisted.

Caleb's lip twisted up. "Is that a fact? For what?"

Leland lifted his casted arm. "You broke my arm."

"Yeah," Phillip added, "And you stole his girl."

Before I could respond, Caleb spoke again. "I can't steal something if it was never his in the first place. As for the arm—" Caleb stared the pretty boy down—"you got what you deserved."

Making a fist, A.J. took a step forward. The large, confident man holding my hand didn't flinch as he continued speaking. "Did Lee tell you what he did to earn that arm?"

A.J. thrust his chin up. "He said you interrupted him and Grace as they were making out because you were jealous."

I gasped, but a simple squeeze on my hand had me biting my tongue. "Really? As I remember it, he was mad at me and decided to take out his anger on Grace by kicking her in the ribs with his steel-toed boots. That's why his arm is currently in a sling."

All three turned to look at my attacker's beet red face for confirmation. Tim was the one to speak, "You actually did that? You kicked her in front of the 'Straight and narrow, don't disrespect a woman, police chief?' Jeez. Even I know where to draw the line."

Leland began to sputter. "You're missing the big picture. She was supposed to be mine this summer, and he stole her from me."

"Tell you what," Caleb said. "I'll let you figure out the true story while we head down to enjoy a little of the party." He tugged and I followed as his brothers turned on their friend.

I let out the breath I hadn't realized I'd been holding. "How could you be so calm? It was four against one, and they were ready to pummel you."

"I'm hurt you think they could succeed." He pressed a hand to his heart and gave a bit of a pout. "Besides, it was hardly four to one. Leland is broken and too afraid of disfiguring his beautiful face. Tim is basically a good kid and tends to be a peace maker. Phil and A.J. both have a mean streak, but other than a few scuffles here and there, neither really knows how to fight."

"Oh, well," I scoffed, "when you put it that way, I suppose there was nothing to be afraid of." I shook my head. "Men."

The Square had been transformed overnight into a red, white, and blue spectacular. Banners hung from every storefront. Children waved flags. The school's band players, who'd marched in a parade earlier, still sported their school colors while carrying around their musical instruments and occasionally starting up their own individual songs.

Rows of tables were set up by the gazebo in the park area, where a pie-eating contest was currently going on, being judged by the council members. Caleb explained it was the last of the contests usually held as next everyone would be heading toward the school for the firework display.

It didn't take long, being amongst the throng of people, for the well-wishers to descend. He leaned down to whisper, "Smile, this is step one in our plan."

And God help me, that's what I did until my cheeks froze in a Joker position. We'd had to have been downtown for at least twenty minutes when I spotted Jake. Hope clung to his arm as she spoke animatedly with her father, while her new husband's pained expression begged to be saved.

"Do you mind if I go say hi to Jake?"

Caleb turned from his conversation with Mark, the teacher from the school. "Of course. See you soon." He lifted my hand, still ensconced in his and kissed it.

My eyes followed his lips as they brushed the back of my hand, the gesture completely unexpected. The tiny hairs on my arms lifted at the simple touch, and I swallowed hard.

This is a farce, Grace. He's playing to the crowd. Go with it.

"Of course, *dear*. I won't be long."

I zipped through the sea of people, needing to escape. Not Caleb, but the surging emotions running through me. He'd only kissed my hand, and for a moment I almost thought it was real. But it was how much I enjoyed his touch which caught me off guard. I thought back to our kiss Saturday night and bit my lip. I couldn't deny my attraction to him even if I wanted to, so if one little brush of his lip against my skin had me losing my breath, what would happen if he kissed me in public?

How far would our farce have to go to convince the town council we were complying with their marriage rules? I sprinted toward Jake and threw my arms around him, pulling him away from the woman clinging to him at the same time.

"Hey, what do you think you're doing?" Hope wailed, but my friend wrapped his arms around me and talked over my head. "We'll be back."

We made quick work of leaving his new wife in the dust and disappearing into the crowd. "Are you okay?" he demanded.

I was now. This was Jake. My best friend. The one person I could truly trust in this socially-backward town. "I guess. And you?"

His stare was intense as he looked me up and down. "I have been worried, and no one would let me see you."

Guilt hit. I should have talked with him when he came to the apartment. "Sorry, my fault. It all hit, and I went into a bit of a tailspin. I wouldn't see anyone."

"I'm so sorry about everything," he apologized. "You warned me not to sleep with her and now we're... you and Caleb... Shit."

"It was all part of their plan, Jake, right down to being caught in a compromising situation. Another few minutes alone with Leland, and he would have made sure it looked like he and I were doing more than we actually were."

He held his hand to his head. "Oh, there were no doubts on my end. When Roger walked in, our pants were off, and I was riding his daughter like a bronco."

I didn't need that visual. "She played you good."

"And that Dr. Todd? Now I know why he freaks you out," he rambled. "Hope spent the entire meeting discussing her menstrual cycle and asking questions because she wants to be pregnant by Labor Day. Gonna be hard because I ain't ever touching her again. How do you feel about another escape attempt?"

"Caleb and I are working on a plan." I explained about the updated security. "Because we are going to be under strict scrutiny for a while, we've decided to pretend to comply and make it look like we are going along with everything, until they lower our security restrictions."

He tugged at the tracking bracelet, but there was no way to pull it off. "To what end?"

"Hopefully, the council will tire of getting alerts every time we leave the general vicinity of the downtown area. We plan to go to the lake and hike and be pretty much obnoxious in a subtle way, but not do anything to raise suspicion. Maybe by the time summer is over, Caleb will be able to get access to our security and disable them to get us out of here."

Jake shook his head. "Caleb said that? I thought he was part of the establishment?"

We pushed through the busy street, talking low so not to be overheard. The sun cast a pink hue in the distant sky. "His eyes have been opened. Helping us is a huge risk. Roger threatened to banish him and keep him from his kids, but he still said he'd find a way to get us out. Trust him, okay?"

Jake shook his head. "I'm not sure I can, but I trust you. I, however, will not pretend anything but contempt for that vile woman and her family for tricking me," he scoffed. "And I thought my ex-girlfriend, Layla, was a psycho bitch from hell. I haven't told you half of what she did to trap me, but she's got nothing on this one."

I spotted conniving witch Hope weaving through the crowd, her sights set on her new husband. "Speak of the devil."

Jake rolled his eyes. "She reminds me of cotton candy. Pretty to look at, tastes good at first, but too much and you get sick."

I held back my laughter as Hope arrived to claim her man, wrapping her arms around his waist and effectively pushing me away. "Jake, honey, it's almost time for the fireworks. Everyone is leaving now."

The petulant siren looked at me, anger evident in every breath. "Shouldn't your find your husband?"

I tried my best not to cringe. I wasn't mentally prepared to say I had a husband when I'm only twenty and a college student. Or was a college student. *No.*

Still a college student. I would be returning in the fall.

Jake gave a pained expression as he continued to look my way. "I'll see you later?"

I nodded as he was pulled away, leaving me alone. Oh, how I wanted to take this time to sink back into my hole. To sneak back to the apartment and steer clear of the residents of Wellington. Caleb came my way, and I waited, wringing my hands. I know I said I would play along, but having people actually comment on our marriage was more difficult than I imagined.

The shuttle buses ran from the side streets to the school, but we followed those walking the few blocks. The heat of the day was dissipating as night began to fall, but it only made the temperature more bearable. I was glad I'd been in an air-conditioned apartment during the afternoon scorcher.

The football and baseball fields, which adjoined, were filled with families settling down on blankets, while the bleachers filled to capacity. We maneuvered around all the children running back and forth, their laughter echoing in the air.

Caleb leaned down and scooped his youngest daughter after she barreled into his legs. "Hiya, jellybean." Shawna squealed as her father nuzzled her neck and hugged her close. "You taste like watermelon. All sticky and sweet. Where's your *Grammaw*?"

"Over there." She pointed a fat finger, and I saw the red of the fruit juice staining her hand. He gave me a nod to follow as he found his mother.

Rita jumped up from the grass. "Oh, darling, it's good to see you. And Grace, too. Welcome."

"Hello." Shy wasn't the word for the way I felt now. Rita knew I'd hidden away, knew I didn't want to be married to her son. This should be fun. But the older woman gave a warm smile and motioned for us to find a spot on the blanket she'd lain out.

Caleb's oldest started to take a seat on the ground but stopped when she spotted me. "What are you doing here?"

I gulped. Not the best greeting.

"Elena." Her father's tone lowered to a warning. "Where are your manners?"

She gave a dark glare back at her parent. "You're the one who married her. I don't want another mother."

"We talked about this. You need to be polite."

I knew what the kid was feeling. I wasn't exactly ready to jump into the role of mother, either. "It's okay, Caleb. This is new for all of us." I looked down at the young girl. "You had a mom, and you loved her a lot. I understand. I have a mom, too. She's still alive, but I miss her. I am not looking to take your mother's place, okay? I am Grace. Just Grace."

Caleb put a hand on his daughter's head. "But Grace is an adult, and you will treat her with respect. Understood?"

She lowered her eyes. "Yes, Daddy."

"Good girl. Now, where is your brother?

She gave a casual, non-committal wave behind her, "He's sitting with Morgan."

He motioned for his daughter to join us. Once everyone was settled, I looked beyond the crowds and across the distance of the field I spotted a sound system with huge speakers.

Caleb shifted so he was positioned beside me, Elena on his other side, while Shawna crawled onto his lap. "I should warn you, this is not a normal fireworks display you are used to," he explained.

"Oh?"

"Nope. The noise of the fireworks scares all the animals so, many years ago the town decided to do a laser light show to music. They still refer to it as fireworks, but, well, as you know, Wellington has their own way.'

I grunted. When the music started, I leaned back on my arms, stretched my legs out, and looked up. I wasn't disappointed.

The music rocked, and the lights flashed in perfect harmony. Whoever put the show together knew their stuff. It was amazing, and while I almost missed the clap and boom of a real firework display, the light show was highly entertaining and I was grinning when it finished.

"You liked it?" Caleb asked.

"I did, actually. Thanks for bringing me."

He stood, taking my hand to pull me to my feet. "I have to bring the munchkins back to my mom's. Are you up for a walk, or do you want to take the shuttle?"

I looked up at the starry sky and the throngs of people loading on to the buses. "Walk, please."

He nodded. Within a moment he had Shawna in his arms and Elena walking beside him. When we located Justin, the young boy was yawning from ear to ear. "I want up, too, Daddy."

Caleb easily scooped the boy up in his other arm, and I watched in amazement as he carried the two young children without showing any sign of fatigue.

Rita fell into step beside me. "I'm glad you came tonight."

I gave a non-committal 'hmm,' not sure what to

say to her. My mind had a lot of questions about her life here and why she didn't question her husband's mandate of how her family didn't want her, but I couldn't. This was her life, and I didn't have a right to interfere.

Although I wish they understood those same boundaries, as Rita continued to speak. "My son is a good man. He'll treat you well."

I wasn't ready for this conversation. "I believe you. Although, this marriage was as much a surprise on him as it is me."

The woman reached over to pat my arm. "Of course. And when the town sees fit, they will locate a home for you, one big enough for the children. Does that scare you?"

Just the thought had my stomach clenching in a knot. Too much, too soon, but I had a part to play. "More than you know. I didn't come here this summer to get married or become a parent."

She gave my arm a quick squeeze before she finally let go. "That may be true, but you'll adjust. I was younger than you when I got married and moved here. It took a little while, but I got to know everyone, and they pulled me into their family as one of their own. You'll find it to be true for you, as well.

My brain was screaming at the woman, wanting to tell her she was a blind fool. That she'd been tricked into marriage; tricked into staying. As much as I wanted to words to come out, I had an end-goal that I couldn't compromise. Instead, I turned my fingers inward until my nails pressed painfully into my palms, and I remained silent.

But when Caleb and I walked back into the

apartment after stopping to grab our clothes from the laundry room, I stared at the tiny space. One bedroom.

How long would he be content to sleep on the floor?

Chapter Six

I woke on Wednesday to the smell of bacon. Caleb had slept on the floor in the nursery again, and I'd taken the bed once more. This time, though, I wasn't staying put. I padded out to the kitchen, watching as he used tongs to flip the frying meat. "Smells great."

He threw me a smile. He wore the same clothes as yesterday, and I realized he'd given me my privacy even with all his clothes in the bedroom.

"Want me to make eggs?" I offered. It was the least I could do.

For the next several moments, we worked side by side, cooking, getting plates, silverware, and orange juice. We were easy companions this morning, and I started to relax a little.

"Only thing missing is coffee," I muttered.

His deep chuckle echoed in the room, giving me warm fuzzies. "Still not adjusting? I'm going to teach you about our teas, then. Maybe you'll find one or two you like."

I mentally shook my head, forcing the weird feelings inside away, instead focusing on keeping things light with our new found truce. Last thing I needed was to mix emotions with my ultimate end-goal. "You can try, but I've been drinking coffee since I was thirteen. I *loves* my dark roast."

He prepared a simple decaffeinated black tea—for

a boost of energy, he said—and I took a sip.

I made a face at the bitterness. "Needs sugar." He turned to a cabinet and pulled down a bottle of honey, but I was quick to interject. "Sugar."

He conceded slightly, handing me a sugar bowl. "Okay, one teaspoon."

"Two," I bargained. "Trust me, that's not much."

He shook his head as I added the second teaspoon of the sweetener. "How much sugar do you put in your coffee?"

I tried to hide my response as I spoke into the cup to drink. "Five." When he groaned, I knew he'd heard my answer. I obviously wasn't cut out for this town's healthier living lifestyle.

As we finished eating, Caleb sipped on his OJ. "So, what would you like to do today?"

I didn't hesitate. "I want Roger's little tracker to ping him constantly. What can we do to annoy him the most?"

His lip twisted up. "Ahh, yes. I do remember you doing that to me as well. Okay, my first thought is to go for a hike up on White Pine Ridge."

"Done."

By the way his blue eyes sparkled, I knew I was back to amusing him, but I was eager to get this farce under way and willing to do anything. Caleb seemed a bit more cautious. "It can be a grueling path, are you sure you can handle it?"

"If it will get us out of this little apartment and cause our current parole officer to regret his decision to track us constantly, I'm up for it."

"It's going to be another hot one. I'll get a backpack and load it with snacks and plenty of water."

The humidity was on the high side, but trekking through the woods helped keep the sun from beating down on us. The path meandered up and over, and there were occasional breaks in the foliage for me to get a distant look at the town, but what caught me more was the view outside of town and how close the fence line was from the top of this almost mountain. I was tempted to keep going. What was stopping me from climbing the fence?

Well, other than a GPS tracking device and a town determined to keep non-Wellingtons prisoners with the intent to build their bloodline?

Caleb stood beside me and I had a feeling he could read my mind. "Are you ready for lunch?"

I turned my back on my mental escape plan and nodded. Within a few minutes, we had a blanket laid out and a picnic lunch in hand.

"I can see your mind whirling in there, Grace. It does look like it wouldn't take long to reach the fence."

I shoved a bite of sandwich in my mouth, suddenly vulnerable, as my thoughts had obviously become an open book.

"We'll get to the point where we can be trusted again by the town." He reached over to pat my leg, and I hated to admit how much I enjoyed even that quick, simple touch. "As police chief, I can tell you current protocol is that if someone leaves the general area of town like we have, and with our high security alert, all officers on and off duty are put on call. If you keep looking, you'll see one of those officers has been assigned to patrol outside the gates. Watch. Sometime within the next ten minutes, you'll spot a Wellington cruiser on the road below, making a pass around town.

Knowing the duty roster, my guess it'll be Tom."

He was, as usual, correct. It wasn't long before a car slowed and came to a stop on the road below us. "Because of our tracking system, Tom can tell we are still inside the gate and up on this ridge. But, if we start to descend on this side, we won't get far."

I took another bite of sandwich as questions swarmed, wanting to be answered. "And you helped bolster that security?"

Caleb brushed crumbs from his lap. "I created the noose which will hang me. Again, I apologize to you. I never realized the enormity of our actions."

I heard the resignation in his tone. "I know. I understand," but I continued to stare down at the fence line at the bottom of the steep hill.

He stood and gathered up the picnic. "I'm glad you are so forgiving. I'm not too happy with myself."

Despite my own misgivings, I felt impelled to say something positive. "You were creating a safe place for your kids. It's understandable with what you went through."

With a gentle tug, he pulled me to stand then he squeezed my hand. "I promise you, Grace, I will find a solution to get you home."

He meant it. His intense gaze promised as much as his words. I wanted to believe him, but there were so many obstacles ahead. With freedom so close beyond the fence line, I couldn't find any more words. As we continued our hike, every now and again I would be in a position to look down on the side of the town line and would spot the police cruiser, tracking our progress. Escape wasn't possible today, but our intent to keep outside of the center of town was a success.

Thursday, we headed to the lake which was much different than when we came in May. It was busy with lots of kids splashing and playing, Caleb's children included. I went in a few times, but mostly I sunbathed or read a novel.

Or sneaked a few glances toward Caleb as he waded while his children swam. He wore nothing more than swim trunks and all the saliva in my mouth disappeared. There was a rumble of his laughter while he played with his kids, and the sound sent a wave of heat through my body.

When I first arrived, he'd been aloof, standoffish even. Over the past couple months, I've seen a softer side of him, like when he is around his kids. This side of Caleb is the one I have a challenging time ignoring, especially when paired with six-pack abs and muscles to rival any of the superheroes in the movies.

He tossed Justin up into the air like he weighed nothing more than a loaf of bread, and my mind wandered. He'd carried me, more than once, as though I weighed nothing. He was strong, no doubt. While I have zero recollection of the first time, that fateful first Sunday, when I passed out. I remembered the time he'd carried me from here at the lake back to his car. He hadn't been mad at me. He'd been—resigned? No, more indulgent, but always kind. Like he'd been on Sunday when he'd carried me on his back out of the woods.

I continued to stare from behind my shades as the sun bounced off the water and danced across his perfectly sculpted, tanned body. He'd carried me. Those arms had been wrapped around me. His chest had been strong and warm. Even when I'd been pissed at him and everyone in this town, he made me feel protected.

I put down my book, tossed my shades beside it, and ran to the water front, splashing until I was deep enough to dive under. It was much warmer than my first foray in late May. My hope was to distract myself from my own wandering thoughts. It failed.

The man is sexy as hell, undeniably, but under the current circumstances with us living under the same roof, I must keep my eye on the prize. *NO! Not him.* I scolded my inner voice. Leaving. Going home. Escaping this unassuming prison.

During my punishing swim out to the rock and back, I convinced myself I could stay on the correct path leading toward my ultimate destination. Until I turned to look at the man in question. I noticed Caleb's eyes on me as I exited the water, and it wasn't laughter I saw on his face.

I gulped as his eyes skimmed down my bikini-clad body, and I stopped mid-stride. I'd seen that look before. On the ball field several weeks ago. Oh, dear God, maybe swimming was not the best choice of activities.

Justin lunged into his father's arms, and he broke the stare releasing me from my frozen-in-time moment. *Shit and two is eight.* I rushed back to the blanket to dry off and throw on my shirt and shorts.

Get a grip, girl. Yes, he's good looking, but you have a goal and that is to get the hell out of Dodge. Not to succumb to a lustful fantasy.

I was thankful for the children. While Elena continued to keep her distance, Justin and little Shawna kept me busy with wanting attention as we picnicked. Caleb and I were both careful not to touch each other in any way, but being together at the lake was another opportunity to have witnesses to us playing the role of a couple.

And, another bonus, being at the lake meant we were far enough outside town lines to have the updated security beeping for hours.

Friday arrived, and Caleb asked if I wanted to go horseback riding. My last experience at Jefferson's farm had me declining. Instead, we walked around town, doing a little food shopping, having lunch at the diner, anything to be seen together.

"Caroline and Aaron return today," he mentioned as I picked at my fries.

That peeked my interest. "Really? When?"

"I was supposed to pick them up at the bus at two, but for obvious reasons, they reassigned the job. They should be back in town by four. My guess is the band will likely be playing tonight. Want to go?"

I really missed my college roommate, but as usual with this place, there were also reasons not to go. "I want to see Caroline, but, Leland and A.J. are usually there."

He brushed off my comment. "They won't be a problem."

"How can you be so sure? The other night they were ready to gang up on you. A.J. always seems ready to start a fight, and Leland is pissed as hell."

He bit into a pickle, barely giving the subject a second thought. "Trust me." I still didn't completely understand his confidence, but I hoped he was right.

We ate dinner at Caleb's parents' house, again, and he spent time with his kids before we headed over to The Hall for the Friday night entertainment. Straight and True hadn't played since before their lead guitarist's wedding, and the band members were more than happy to put on a rocking night.

I spotted Caroline immediately and nearly sprinted across the room to envelope my friend in a hug as she gushed in her usual exuberance. "Grace, I have so much to tell you."

"Same here. Let's find a table."

She looked great in a simple, cotton sundress. It wasn't the clothes, though. My friend glowed with contentment. I looked down at my own shorts and tank. We didn't go back to the apartment when we left Caleb's folk's house. At the time, I hadn't cared. Now, next to my beautiful friend, I felt under-dressed.

She looked from me to Caleb as he joined us at the table. "Are you in trouble again?" she asked under her breath.

"Nope. Part of what I need to tell you."

"Then you go first."

Even though it had been a week, I still struggled saying the words. "Caleb and I are, um, well... We're married."

"Shut the front door. You're lying."

I shook my head. "Jake and Hope are also married, but believe me, it was not like the wedding you had."

I filled her in, answering all her questions. "Oh, my. Oh, dear," she kept repeating.

I spotted the other newlywed couple enter and knew Jake would be joining us in a few minutes, his ball and chain in tow. Our detailed conversation was about to be curtailed.

"Enough about me," I said, taking Caroline's hands in mine. "Tell me about your trip back home."

Her mouth twisted. "To say my parents were shocked is an understatement. My father nearly had a heart attack, but after a couple days, they warmed up to Aaron. In the end, they said they're happy for me."

I kept myself from saying *I told you so*, mostly because the past week had shown me it wouldn't have mattered if they'd wanted to wait. So, I lied. "I'm happy for you, Caroline. It sounds like a positive trip."

Jake sat down across from me, with the wonder twin pouting beside him. With the way she kept looking to the other side of the room where her brother sat, I knew we were not her first choice of people to sit with.

Jake and I could look at each other and know what the other thought, and tonight is no exception. He was dying a slow death. I could almost see the invisible rope his new bride had attached to him.

The easiest way to get time alone with the soon-to-be corpse would be to get out on the dance floor. I motioned to him as a rocking number played, and he nearly tripped over his own feet in his haste to escape from the blonde albatross.

"Don't you think your husband is going to get mad with us out here?" he yelled into my ear as we gyrated together.

I laughed. "Not nearly as much as your wifey."

We both let loose, needing to escape into the music. When it ended, Caleb stood and led me back to the floor, this time, the music changed to slow, and he pulled me into his arms. "My turn."

With Jake, I'd been free and loose. Now, I suddenly felt shy and insecure as I tried to decipher Caleb's current mood. "Are you mad at me for dancing with Jake?"

"No, you're friends. You have history," he rationalized. "But we have a part to play."

Right. A part. He moved me smoothly across the dance floor, his hand at the small of my back. With each step, I became more and more confused. When I'd danced with Jake, we'd let loose with our dirty dancing. While almost sexual in nature, for us it had been all fun and games.

This dance was different. For a large man, Caleb moved with a casual grace, sweeping me across the wooden floor of the room. He held one hand with his larger one, his other stayed in one place on my lower back. No funny business. Yet, he had my complete attention. He was all heat and quiet authority. Every brush of his thigh against mine was more intimate than the gyrations with Jake. My face flamed, and I looked up to see if he felt the same as me.

He looked down at the same time, and I lost myself in his cobalt eyes. As usual, with him, the air around us thinned, and I had difficulty finding my breath. Why could this man send my senses into instant overload with a single look?

Another couple bumped into me, and his arm tightened, pulling me closer as he turned in another direction. I was now pressed against his massive chest, as we spun around the cavernous room. Dear God, I could almost get dizzy. Not from the spinning, though, but from losing myself in his unwavering stare. Could he read my mind? I certainly couldn't read his.

The attraction I'd felt earlier in the summer washed over me again. The memory of the kiss we'd shared in the woods hit me, and I was a young, naïve girl wildly attracted to a man I couldn't have.

Except now the unattainable man was technically my husband. But he wasn't. Not really. I still wanted to leave in six weeks, and he was still in love with his dead wife. I stumbled over my feet.

"Am I going too fast?"

I licked my lips. He had no idea. "It's not you," I murmured.

The song ended, and we stood for a single moment longer. Only a second, but it could have been forever as I continued to look up. His blue eyes darkened. It was a perfect moment for a kiss, we both knew it. We both wanted it.

"We should join the others," Caleb said, and a rush of reasoning crashed into my irrational thoughts.

This was all a game. Damn. Why did I keep forgetting about our pact? "I'd like some water first."

Maybe he sensed the need to put a little distance between us as he was quick to respond. "I'll get it for you. Want to meet me at the table?"

We both moved to opposite sides of the room. My skin still tingled where his hands had touched me. My brain was in sensory overload, and I welcomed the distance.

Jake and Hope were in the midst of an argument when I arrived back at the table near the front of the room by the staging. I went to stand next to Caroline to watch, welcoming the distraction.

"Why won't you dance with me?" Hope whined.

"I've said this before," Jake scoffed. "You and your family tricked me into a marriage. I want nothing to do with you."

The leggy new bride grabbed at Jake, forcing him to stay and listen to her. "You've been trying to sleep with me all summer, but the moment we do, you abandon me like a cheap whore."

He pushed her arm away. "Well, maybe that's what you are."

I cringed at the harshness of Jake's words and tone, even if I thought the girl deserved it.

She swiped at the tears filling her eyes. "How can you be so hateful? You're the first man I ever slept with, but I know I'm not your first. How does that make me the whore?" Her voice began to get loud, and despite the music, she was drawing attention. She reached out to him again, desperate for a connection. "Do you do this to all your girlfriends? Sleep with them and then discard them like garbage?"

"You're making a scene." He pulled from her grasp and started to go, but she went after him, spinning him back around. That's when I spotted Leland making his way across the room toward them with a determined step and my immediate thought was to intervene.

Caroline grabbed my wrist. "Maybe you should stay out of this, Grace."

I shook my head as Hope's voice got louder. "Let's clear this up right now, Jake Wellington, you…"

"Hold on," he said, raising both hands in a stop position. "I am *not* a Wellington. I don't give a flying fuck about the your town rules; my name is Collings. I don't care what we did before the stupid ceremony, we have not consummated the marriage, and I have no intentions of doing so."

When Leland rushed to his sister's defense, I shook Caroline's hand away so I could move the few steps to be there for my friend, as the two men were already nose to nose. "You screwed my sister, you marry her.

End of story."

I tugged at Jake, feeling the anger trembling through his body. "Let it go before this escalates any further."

He was beyond caring. He brushed my hand away as his voice raised to a shout. "I don't care, nor do I consider myself married. I am not going to spend the rest of my life with this bitch."

That was all Leland needed to hear. He grabbed Jake with his good hand and shoved him back. Jake responded by doing the same. No one was dancing anymore, instead they circled around the two men. Watching. Waiting. But no one intervened. So I did.

"Stop." I cried out, trying to be heard above the music. Leland, one handed as he was, decided to head butt Jake, but at the same time I moved in front of my friend. Leland's head connected with my ribs, and I stumbled back into a table.

That's when Caleb arrived. "For Christ's sake." In a matter of seconds, he had Leland by his shirt in one hand and Jake by his in the other. "Quit *jaggin'* around. You all need to go home. Now. Without any more fights. Is that clear?"

Hope moved forward, sobbing. "It's all his fault." She pointed at her husband. "He called me a slut."

Caleb, still holding the two men rolled his eyes. "Seriously, Hope, you played the man like a fiddle with the intent to trap him in marriage. Can you blame him for being mad?" He looked back between the two seething men. "Brent was called away about ten minutes ago, so there doesn't have to be a report on this if you all just head home now."

He released the two men, watching to make sure

they stayed apart before he strode to me. "Are you okay?"

His voice was rough, and I couldn't tell if he was just frustrated at the fight of if he was somehow mad at me. I rubbed my side. "Other than these ribs taking another direct hit? Yeah. I'm good."

Straight and True finished their song, and the music didn't continue. Aaron spoke into the mike. "Is the night over, Chief?"

Caleb didn't look up, his narrowed eyes not leaving mine, but he raised his voice to answer the band's leader. "I'm officially on leave. I think things are resolved here, so I'll leave it up to you."

Aaron spun his finger to have the music continue. Caleb looked down at me. "Want to call it a night?"

I wasn't in the mood for dancing anymore. We exited the stuffy hall onto the sidewalk, and I spotted Leland walking away. Going the opposite direction was Jake while Hope huffed behind him.

I rubbed my side again, and eagle eyes was quick to notice. "Damn it. How bad?"

Wow. Second swear tonight from the straight-laced man of law. "I'm fine."

"What were you thinking jumping in between them?" he barked.

I didn't care for his tone, so I immediately went on the defensive. "Same thing you were, I believe. I was hoping to stop things before they got out of hand."

"They're twice your size. You stepping between them has the effect of spitting into the wind."

I picked up my pace in a sorry attempt to storm away, but not before I had what I hoped would be the last word. "Well, in a room full of pacifists, this little piece of spit, was the only one to do anything."

He took my arm and stopped me, but I refused to look at him. "You're right. I'm sorry."

Damn him. Why did he have to apologize? And use a tone that begged for forgiveness. I felt my anger dissipate.

"You keep rubbing your side. The same place where he kicked you."

It was and it hurt like the dickens but I didn't want him to make a fuss. I lowered my hand from my ribs and instead took Caleb's hand, hoping to distract him. "You're never off the job, are you? Quite the display of authority in there."

My change of subject didn't go unnoticed, but he went with it. "They both needed a swift kick in the ass, but it did the job."

"Guess Hope didn't quite get what she wanted." I noted. "Of course, neither did her brother, so I guess they're both a little pissed these days."

Caleb gave a little 'hmmm,' and I walked beside him back toward the apartment. I could still feel the tension emanating from him, so I continued my attempt at distraction. "You always come to my rescue, though. Thank you."

His paced slowed a bit to match mine. "I wish you would stop getting into trouble where you need to be rescued."

I shrugged, still holding his hand as we walked, while crickets chirped their goodnight song around us in the still night. "Tonight wasn't my fight. I was only trying to help."

Caleb grunted. "By standing between two men twice the size of you and their swinging fists? Hardly the best plan."

Back to this? "Well excuse me. So I don't have your brawn or strength. At least I tried." I released his hand and stomped away.

The moment we entered the apartment, Caleb turned on me. "Let me see your side."

I moved past him, flipping on the overhead light. We'd left the air conditioner running throughout the day so after the warmth of the summer night, the cool interior was welcome. "There's no need. I'll be fine."

"Grace, are you really going to fight me on this?"

I froze. I knew that voice. It was his, 'you can argue, but you won't win' attitude I remember from the early days of arriving in Wellington.

I slowly turned to face him only to find him leaning against the closed door, one eyebrow raised as he looked ready to advance.

I felt the hairs on my skin rise. "There is nothing to argue about. I said I'm fine, and that's the end of this conversation."

He pushed away from the door, and his move across the room was slow and deliberate. Part of me screamed to run, but the other part, the stubborn part, held ground. I lifted my chin to look up at him and put my hand out. He stopped when his chest met my palm.

Me stopping him? Unlikely.

"Lift your shirt, Grace."

Adrenaline pumped swiftly through my body. I hadn't seen this side of Caleb in a while. "You're making this a bigger deal than it has to be."

He took another step forward forcing me to step back. He took two, I took two, my hand never leaving his chest. "Caleb."

He had the upper hand, and he knew it. Larger. Stronger. But my fight or flight instinct—or my plain stupidity, who knows—kept me glaring at him. The glint in his eyes spoke volumes. I took it to mean he enjoyed this cat and mouse game.

The arm I held out only kept the distance between us because he allowed it. He took another step, and I moved back, this time coming in contact with the wall behind me.

I gulped.

"What will you do now, Grace?" He stood his ground. "Who is actually making this a bigger deal?"

I struggled to find reason in the face of his impenetrable stance. "It's my body. I decide…"

"Not when your health is concerned."

My temper flared. "No. That is exactly when it is my decision. That's what started everything bad about this place. No man. No doctor. No bloody town. No one but me gets to decide. If I say you are not going to see my side, then you need to respect my decision."

"You're my wife."

I was about to go over the deep end. Way over. I didn't yell, though. My words were slow and deliberate. "Stop right there. Don't even think of pulling the husband card. We are *not* married. Not in the proper sense of things, and you have no rights over me."

I saw a slight bending in Caleb's stance. His eyes, which continued to bore into mine, went from steel to a flash of something else. Pain? Compassion? I still didn't know this man enough to read him.

"Fine." He took a single step back, and I slowly lowered my hand. Had I actually won this battle? "I know what happened with Dr. Todd on your first day here scarred you. I won't repeat the same mistake. However, I will ask you to tell me the truth, at least. Do you have any broken ribs?"

I had won. He was capitulating to me. I had to take a moment to recollect myself before answering. "Tonight was nothing compared to last week, and you already determined on that night I was fine."

"Any pain when breathing?" he continued.

"No. Jeesh, Caleb, he just head-butted me where I was already bruised."

His eyes darkened again, and when his jaw tightened, I knew I'd revealed more than I should have. My mouth dried.

"You never told me about the bruising." He sounded sad at my revelation.

"Ah, well, we've been a bit preoccupied with being forced to marry, moving into an apartment, and then playing out our plan for redemption with the elders of this freaking town."

He ran a hand over his head and while I knew he was completely frustrated with me, his eyes kept going back to my side and there was no denying his worry. "Really, Caleb, it's not a big deal. Nothing appears to be broken. I've gone an entire week without any complications. The bruising is part of the healing process." He remained silent, and it was my weakness. "Oh, for goodness sake. Fine. Look."

Chapter Seven

I pulled up the side of my shirt, revealing the hues of purple, blues, and greens. "It's healing."

Caleb's eyes closed for a second before he fell to his knees on the floor before me and gently placed a hand on my bare skin. I sucked in my breath with an audible sound.

His hand snapped back. "Did I hurt you?"

"No." My voice was little more than a whisper. "You startled me."

And surprised me with the level of compassion. His hand hovered again at my rib cage, and his eyes asked for permission. This time I nodded. His fingers first traced the outline of the bruise before he pressed his thumb down and checked, like he had the week before, that nothing was jutting out.

"Promise me that if you have any difficulty breathing, you will tell me." He looked up at me, and I melted at the sea of emotion I saw in his eyes. Sadness and even a hint of vulnerability. "I don't care how much you hate our doctor here, I need your promise."

I gulped. Damn him. He knew the last thing I wanted was another trip to the clinic; knew I'd endure any amount of pain to avoid it. But he cared. He truly cared if something happened to me. I slowly nodded, but when he raised his eyebrow, I knew he needed to hear the words.

"I promise, Caleb." I tentatively reached out to cup his face in my palm. "I also meant what I said. I'm fine. It's tender, but there's no need to worry."

"I don't like to see you hurt." Then he leaned forward and kissed my bruise. Both the admission and the kind gesture rocked me to my core, and I leaned back against the wall as I tried to comprehend what was happening.

Gone was the fierce, over-protective police chief determined to have things done his way. The man on his knees, brushing his lips and fingers across the rain-bowed skin to soothe away my aches and pains was a man I could fall for if given the right circumstance.

When he stood, his hand stayed on my bare skin, but the rest of his body brushed up against mine, pressing me, albeit lightly, against the wall. "Thank you."

I stared up at him, at his blue eyes, dark with an emotion I couldn't understand. "For what?" My voice was as soft as his. I didn't know how to take this moment. First, he'd been mad, then determined. Then he'd been amazingly gentle and sad. Now his apology had my head spinning.

"For allowing me to see that you are okay."

The cracks in my defenses splintered. I'd been so completely wrong about him. He wasn't a stone wall. He was a river, weaving around my heart and sending me rapidly toward a waterfall.

"I really am okay." I placed my hand on his at my waist where his thumb continued to rub gently sending spirals of sensation through my body, making it hard to get more than a few words out at a time.

Caleb gazed down at me, his eyes deep and dark

with emotion I didn't recognize. "Grace, I really want to kiss you now. Please?"

Oh, dear God in heaven. This man was asking permission? He wanted to kiss me? *Okay. Yes. Yes.* My brain screamed the answer, but I couldn't respond. It seemed I was doing that a lot lately. Losing my ability to talk. "Mm hmm."

"Say yes." It was an order, but also a plea and I tried to swallow around my dry mouth.

"Yes."

His mouth captured mine. Gentle at first. Tasting. Exploring. Sending sweet sensations throughout. I was aware of every place his body touched mine. His left side from shoulder to toe pressed against my right, while his right hand still pressed gently against my bare skin under my shirt. My hand moved from his to roam up his biceps, across his shoulder, until I reached his firm chin. I leaned in more, silently asking for him to deepen the kiss.

It was all he needed. His hand moved to my back, pulling me closer as he pressed against me. His tongue plundered deep, and I answered its call to action. This wasn't our first kiss, but this was the first where we didn't hold back. This was more than the mere attraction we'd been courting for weeks. We'd moved along to an almost desperate need.

I was panting by the time his lips moved to my neck, and I threw my head back to give him access to my throat. His hands roamed my skin beneath my shirt until he reached my bra. With a quick twist, he released the hooks. Seconds later, he was back on his knees, my shirt pulled up, and his warm mouth attached itself to a nipple.

I moaned. My hands curled into his hair, as every erogenous zone zapped to life. I didn't know how much longer I could stand, so I pressed against the wall as his mouth licked, then sucked while his fingers prepared the other nipple for the oncoming onslaught.

When was the last time I'd let myself succumb to these feelings? I'd lost my virginity to my boyfriend in high school, and he'd broken my heart. I'd taken things slow with the guy at college, and he would have raped me if my friend hadn't intervened.

Deep down, I knew Caleb wasn't like either of them. Yes, I found him attractive. Yes, I'd been having lustful feelings toward him for weeks, looking for any opportunity to see him. Five minutes ago, I was mad as hell at his overbearing nature, but when he'd dropped to his knees, my anger had dropped away with him.

When he stood again to capture my mouth, I nearly lunged forward to meet him. I needed this tonight. I needed to feel something other than fear and anger and resentment that had been keeping me going for the past two months.

He didn't meet me with the same intensity. Instead he pulled just far enough away to place a kiss on my forehead. "As much as I want you, we can't do this."

His words stung me like a thousand bee stings. Why was he doing this to me? Why had I allowed myself to feel anything for him? I couldn't help the sudden onset of tears that welled in my eyes.

"Shh. No. Don't cry." He kissed the wetness on my cheek. "I'm sorry." In a swift movement, he swung me into his arms and carried me into the bedroom and somehow managed to pull the covers down before placing me in the center of the bed. "I didn't mean to make you cry."

As he went to pull away, I reached out and grabbed his hand. "Don't go, Caleb."

The enormity of my words hit me. I didn't want to be alone. I didn't want him to leave. I didn't want to fight my feelings any longer. We may have only been married, so to speak, for one week, but the past months had weighed me down and those few moments in the living room had almost made me forget everything else.

His fingers tightened around mine. "What are you asking for, Grace?"

I scrambled to my knees and took his other hand in mine as well, as I looked up into the depths of his blue eyes. "Stay with me. Make me forget what's outside these doors. Kiss me again and take all this craziness away. Please."

When he closed his eyes, I thought he was going to refuse. But when they opened again, he couldn't hide the desire in the dark depths, or in the huskiness of his voice.

"From the moment I met you, I've been trying like hell to not want you, but as much as you frustrate me, you also make me laugh." He squeezed my hands, and I wondered where this was going. "Every day since your arrival, I have marveled at your spark, at your energy, but I've also seen the sadness in those gorgeous brown eyes. Every instinct in my body is urging me to do whatever I can to erase those tears."

"Then stay with me," I pleaded. "I just need this one night. When you touch me and kiss me, there is a part of me that feels there is at least one thing right in this messed up summer internship. I need you, Caleb. I need the feelings you stir up in me."

"God help me." He ground out before capturing my mouth while he moved to kneel on the edge of the bed with me. The tears that rolled down my cheek now weren't from sadness. Relief? Maybe. All I know was I couldn't get enough.

He pulled my shirt and bra up over my head to throw them on a heap on the floor while I struggled to get the buttons of his shirt to cooperate with my hasty fingers. With each button released, I pushed the fabric aside to kiss his skin until I stopped caring and finally yanked the remaining fabric aside, the final few buttons flinging across the bed.

I'd admired his muscles from afar, but up close? I ran my fingers across his body, marveling at the ripples and ridges of perfect pecs and abs.

"Lay back," he ordered.

I did, lying across the bed diagonally, as Caleb worked the buttons of my shorts before pulling them and my panties down in one smooth motion, taking my shoes off at the same time. While we'd never turned the bedroom lights on, the light from the living room streamed in, giving me more than enough light to see how his gaze traveled my exposed body. The blue in his eyes darkened causing my body to melt like an ice cream cone under the sweltering heat of the sun.

He turned from me, sitting on the edge of the bed to quickly remove his boots. My brain told me to move, to take that time to press against his back, to kiss his neck, to wrap my arms around him. But I stayed and a moment later, he joined me, both of us lying sideways across the expanse of the bed. He still wore his jeans, the denim rough against my legs while his bare chest slid tauntingly against my rigid nipples as he claimed my mouth in another kiss.

I couldn't let him have all the fun. My hands went around him, touching and learning the contours of his body. From his back, around his sides, and between our bodies. I skimmed my fingers up his chest until I found his nipples and I let my thumbs replay what his had done to mine earlier, eliciting a deep moan from him.

Between the tangle of our legs, I felt his arousal pressing against his zipper. I shifted, bucked up, asked for more. Caleb answered by moving against me, his lower body gyrating in the most intimate way possible, and I felt the moisture pool at my apex.

We continued our movements as our mouths and hands set each other on fire. It had to be a hundred degrees in the room, despite the central air working furiously in the summer heat.

My hands went to his waistline, unbuttoning his pants. His hands stopped me. "Not yet." The air conditioner cycled on sending a blast of cool air over my heated body. I wanted to curl into Caleb, instead he leaned back. With gentle fingers, he turned my chin so our gazes met. "You're beautiful, Grace. I want you more than you know. I've wanted you for some time. This summer isn't what you expected, I know that. It's not what I'd planned either. So if I can help you forget everything about this place that makes you sad and replace it with something better, even for a night, I'd like to do that for you. Do you trust me?"

Did I? I desired him. I was attracted to him. I wanted him to finish what he'd started. But trust? Caleb was a good man. He'd shown that time and again. I'm not sure why he was asking, but deep down, I knew I could answer truthfully.

"Yes, I trust you."

He pushed back and stood at the side of the bed, and my heart cried out thinking he was leaving me. Then he lifted one leg, sliding his hand down my calf, then under my heel, lifting it to place a sweet, tender kiss along my arch. Placing my legs over his shoulders, his lips trailed a path of meteor showers as he moved inward. I was lost, gone in another atmosphere.

I'd asked for this. The past eight weeks disappeared as I escaped into this world of sensation, of hope, of one night of passion. The future was bleak, and not something I wanted to think of. Caleb was here. Caleb was now.

And Caleb was as sad and twisted up inside as I, forced into a situation neither of us had ever expected. Maybe this night had been inevitable, marriage or not.

As though he could read my thoughts, he stopped long enough to say those two words again. "Trust me." Then he buried his face at my center.

I sucked in my breath as his tongue darted inside. My entire body reacted, every nerve jumped to attention. Tension coiled in my stomach as he continued. My hands gripped at the cool cotton bedsheets, as his tongue swirled and plundered.

"Caleb," I gasped his name. One word. I couldn't think enough to put more than that together. My body pulsed where his lips touched.

While I continued to pant, his mouth worked its way up my body, but he wasn't done with me. His fingers took over where his tongue had been moments ago. "Let it happen, sweetheart," he murmured before his lips captured mine.

I groaned into his mouth that tasted of sex. Yes, I

needed this. I needed the rest of the world to disappear. I needed to feel nothing more than what he was doing to my body. I closed my eyes and forgot about everything except the here and now. My fingers pressed into his shoulders. His lips left mine to trail a fiery path along my neck.

My hips lifted to meet the rhythm his fingers made inside me, tantalizing me, pushing me, until the orgasm hit me hard and I cried out.

It took a moment before my heart rate slowed enough for me to open my eyes and become aware of my surroundings again. We were in the bedroom, not on some higher universe that Caleb had sent me to. My body was still shaky as was the smile I sent his way.

"Hi, there." Those two words he uttered came with a satisfied grin, as though he knew I'd traveled to another world at his behest, and had just returned.

"Mmm. I'm back." That had him chuckling as he shifted, moving to my side, and I felt the scrape of denim against my bare legs and I realized I'd been the only one on the trip around the world. I reached between us to work at the zipper, to free him, to touch him.

"No, Grace."

"But…"

His hand closed over mine. "This was for you."

Trust me, he'd said. Now I understood. He'd made a promise to get me home, and this was not part of the agreement. Part of me though, the part still basking in an afterglow, felt I should reciprocate. I moved my hand from the waistband of his clothes, up his bare chest, taking a moment to explore. My finger brushed across his nipple and he gulped. While he said no, for my sake, he was not immune. My hand drifted downward, cupping at the hardness behind his zipper.

"Grace." It was a warning. A plea. But instead of pushing me away, his hand went to the back of my head to pull me closer. He spoke to me with his mouth, telling me how much he wanted me. How much he needed me. But as he pulled away, he was also telling me he wasn't going to take it any further.

I didn't want to think anymore, didn't want to discuss anything. I wanted to spend the night in this man's arms, doing the very thing he'd promised not to do. I pressed my lips to his corded neck.

He didn't push me away, and I continued my exploration down his collarbone as Caleb's tone remained tight as he spoke. "Let's face it, Grace, once we cross this line, I won't want to stop. It won't, it can't be, a one and done between us."

His words dove into my heart. A part of me knew he was right, but what he'd done to my body with his mouth and fingers had left me wanting more, not only for me. I wanted to give, too. I moved down to pull his nipple into my mouth.

"You aren't making this easy." I heard his words, but he didn't stop me.

"But am I making it hard?" I ran my hand down past his stomach and pressed it to the bulge. "Yep."

He growled and again took charge. He swung me around to my back, pressing my hands against the bed. His voice was husky, but stern. "Don't you get it? There is no birth control here, Grace. That's why we had to throw away your pills when you arrived. I made you a promise to get you home to Vermont, but if we don't stop now—and God Almighty knows I am struggling to not sink myself inside you and forget that I'm a man of my word—there is always a possibility of getting you pregnant."

I sucked in a breath. He was right. Roger had made it clear that a child would tie me to Wellington. There would be no going home after that. It was the whole point of this summer internship and then our shot-gun wedding. The town council was betting on the natural course of events of our forced cohabitation.

I sunk back onto the bed and closed my eyes. What did that make me? Damn, I was a fool, letting my emotions get the best of me. The past eight weeks had been a roller coaster ride of ups and downs. Hating this place. Accepting I had to work out my contract. Watching my college roommate marry the man of her dreams. Lusting after the man who'd been sworn to protect me, but also under orders to make sure I didn't leave. Getting a promise that I could go home, and then forced to marry so I'd have to stay.

"Damn it, Grace," Caleb's voice softened as did his grip on my wrists. "This isn't how I pictured tonight. Come here." He gathered me to him so that my head rested on his shoulder while he wrapped the sheet over us. "Under other circumstances—" He kissed my forehead. "Ahh, forget it. It doesn't matter. Go to sleep."

I lay against him. What the hell had happened? First, I'd made it clear that I made my own decisions and he wasn't to touch me, but then, with one simple please, and an innocent touch to my bruise, I'd agreed to let him kiss me.

One kiss—albeit it was one hell of a kiss—and I'd forgotten my entire reason for staying strong. That one kiss had broken down my protective walls and opened me up like a cracked egg.

He'd asked me to trust him, then he'd proven, in no uncertain terms, that he was a man of his word.

Did he have to be so freaking caring and protective and moralistic? If he hadn't been so determined to keep his promise, where would that have put us? Because, obviously I wasn't thinking clearly anymore.

Chapter Eight

I woke wrapped in Caleb's arms, my head nestled in the crook of his shoulder. I took my time opening my eyes, wanting to prolong the inevitable start of the day. Everything had changed, and I wasn't sure what lay before us.

When he shifted, I knew he was awake, waiting for me. The time had come. I lifted my gaze to meet his and saw one of his rare smiles. My heart did a flip flop.

"Good morning."

I brushed my hair away from my cheek, trying not to think about what the deep timbre of his voice did to my insides. "Morning."

My hand was on his chest, and in a moment of shyness, I fought the urge to run a finger across the sculpted work of art. Instead I remained still, noticing how pale my hand was against the rich tan of his skin. "Did you sleep well?"

Loaded question. I wasn't about to tell him the truth. It had taken me forever to fall asleep, wondering what this latest turn of events would mean for our relationship. However, sleeping beside him had felt wonderful. I'd go with that as my answer. "Um, yeah. And you?"

He scrunched his nose. "It was difficult over your very unladylike snoring."

Shy no more, I thudded his chest. "I don't snore.

What a horrible thing to say."

Caleb grinned, and my heart did a quick pitter patter at his carefree manner. This was definitely a new side to this man, and I kinda liked it. "Okay, you don't snore, but you do talk in your sleep."

I froze for a moment and twisted up to lay more on his chest trying to ignore how my nipples puckered as they brushed against his skin. "What did I say?"

He let out a rumbling chuckle and this time, I couldn't ignore how my pulse quickened. "Ah, that she doesn't deny. I will have to pay close attention in the future."

"Oh, you…" I went to swat him again, but he grabbed my wrist and brought it to his mouth to kiss it, and my mouth went completely dry. Things could go from fun to serious in a nano-second, and I was already naked; already half way to wanting to pick up where things left off. The dark flecks in Caleb's blue eyes echoed my own wayward thoughts.

He'd made it clear last night we couldn't go down this road, so I did the only thing I could think of to change the course of direction. "If you want to shower first, I'll make us breakfast."

With a blink of an eye, he was back to the casual, fun man of a few moments ago. "Deal."

As I rolled off him and sat, holding the sheet to my chest, He swung his denim clad legs to the edge and stood. He opened his bureau drawer, retrieved clothes, and gave me a heated look before exiting. He knew I'd been watching, and he didn't care.

I pressed my hands to my flushed cheeks. What the hell had I done? Had we done?

Gave in to attraction? Sure. Had a mind-blowing

orgasm? Absolutely, and it was worth it. Oh, my, it was worth it.

If I didn't get up this moment, I would never get out of bed. I moved quickly, donning a tee and shorts and headed to the kitchen. It was a pancakes and sausage type of morning, and I had the batter mixed and ready by the time he joined me.

He took over with the sausage, and we moved through the kitchen like a well-practiced duo. Before we sat, the phone rang and Caleb answered it. "It's Aaron. He wants to know if we're up for baseball later today."

Up for it? Hell, yeah. I needed something active to occupy my mind and whacking a ball across the field was just the right distraction. "Sounds good."

He put a hand over the mouthpiece of the phone. "Are you sure? What about your ribs?"

I didn't know whether to be mad or just completely frustrated with the man's obsession with my bruised side, so my tone may have been a bit on the curt side. "Tell Aaron we're playing the damn game." I'm pretty sure I made my point when I noticed Caleb's lip curl up in his amused smile.

Once breakfast was over and dishes washed and put in the strainer to dry, I headed to take my own shower while Caleb made calls to get his side of the team together, but when I returned the call he was on sounded serious.

I hovered by the table, not sure if I should be eavesdropping or not. He turned to me when he hung up the phone. "That," he motioned with his head, "was Frank. We have been summoned to choose our wedding bands by Monday morning."

I looked at him. "Or what?"

"Or he puts in the order on our behalf."

I wrung my hands and nodded before turning to the kitchen, looking for something, anything to change my focus. I found the bottle of cleaning chemical under the sink and sprayed the already spotless stove top, and got to work scrubbing at non-existent grease.

"This doesn't change anything."

What did he mean by 'this?' Putting a ring on my finger? That doesn't change our plan to pretend to get along. No, that's pretty much in line. 'This,' meaning what we did last night? That actually changed a lot. At least for me. I played along. "No. You're right."

Caleb took a few steps in the tiny apartment and was at my side in a flash. "Grace, last night…"

I continued at my task, avoiding him, not wanting to see him if he was going to say it was a mistake. With a gentle touch, he stopped my useless fiddling. Once I put down the sponge, he turned me so he could lift my chin and I looked up into his amazing, confident eyes. "I don't regret a moment of what we did last night, and I hope you don't either."

Oh, thank God. Hoping he couldn't see or feel the trembling of doubts that had started. I pushed my nails brutally into my palm and instead shook my head.

"No? Good." He leaned down and tore my breath away with his mouth. "Good," he said again when he finally released me.

The man confused the hell out of me. I didn't know what to say. What to do. What I wanted to do was return the kiss and explore the emotions he'd surged inside me the night before. But he'd made it clear we couldn't walk that path. Instead I ducked around him and walked to the living room, getting the space I needed to breathe, but his next question stopped me. "So, now that we are technically married, you are planning on playing on my team today, right?"

Back to the game. The topic change had my head spinning, but I threw him a grin over my shoulder. "If you think a little ceremony changes anything, you're mistaken. You, sir, are going down."

****

Baseball, my passion. My solace. The activity focused my brain and kept me from over thinking this past week. Both teams played well, and we were an even four to four going into the seventh inning.

I was first at bat, and I ran from the field to the dugout to grab my helmet and bat as the teams changed positions. I was focused and didn't see Caleb come up behind me.

"Whoa." I nearly lost my balance as he spun me around, took my face in his hands and planted a long, deep kiss, curling my toes and rocking me back on my heels.

"That's for luck," he murmured before bending to grab his mitt he'd dropped on the ground and headed out to first base.

"Oh." I walked to home plate, head reeling from the unexpected, totally hot kiss, and swung at the first throw. When the third strike was called, I glanced and spotted Caleb with a shit-eating grin. I got it. The 'for luck' was for his benefit. Game on.

I headed toward the ice buckets of water. No amount cold liquid would quench the thirst that man had started in me, but he'd started a game, and I wasn't about to back down. I turned my attention to my team captain, watching me with a raised eyebrow.

"That kiss?" I mentioned as I lifted my cup. "Was a distraction. It won't work again."

"Really?" Aaron was amused by the whole thing; must be because he was happily married and liked to see things for more than what they were.

I pulled my ball cap back on, pulling the rim down to lower the bright glare of the sun. "How can we turn the tables? Make him lose focus?"

He snorted. "Have you met Caleb? He's a robot. It's not going to happen."

I pursed my lips and sat down to watch the game. Somehow, someway, I would get the better of him. I spotted the pad of paper and pen Aaron had been using to plan the batting order and began to scribble.

Caleb, I can't stop thinking about last night. It was amazing. How about we up the ante on the game? If my team wins, we have a replay of last night. If your team wins, I get to do similar things to you. How ya gonna play it?

I folded the paper in half then half again, scribbled his name on it, then asked Pete to deliver the note at the inning change.

I was already at second base, glove in hand, when the note exchange took place. I watched as Caleb read it then his head slowly raised to stare at me across the field. Dry lightning could have flashed in the afternoon sky, and it wouldn't have been as hot as that look. He slowly folded the paper and pocketed it. This time I was the one who grinned.

I had to wait for four players before Caleb came to bat. He waited two steps back from the plate as he did a practice swing and took another moment to glance my way. I blew him a kiss and even from my position I saw his eyes close.

The first pitch was called a strike. The second a foul, the third another foul. I couldn't resist. "What's going on, Caleb? Your mojo seems a little off."

Instead of distracting him, he gripped the bat and the next was a solid hit into outfield, but the pop up was caught, and he sent me a salute before heading back to his dugout.

Eighth inning both teams earned another run, and Caleb made his way to me as he came off the field. "Hope you're ready to keep your promise, sweetheart."

I pretended his deep tone didn't turn my insides to liquid—not an easy feat to do. Instead I patted his chest. "Game's not over. Too soon to determine the winner."

He leaned down and whispered in my ear. "Either outcome, I win."

Well, hell in a hand basket. I was way out of my league with this man. It was the top of the ninth with an even score. I was still a bit off my game when I came up to bat next, but I was determined to show that he couldn't put me off balance so easy.

I was ready. Focused as much as I could be. The ball left the pitcher's hand and I swung—at the same moment that a little girl screamed from the bleachers. "Justin, you little turd. Look what you did."

Like any good father who hears the shrieking of his child, Caleb looked away. The bat hit the ball and made a line drive to first base. Caleb never saw the ball coming.

It hit his shoulder, spinning him around and down to the ground.

I dropped the bat and sprinted down the base line

to kneel beside him, taking his ball cap off so I could see his face. "Oh, my God. I am so sorry. Are you hurt? How bad?"

Other players surrounded us as Caleb rubbed his shoulder, grimacing in pain. "I think it's dislocated."

I put my hands over my mouth. "That sounds painful. Can you put it back in place? They do it all the time in the movies."

With an unexpected move, he grabbed me by the shirt front with his good hand and swung me around to sit on his lap. "This is your fault. You planned this."

I huffed at his sudden attack, not quite sure how to take him. "How am I to blame? It's not my fault you were distracted."

He looked up at Aaron, now standing beside us. "She planned this. I can prove it. I think the game should go to the blue team on a technicality."

The pitcher shook his head, put his hands up in surrender. "I'm not touching this. It's between you."

"How did I plan this?" I asked, staring up into Caleb's laughing eyes.

He cocked his head to his side as he spoke. "I specifically remember the words, 'you are going down' coming out of your mouth this morning."

I giggled as I finally knew he wasn't mad. "Uh, yeah. I do believe I did."

Then his lips were on mine. His kiss would have knocked me off my feet with its lightning bolt intensity had I been standing. Perhaps the foreplay on the field, or the note, was the cause, but I grabbed his shirt and hung tight as my world spun out of control.

"Newlyweds. Jeez."

"Get a room."

"Player down." One of the umps called out. "Time to call the game. Tied in the ninth."

"Daddy."

The kiss ended, but Caleb held me in place as we both looked up at his oldest daughter who stood at our side, hands perched on her hips. "Hey there, princess."

How his voice could sound normal after a kiss of that magnitude, I don't understand. I was still reeling.

"Your *son* is annoying everyone."

I spotted the quick tip of Caleb's lips. "I'm sorry to hear it. What is *your* brother doing?"

Elena gave a deep dramatic sigh. "He won't sit still. He climbed on everything, making noises like a tractor. Then, he had the baby doing the same."

"Boys do like to move around." He shook his head in mock agreement.

"All I wanted was for him to sit still and color. Instead he got louder and then he spilled Shawna's juice all over us."

"Ahh. That explains the yelling."

The child continued the oblivious to her father's mirth. "So *Grammaw* took the two of them home to change before we go to Aunt Karen's house for supper. I told her I would wait for you."

Caleb gave her a serious look, but the humor was still in his eyes. "Then, I guess we should get going. Why don't you grab my water bottle and I'll meet you at the dugout?"

The young girl gave another sigh before stomping off. Then Caleb gave me a casual, almost distant smile. "I think that's enough of a show, don't you?" he said and in a swift move had me off his lap.

Chapter Nine

I sucked in my breath. Of course. Today had all
been a show. How could I forget? Why did I think last
night had changed things between us?

Last night I had asked him to stay. I'd practically
begged him to make love to me. He said he wouldn't
because I could get pregnant. Neither one of us wanted
this marriage. What if there was another reason he
wanted me gone? What if Caleb was still in love with
his first wife? Maybe he didn't want a replacement, or
more kids?

Not that I was looking to have any of that, either,
but in the heat of the moment, I wasn't thinking about
the false front we were putting on for the townsfolk.
Maybe cool, always controlled, Caleb never forgot the
end game.

I walked to the dugout for my glove and water
bottle and then took my time to join Caleb and his
daughter at the bleachers where he spoke with Aaron.

"Pull it straight up," he instructed as his cousin
lifted his arm at a ninety degree angle. I heard it pop
into place, and my stomach twisted at the sound.

"Oh, God." I quickly sunk to the bleacher grasping
my waist, silently begging my insides not to hurl.

"Grace?" Caleb immediately bent to his knees in
front of me. "What's wrong?"

I held my hand up, not able to talk yet. I breathed

through the nausea.

"Grace?" I heard the urgency in his voice, but it still took me another minute before I could lift my head.

"Sorry. The sound... It... Ugh." I struggled for words. "Reminded me of what happened with Leland. Guess I'm not good with broken bones." I got my composure back as I took another steadying breath.

"It's not broken," he assured me. "See? Good as new." He moved his arm around to show me.

He was right, it wasn't broken and seemed to be back in working order. I needed to get myself back under control, emotionally and physically, so I rushed to reassure him I was fine.

"Okay. I'm good." I went to stand, and he took both of my hands, maybe to make sure I was actually steady on my feet, but I was still mad at him, so I pulled away. "I've got it."

His raised eyebrow let me know he caught the curtness in my tone, but before he could ask, Elena tugged at his shirt. "Daddy, are we leaving yet?"

I responded for him, trying to keep my frustrations at bay for the sake of the child. "Yes, we're leaving." I turned to her father. "I'm going to head back to the apartment and clean up. Plus, I want to get a dish ready for the meal tomorrow."

Caleb stood, his hand on his daughter's head, stroking her long blonde hair, but his attention was still all on me. "Are you sure you're okay?"

I gave what I hoped was a 'do you really need to keep asking?' look and he bought it because he turned his attention back to Elena. "Let's get you home and fed. Want a piggy back?"

I gave a pointed look to his shoulder, but he didn't

even flinch when his daughter stepped onto the bleacher, flinging herself onto his back, her arms hugging his neck.

"Come join us when you're ready," he instructed then pressed a quick kiss to my lips before heading off with his daughter, talking to her as they left. "So today was a tough day to be a big sister, huh?"

"You have no idea," the young girl agreed.

I took a swig of water as I walked back to the apartment. What the hell was I doing? I let myself get too close. I let my emotions get in the way of the mission to escape. I let my attraction for that man cloud my judgment.

Caleb had children here. A family. He claimed he wanted to help me leave, but why would he? He wouldn't do anything that would jeopardize being with his kids. I should have seen it before. Pretending to get along had to be a game; a way to get me to believe the result would be to help me to escape, but what if it wasn't? What if it was to have me fall for him so I wouldn't want to leave?

And last night, I'd been the one to beg him to stay with me. He could have had sex with me, and I wouldn't have said no. Why didn't he? By not consummating the marriage, was that part of his ploy to prove he was trustworthy? So I'd continue to believe he'd help me leave? If so, it had worked. I berated myself all the way back to the apartment wanting nothing more than to wash the day away.

I'd just stepped from the shower when I heard knocking on the apartment door. "Who is it?" I yelled from the bathroom door.

"Jake."

I wrapped a towel around my body, another around my hair, and strode across the small apartment to let him in. He barely looked at me as he stormed into the room. "Is he here?"

I closed the door and waved my hand. "Caleb? No, he's with his kids."

"Good," he muttered before turning on me. "You slept with him, didn't you?"

My jaw dropped at the unexpected inquisition. I sincerely prayed my face didn't become a beacon of truth. "What? Why would you say that?"

Jake came to stand in front of me, staring down from his taller height. There were times I hated being short. This was one of them. "I saw you today. You and *him*." He spat the word 'him' like it was poison. "The two of you were on each other like white on rice."

Feeling vulnerable, I clutched the towel closer against my middle. "What you saw was nothing more than a show." The words tasted bitter on my tongue. "I told you before, we need to convince everyone we're together so Roger will lower the security on our tracking back to at least a normal level. Until then, getting out of here will be impossible."

He shook his head as I spoke. "I've slept with enough girls to know the difference between the looks and exchanges a couple gives off before they've had sex and after. Today was definitely an *after*-sex day."

He put his hands on my shoulders and pulled me into a fierce hug. "Don't get involved with him, Grace. He's the reason we are here in the first place."

It was a plea, but there was something more in his tone. I was pressed against Jake, but my hands still clutched the damp towel. When he pushed the other towel off my hair and leaned down to kiss the top of my head, I froze in place.

Why did I feel like I was cheating? This was Jake. *Jake.* I'd known him forever. We were friends. Besides, Caleb had made it clear that what had happened last night was nothing more than a perk for pretending to accept our marriage.

Jake's hands burned on my bare shoulders. Why did this feel so wrong? He'd been in my dorm room plenty of times when I'd showered, coming back into the room in nothing more than a towel or tee shirt, scrambling for clothes. He'd seen me in my bikini, which probably revealed more than this. We were usually so comfortable with each other.

"You have to stay away from him," he pleaded, his mouth still pressing down onto my head.

"Jake, I…" I bit my lip, stopping myself. "Let me get dressed, then we can talk."

He followed me to the bedroom and stood outside the closed door as I changed. "He's trouble, Grace. You need to stop this thing, whatever it is between you. You know he's manipulating you."

I looked in the mirror as I pressed my hands against the bureau top. Was he right? My own doubts still echoed in my head, but a part of me wanted to believe last night meant more to Caleb, as much as it meant to me. The other part, the one still reeling from his cold words on the baseball field, had Jake's words swirling in the forefront.

Why had I allowed myself to fall for Caleb? Was I a sucker for a good-looking man with moody blue eyes and killer abs?

I think that's enough of a show, don't you?

Yes, we'd put on quite the show today. No one would question our relationship. No one outside of these doors. But I couldn't do it again. I can't let my heart get involved.

I dropped the towel on the floor, grabbed whatever clothes I found, and used my fingers to comb my hair. Last night was a mistake. Today was nothing more than a convincing act for the public.

I opened the door, brushing by my friend. "I'm telling you, what you saw today was a farce." My words were as much to convince myself as anyone else. "Caleb is the one who is going to help us escape. Don't alienate him."

"Is that why you slept with him? So he'll help?"

The words felt like ice. I whipped around and gave him a solid push, forcing him back a step. "You know me better than that. I don't use people."

Jake put his hands up in surrender then turned to pace around the room. "Yeah. I know. But this place—"

I knew where he was going and let out a defeated sigh. "It's like a ball of contradictions?"

"Exactly." He continued to pace, making a figure eight around the furniture. "On the outside it appears completely normal. Okay, maybe nineteen sixties All-American-apple-pie-wholesome normal."

"Until you get inside and see the absolute control they have over all the residents," I said. "Where tracking everyone is termed safety and security measures. Monitoring your sex life disguised as a need to keep their legacy alive for future generations."

"That's what I mean." He grabbed my hand and squeezed. "But forcing marriage on someone because of a sexual indiscretion is absurd."

"It is old-fashioned," I admitted.

He rolled his eyes. "Completely. Yes, I had sex with Hope, but who the hell doesn't have unmarried sex these days?"

I let me hand slip from his as he went back to his anxious pacing. "You said it yourself, Wellington is stuck in a less progressive time."

He didn't stop his tirade there. "Sure, but you were stuck in the woods with the chief and nothing happened at all, except keeping safe and they forced you two to marry because you were alone all night. That's not nineteen-sixty, that's eighteen hundreds' mentality."

I needed to keep busy, so I headed to the kitchen. I'd planned on making a peach cobbler to bring to the fellowship meal, so I grabbed all the ingredients and lay them on the counter.

"Roger drove the bus on my marriage," I said. "It was payback for me rejecting Leland, and for Caleb breaking his arm."

"It doesn't matter who forced the marriage." He finally moved to sit in a chair at the counter separating the living room and kitchen areas and leaned dejectedly onto one hand. "You can't forget it has been the police chief taking charge of keeping us here."

"Well, technically, yeah, but he was under direct orders from the council. Did you know we are the first group of college students to be bussed in? In the past, they've basically gone and searched out runaways looking for a safe haven."

"See what I mean," he huffed. "Lover boy was a part of it all."

My chest tightened at the term. "Please don't call him that. Like I said before, it was Roger's doing." As mad as I was at Caleb, I felt an intense need to defend him. "Roger wanted a better class of people to marry his children to. He figured runaways would have too much baggage or be drug addicts. Plus, by recruiting at the colleges, they hoped to bring in several people at once, not one at a time."

"So they lied about a work program to get us here? They never had any intention to let us go?"

"They were relying more on everyone loving Wellington so much they wouldn't want to leave," I explained. "And for the most part, they're right." I waved my spatula in the air. "Have you seen the others who came with us? The one's I've spoken to are awestruck. I mean, what college student wouldn't want to move to a place where everything they wanted was handed to them.

"Sure, they work," I slid the cobbler into the oven as I spoke. "But they walk into the diner and swipe their wrist band and, voilà, food appears. No money changes hands. Want to go to a movie? Bowling? Just a swipe of the arm as you enter. It's easy."

With the dessert cooking, I couldn't sit still, so I grabbed the bananas and started on bread. I got why my parents cooked. It was soothing; combining ingredients; following instructions; having a finished product to share with others. Focusing on the steps helped distract me from what was happening in my life outside of the kitchen. Or would, if Mr.-Regret-My-Decisions wasn't front and center telling me my almost indiscretion was worse than his major faux pas.

Jake stood and watched. He hated cooking, so never offered to help. "I guess I never gave it a thought. It is an easy lifestyle here, and I suppose it would sound appealing. So are they all in? They've all fallen for it?"

I filled him in on my observations so far. "Kevin has. He doesn't have a good family to go home to so he loves it here. Isabelle has blossomed. She's no longer the quiet girl who came. She has guys fighting over her. Caroline is already married. Marcus has been practicing with the band and isn't in any hurry to head home. I haven't really spoken with the others."

"How come we're the only ones who see what is happening?"

"Caleb does. Now."

Jake scoffed. "What took him so long?"

I hesitated. "It's not my story to tell, but when you grow up here, all of this is normal. He didn't know any different. His eyes have been opened to the reality."

In a few quick steps, he moved around the counter to stand at my side and grip my shoulders. "You keep defending him, but I still don't trust him to follow through. You need to watch your step and don't sleep with him again. If you get pregnant, he'll never let you leave with his kid."

He didn't know how true his words were. But pregnant? Not a chance. I turned my back to Jake as I searched out bread pans. Caleb had kept his promise last night, but in the heat of the moment, I'd been ready to give in. Now, knowing Caleb still thought of all of this as nothing more than show, I should be thankful he'd been strong.

Or conniving?

I was the one who'd wanted more. I'd thought what we had experienced together last night had meant something, or at least changed the dynamics. I was wrong. Damn. I guess I still had a lot to learn in the relationship department. The man I was forced into a marriage with was ten years older than me and a hell of a lot more experienced. As I switched out the pie for the banana bread to bake, I told myself to grow up. The wedding was a sham. What had happened—and what didn't happen—was a lesson learned.

Jake was still in the apartment when Caleb got home. By the way he slowly closed the door, I could tell he was surprised at my company. "Hello."

He bent to pick up the towel I'd forgotten about. Oops. I really should get better at cleaning up after myself. "Ah, hi." It was all I could manage. I was still hurt by his words earlier, and my friend's warnings still swam in my head as Jake barely acknowledged the new arrival home.

My eyes followed Caleb as he stepped into the bedroom, my guess to put the towel in the hamper and I'm sure he discovered the other towel on the floor. I could only imagine what he thought. I worried my lip as I suddenly didn't know what to say or do around the man who'd turned my world upside down and then inside out in less than twenty-four hours.

Jake stood to leave. He came around the counter where I was now doing dishes and kissed my cheek. "Thanks for earlier," he said loud enough for Caleb to hear as he came back into the room, but then he leaned down to my ear. "Remember what I said." Then he quickly left the apartment.

"He doesn't look happy," Caleb commented as he strode to the counter. "Wow, you've been busy."

I looked over at the cobbler, two banana breads, and three dozen sugar cookies, all a testament to my current stress level. I saw he was about to come around the counter to give me a kiss, but I turned my back to him, putting away the pans as an excuse. "Yeah, I got a bit carried away."

He stopped at the corner, obviously noticing my avoidance. "I thought you would join us for supper. Did you eat?"

"No. Guess I forgot."

That's all he needed to advance in the tiny confines of the kitchen. "How do you forget to eat? Here, I'll make you something."

The gesture was sweet, and I could quickly get used to his nurturing side, but Jake had been right. I need to keep emotions out of it. I need to concentrate on the plan to escape. And I needed space. "Nah, that's okay. I have a headache and was about to head to bed."

Caleb, being Caleb, didn't let it go. "You probably have a headache because you didn't eat."

I grabbed a cookie and took a bite. "There. I ate." I forced a yawn. "I really am tired."

He stepped in my path. "What's going on, Grace? I thought we were in a good place?"

No, you thought you could have a little fun while we played house. I couldn't help the snide thought. Jake was rubbing off on me.

"We're fine. Everything is status quo," I insisted. Which was true, with status quo being where we were before our little romp in the bedsheets the night before. "How's the arm?"

His hesitation was enough for me to know he wasn't buying my excuses, but he let it pass. "Nothing a few days won't cure."

"Help yourself to cookies, but the pie and breads are for the meal tomorrow. Good night."

He didn't push any further, and I quickly changed and curled up on one side of the bed. I heard him moving around and a part of me wondered if he would take the hint and sleep back on the floor in the other room again.

He didn't. He came in, stripping off his clothes in the dark and sliding in beside me. I pretended to sleep, keeping my breathing slow and even, but I was aware of every move he made. Aware of the length of his body under the same blankets. Aware of the immediate heat he generated.

He'd been the one to remind me we were still playing a game. Jake's visit had only reinforced how important it was to play it cool and keep emotions out. Game on.

Maybe.

Chapter Ten

Caleb was in the shower when I woke. It gave me a couple minutes to prepare for another day. I needed to get my head back in the 'game' of this pretend marriage.

Jake was right. I needed to keep a distance from the man I'd been forced to marry. But would I keep myself away and still convince everyone we are happy newlyweds? How do I convince Caleb nothing has changed either?

I'm not a natural flirt. I haven't had a succession of boyfriends, but I'm not a virgin either. I heard the water turn off in the other room and knew my time was up. I could do this. I could handle the kisses and touching and show the town we are close, but it would stop there. No repeats of Friday night.

I grabbed clothes to wear to church and was ready when the bathroom door opened. "Don't you look nice?" I plastered a smile on my face as I looked him over from his Khaki pants, white button-down shirt, and plain tie.

"Thank you." I saw the look he gave me, assessing my mood. I touched his arm as I brushed past him. "My turn to clean up. Be out shortly."

I closed the door and leaned back against it. I did it. Friendly and casual. I've got this.

Sitting in church and eating the fellowship meal

was easy because there were three children who demanded time with their father and managed to put space between us, maybe with a little coordination on my part, but I made sure to look across their little heads to smile up at my 'husband' and maintain the look of family to the world around us.

Halfway through the meal, Shawna demanded, "Daddy, I want to go to the park."

Caleb looked down at her plate. "You have to eat first before we play. Justin, if you want to go on the swings, you need to sit still and eat, as well."

"See, Daddy," Elena shoved a forkful of food in her mouth, talking over it, "I told you yesterday he won't sit."

Rita, who sat across from me, rolled her eyes at Elena's uppitiness about her siblings, but their dad took all their antics in stride.

Once the meal ended, Rita and her husband, Conrad, left while we took the kids to the park which gave me another excuse to have separation as we chased the little ones in opposite directions. I pushed Shawna on a swing, while Caleb was off with Justin. Elena was old enough to roam between us. There were lots of other families there, too, and I hoped the five of us together presented a normal relationship of a couple out with their children.

We weren't alone again until after dinner when we finally left Rita's home to walk back to the apartment. I'd grabbed Caleb's hand as we walked out the door, a perfect sign of unity, but Eagle Eyes hadn't been fooled by my antics. "Want to tell me what's going on?"

I'd been waiting for this all day, playing it out in my mind. I gave an innocent look up at him. "What do you mean? I thought today went well. I think everyone saw us as a good family unit."

"Ahh."

No arguments? No more than a single non-committal word? And silence. I can't stand silence. Or this man's penchant for non-committal, one-word revelations.

Nope. I wasn't going to engage. Nope, I was going to leave well-enough alone. I didn't want to argue. I made it half a block before I pulled my hand from his, turned to face him and stopped him from moving forward.

"What do you mean by 'ahh'?"

He raised an eyebrow and continued to remain silent. Fine, he had learned which button to push. "Don't ignore me, Caleb."

"Why don't we have this conversation back home?" His tone was quiet and non-engaging. He was maintaining the calm I'd hoped to do moments before but lacked the control to do so.

"Why? So no one sees us arguing? So we don't blow our cover?"

While my voice had risen with my sarcastic comment, his remained low and annoyingly controlled. "May I remind you who stands to lose if we are not seen as a loving couple? The town council has eyes and ears everywhere, reporting our behavior."

I opened my mouth to make another sarcastic retort, but he was right. We weren't the only ones on the street, and any one of the neighbors could be reporting in to Roger or his blind followers. I turned on my heel and strode ahead, Caleb only a step behind.

"Let's wait until we get home, he says. There are

people watching, he says," I muttered under my breath. "The apartment is not my home, it's just a freaking temporary living arrangement. Oh, and he always answers with a single word, like he knows what I'm thinking, like that isn't annoying."

"You know I can hear you, right?" he said from beside me, and the quick glare I threw at him had me fuming more. Did he think this was funny? That's it. The man was toast. I couldn't wait until we were back in the apartment.

I stopped short and turned on him. "Stop smirking. Ugh, you are so infuriating."

Caleb pressed his lips together; my guess was so he could suppress another smile. I poked the bear in the chest. "I don't know what you find so funny? I'm not finding any of this humorous in any way."

Now he raised his hands in surrender. "I'm not laughing."

"Not out loud, but I saw you." I poked him again. "And what's with the single word answer? Why do you always have to be in control of everything?"

He continued to hold his hands up in the air. "What has you so hot and bothered today? What did Jake say last night to have you in a tailspin?"

He was too close to the truth, and my skin prickled with tension and pent up frustration. "Why do you think Jake has anything to do with this? He has nothing to do with this." I poked him again, this time his eyes went dark and maybe I sensed he was no longer laughing but I didn't quite process the change. "We had a good conversation last night, but he didn't say anything I didn't already know."

"And that would be what exactly?" His voice

dropped. My brain sent a quick *'Danger, Will Robinson,'* but my mouth had already engaged.

"Why don't you tell me, Mister I-know-where-this-is-going, sputtering out a single non-committal word?" I went to jab him once again, but my hand was captured in his larger one.

"Be careful, Grace," he warned in an ice-cold tone, one that I didn't heed.

"Or what?" I stared up at him. "Jake thinks you're part of the conspiracy. He said you are playing me like Hope played him. That...that...that you are like all the others and plan to seduce me until I no longer want to go home."

Caleb's head snapped back, and the air between us darkened. "And you believe him?" He released my hand and stepped back. "Of course you do. You've known him a long time." I don't know how he does it, but it was like a curtain came down over his expression. There was no emotion. He motioned with his arm toward the sidewalk ahead. "Let's head home."

"Oh, yes, let's go back to the *apartment*." I enunciated the word, making sure he understood I wasn't calling it home. I stomped ahead, while he maintained his quiet control. The man didn't even make a sound walking, which made me want to stomp harder.

We were half a block away from our destination when someone called out to Caleb. "Hey there, Chief. Enjoying the sunshine?

He took time to stop as though we were out on a casual evening stroll; as though we weren't in the midst of an argument that I was oh so ready to continue. "Evening, Shelly. Your rose bush is exceptional this year. Did you do anything different?"

I wanted to move forward, but if I left Caleb behind to talk with the neighbor, it would send the wrong message about our relationship. Instead, I made sure to stand a foot away from him, half hidden from Shelly's view, and tapped my foot, until he finally waved goodbye.

Finally. Now to get back so we could have our conversation in solitude. Before we could get to the apartment complex, we were interrupted a second time. Officer Brent pulled up alongside us in a patrol car.

"Hey, Chief, we have a situation, and I was wondering if I could pull you back on duty to give a hand."

Caleb stepped off the curb, and I stayed where I was, more so because I was curious of what 'situation' would be cause to pull someone off their honeymoon leave.

My ears perked up at Brent's words. "Sam spotted kids out behind his corn field. He chased them away but found a half-gallon of hard cider."

I knew where this was going; I suspected the chief did as well.

"I looked on the tracker, and it was A.J. and Leland," Brent continued. "Looks like they have two of the new girls with them, as well. Penny and Christy."

Caleb looked back at me, and the tightening of the jaw said more than words that our conversation was far from over. "I'm going to be late," he said before circling the car and got into the passenger seat. Brent handed him his phone so he could use the tracker, and the two drove off.

I headed upstairs only to realize I was itching for an argument but couldn't fully rationalize where the emotion stemmed from.

****

He didn't come home.

I woke to an empty bed and empty apartment and dragged myself to the shower. I hadn't slept well, wondering when Caleb would get back and if he'd want to continue our discussion.

The shower pounded on my shoulders as I contemplated the issue at hand. I knew why I was mad at him. After swearing to myself I would not get emotionally involved with my forced roommate, he'd gone and shown a sensitive side, kissing my bruise, then making love to me, but also keeping his word to not jeopardize my leaving. Despite his role in bringing us to Wellington, despite his job to keep us locked inside, I'd seen a softer, gentler side.

My anger wasn't Caleb's fault. No, that was on me. I had turned around and thought I was falling for him. I let myself believe I might have feelings for him and, *gulp*, believed he felt the same way.

I was obviously wrong. He'd made it clear after the game on Saturday that it had all been for show. That had hurt. More than I wanted to let on, so I'd tried to stuff it all down, but that's not how I'm wired. I need to vent, to let the emotions out.

We'd almost had sex on Friday night. Almost. The angry part of me said the reason we didn't was because Caleb wanted me to trust him, to give me a false sense of hope. The rational side knew if Caleb wanted to have a hold over me, he'd have consummated our marriage.

I had let him get too close, but I could hardly tell him the truth. No, that would give him too much power. Better to let him think I regretted Friday night and still blamed him for bringing me to this town than to let him know he'd slipped past my defenses.

I wrapped a towel around my body and another around my hair and opened the door to go back to the bedroom and instead walked into Caleb, who'd been about to knock.

I didn't scream at the unexpected arrival but did let out a squeak. "Jesus, Mary, and Joseph, I didn't hear you come in."

He stepped back quickly, his hands up in surrender. "Sorry, I didn't want to startle you."

I licked my lips, still not sure what to say, knowing there was already so much unsaid between us. "Um, did everyone stay in jail like last time?"

"Penny is at the hospital. She drank too much, but she'll be fine. Christy is home. The rest continue to stay at their new hotel for at least another day."

I raised my eyebrow at the extended jail time, and he answered my unasked question. "Second offense this summer. I'll head back there in a little while. After I clean up, we need to keep our appointment with Frank."

Shit. I'd forgotten about the wedding bands. I wasn't in the best frame of mind for putting up a show in front of someone I'm sure was a spy for my dear friend, Roger. "I'll get dressed."

I found clothes quickly, not wanting Caleb to walk in while I was still naked. I heard the shower still running as I moved back into the living room and headed to the kitchen. If ever there was a need for a strong cup of coffee, it was now. I was at a loss for something to replace the immediate craving, and with the tension between me and Caleb I was far from hungry.

But I was brought up around chefs, and chefs feed people, even if they are mad at them. By the time my male roommate—as that was all I considered him—was dressed, I had a hot plate of food ready. I munched on an English muffin while I cleaned, leaving Caleb with the impression I'd had more to eat.

I'd thrown on shorts and a casual top to combat the heat of the day. I found it twice as hot here as at home, maybe because of all the flat farmland around. I was used to more mountains and a lot more trees. Maybe that's why I liked the far end of town where it butts up against the woods. That area reminded me of home. I needed to go back there to rejuvenate soon. I grabbed my sunglasses and walked with a silent Caleb out the door and headed toward the hustle and bustle of activity at The Square.

I'd hoped for silence, hoped for a bit more time before we continued our discussion that had been interrupted the night before, but Caleb wasn't one to wait. "Grace, we need to talk about Friday."

Shit, shit, shit. I wasn't ready. "Now? I mean, we need to play nice in front of Frank. You know he'll report to Roger and the rest of the council."

He ran a distracted hand over the scruff at his jaw. The fact he didn't seem to have everything under complete control made him almost human. "Exactly my point. The tension between us is visible. We won't be fooling anyone."

I plastered a smile on my face. "Sure we can, *dear*. One united front and all that shit, right? I'm sure we can put our differences aside for now and do whatever it takes to convince everyone we're fine. There'll be plenty of time after, when we don't have to rush out."

After a long pause, he finally opened the door to the store. "Okay. Whatever it takes." He put a hand on the small of my back as he led me to the back to the jewelry department. I know it is a simple gesture, Caleb being a gentleman, but the heat of his hand seared my back. I couldn't stop the wishful side of me from wanting Friday night to have been real, and to have his touch be more than a necessity.

I gulped as Frank spotted us and joined us at the jewelry counter. "Good morning, newlyweds, and how are you this fine morning?"

Let the game begin. I pushed my sunglasses on top of my head. "We're doing fine, but poor Caleb worked all night, so he's a little off his game today." I spotted the spark in his eyes as I put the ball in his court. "We'll be quick with our decision, so he can get back to work."

Caleb's hand moved from my back to take my hand. "Not too fast, though. We need to find the perfect ring for this beautiful woman." He kissed my knuckles, and I felt a blush tinge my cheeks. Damn, he was good.

There was tension, for certain, but I almost felt a spark of what had been between us out on the ball field on Saturday. Pure sexual tension. I bit the inside of my cheek, the pain reminding me not to lose focus.

"Lovely." Frank bobbed down off his step to reach into the locked case then spryly jumped back into position with a tray of sample rings. His gnome-like face sporting a look of determined intent. "I already have your sizes, so now all you'll have to do is pick a design."

Caleb pointed to the first one with an intricate webbed design. "This one matches your personality." He leaned down and whispered into my ear.

"Complicated and confusing."

Two could play. I pointed to the ring on the opposite side. "And this one matches yours." Like him, I leaned in so only he could hear the rest. "Plain and simple. No muss, no fuss."

Frank watched the display between us, and I hoped he was only seeing what we wanted him to. Caleb slid his finger toward the center of the collection and his tone changed to something softer and his eyes met mine, freezing me in my spot. "Maybe we could meet in the middle?"

I sucked in a breath. Was he still talking rings? I didn't think so, but I turned my focus from his intense gaze onto the ring he pointed out. It had a beautiful knot design, not unlike the one on the far end, but it was only along the middle of the ring, while on either side the band was plain. A perfect blend of simple and complex. Much like our tumultuous relationship.

Meet in the middle? If he could, then I would too. "That could work," I agreed. I hoped he got my message. I was ready to talk and work things out.

He took my hand again, giving it a light squeeze, and I knew we were both talking the same language. "We'll take this ring, Frank."

"Excellent. I'll order it today, and it should arrive by Friday."

"Caleb!"

The shriek rang through the entire store. A short woman with platinum blonde hair, a massive bubble butt, and a Jessica Rabbit chest, made a beeline toward us. "I've been looking all over for you."

Chapter Eleven

The woman gave the jewelry counter a disgusted glance, pointed an exasperated stare at me, then turned her considerable venom on Caleb. "My son is in jail while you are in here, shirking your duties."

I didn't know who she was, but I immediately became defensive. I stiffened and took a step toward the woman, putting myself between her and her target. Before I could say or do anything, I felt a large hand on my shoulder and a gentle squeeze.

"Sylvie," Caleb's voice was quiet and calm while I wanted to get in her face. "How can I help you?"

"First, you can get back to your job and release your brother, Austin, from that jail cell." The woman's voice was shrill and demanding, and I was in no mood for the scene.

"First," I repeated, stepping into the woman's personal space, "Caleb worked all night; he's on his dinner break. Second, he is technically supposed to be on leave but went back to work because of *your* son and his penchant for breaking the law."

The hand on my shoulder tightened a second before I was turned around. With a gentle, but nonetheless forceful tug, he pulled me a few steps away in a little dance maneuver that put himself between me and the shrew. "While I appreciate your loyalty, I'll handle this."

"But she—" I tried to look around him, but he continued to block my view.

"I'm used to dealing with my stepmother." He leaned down and kissed my cheek, and I spotted the twitch at his lips, the little spark of amusement he couldn't hide. "I have to go back to work anyway. Why don't you go home, and I'll meet you there later?"

Caleb let me go, but as I moved away, I used my fingers to indicate to Sylvie I was watching her. The woman glared at me but was too busy tapping her foot during our exchange. "Are you quite finished playing house?" she demanded. "My Austin has been rotting away all night."

"He's hardly been rotting, Sylvie. Sitting in his own stench from his excessive alcohol binge, perhaps, but that was his own doing." Caleb took the woman by the arm to escort her out the door while I watched from another aisle.

I didn't want to go home. I was too wired, both from my exchange with Caleb and with his ex-stepmother. Dear God, his father had cheated on Rita for that…creature? Poor woman.

I decided to load up on groceries while I was here, brought them back to the apartment, and couldn't sit still. Caleb would be a while, so I headed back out and soon was on a shuttle out to Jackson and Amelia's farm. I needed my best friend.

Caroline was working inside, packaging and labeling herbal mixtures to be shipped out for on-line orders. Another reminder of how up on the times this antiquated town is; another reminder how us newbies are unable to access it.

"Gracie." Caroline greeted me with her usual

excitement. How we are friends sometimes amazes me as I am nowhere near as positive as she, but then again, I need that from her. Especially today.

While Caroline is usually the one to give hugs, today, I walked over and wrapped my arms around her, and she knew in an instant I was on the brink. "Oh, honey, what's wrong?" After a moment, she pulled back slightly. "Give me one sec, okay?"

She walked to a door on the far side of the room and opened it. "Amelia, I'm going to take lunch a little early." Then she came back and led me outside to a picnic table away from the building and in the shade of trees.

The herb farm abutted Jackson's horse farm, close to the woods and trails. The shade was welcome from the mid-day heat, and I sank onto the bench, twisting my fingers.

"Talk to me," she ordered.

It took me a moment, but finally the words gushed out. I filled her in on almost everything. Except the plan to escape at the end of the summer.

"…and then we had sex on Friday, well, kinda, ah, it's complicated. But on Saturday, he said something that, well, it hurt, and then I sort of accused him of being part of the whole conspiracy and using sex to keep us here against our will, and…"

"Ouch." The male intervention had me spinning around to see Aaron approaching.

Caroline made shooing motions with her hands. "Private conversation, husband."

"Public location, wife," he retorted. "I didn't mean to eavesdrop." He came closer and gave his wife a kiss before turning to me. "May I offer a bit of advice?"

I nodded, knowing he would anyway.

He took off his Stetson and swiped a bit of dust from his jeans with the brim of the hat. "Caleb is as good as they come. Fair to a fault. But things can be black and white with him, especially when it comes to a moral compass. If you accused him to his face of using sex against you, you may as well have accused him of, to put it bluntly, raping you."

My jaw dropped. "What? No. It wasn't like that." With my past history for relationships, had my brain automatically gone in that direction? Had I jumped to the wrong conclusion with him?

"I'm sure it wasn't," Aaron reassured. "You said this all happened on Saturday? Caleb's not usually one to let things simmer this long. He likes to settle things immediately."

I'd seen that side of him. "It happened yesterday, and while we were in the middle of the argument, he got called into work, and other than an hour this morning, he's been there."

"Don't let it wait any longer. Go talk to him. I'll leave you two to talk." He gave Caroline's shoulder a squeeze then took his brown bag lunch and left us alone. There was genuine love between the newlyweds. They were lucky. As quick as the marriage had occurred, and as much as I had protested, my former college roommate had found a good man.

When my friend's lunch break was over, I nodded to the gardens. "Mind if I walk around?"

She waved a hand toward the rows of leafy plants. "Of course not. This place was meant to enjoy. You might find it therapeutic."

I roamed the gardens for a while and ended up on a

path in the woods. Before I realized it, time had passed, and I was no longer near the herb farm, but high up on the hill behind overlooking the steep drop to the other side and, in the distance, the fence line to the outside world.

Oops. With my current restrictions, I wondered how long before I would spot a cruiser. I should head back, but truthfully, I wasn't quite sure which way would be faster, going back or continuing forward. If I got a little bit higher, I might be able to see where the paths went.

I found a tree I could scale and climbed as high as I dared. From my perch, I couldn't make out which direction I should go back down, but the view beyond the town gates was beautiful. The land beyond the road below was flat giving me access to see for miles. I could see a farmhouse far off in the distance, fences along farmlands, as well as a few scattered cows. I saw the back end of a vehicle in the distance and wondered if it was a cruiser, making its path on the outside, ensuring I didn't wander past the fence.

The quiet calmed me, and I stayed for a while longer than I should have. I was still sitting on my elevated perch when I heard hoof beats coming closer. Yikes. Had my rambling ensued a search party? The last search and rescue hadn't ended so well.

The horse and rider appeared below and came to a halt as Caleb swung to the ground, looking around. I took pity on him and called down. "I'm up here."

He looked up. "What the hell are you doing?"

"Solving all the world's problems and not telling anyone." I swung off the branch and began my descent. When I was in reach, Caleb grabbed my waist and swung me down to the ground.

"Do you know how many times that thing has pinged? Roger's been on my ass for hours to fetch you."

I felt a sting of tears behind my eyes. After my lunch conversation and meandering walk, I'd been ready to apologize to Caleb. Instead, I'd gone and frustrated him again. The hair on my arms rose as did my hackles. "All I did was have lunch with Caroline."

"I know." His hands slid up and down my arms. It wasn't the gentle caress that confused me, but his low, easy tone. He didn't sound mad, but there was a hint of some other emotion I was too wound up to decipher. "I saw that earlier, so I wasn't worried then, but when you wandered off alone, and well…"

My lip trembled as I looked up into his concerned stare. No, it wasn't mad or frustrated. It was… "You were worried about me?"

He closed his eyes for a moment, as though to gather strength. "Grace." From the way he said my name, I knew there was still some frustration, but he was far from angry. His hands continued to move up and down my arms; part of me wanted to press forward against his chest; wanted his strong arms to wrap around me. There was too much still unsaid between us.

"We need to talk," I admitted, pulling away.

Aaron's words echoed in my head, and I knew I needed to clear the air. But I'm not usually one to formulate my thoughts and talk like a reasonable adult. I usually spit out my feelings in the heat of the moment, much like a firecracker that explodes in the sky before fizzling out with a curse word or two. Maybe it was time to act my age and start to do the whole adult conversation thing.

I walked away, not able to face him. It was too hard, too personal. I looked out to the distant fields, far beyond the fence line, trying to avoid the inevitable. Or gain a bit of courage.

"Friday night was…"

Gawd, talking about what we did was going to kill me, but if what Aaron said was true, I couldn't let Caleb believe I thought that he was the type of man who'd take advantage me like my former boyfriend.

"It was great. Amazing, actually, even though we didn't…couldn't…" While my back was to him and he couldn't see my face, I wondered if the heat enveloping me could be seen on my neck, too. I pressed my nails into my palms, letting the slight sting of pain bring me back into focus. "What I'm trying to say is, I read more into it than I should have."

I felt him move behind me, I felt his heat at my back, but he didn't try to make me face him, which I was thankful for. "What are you saying?"

"Let me finish, please." I wrapped my arms around my waist as I talked, thankful for the overhang of branches blocking the afternoon sun. "I think we both got caught up in the moment. I'm not… I don't… What I'm trying to say is I don't take relationships lightly and I don't sleep around."

"I never thought you did." I heard the question in his voice, wondering where this was going, and I knew I was butchering this. I still couldn't face him, and Caleb, while close, continued to wait.

"I think you know I'm attracted to you. I like you, Caleb, and I enjoyed Friday night. A lot." I gulped. "But what you said on Saturday really caught me off guard. I was hurt, and I lashed out."

"What I said? What did I say?" He put his hands on my shoulders and finally turned me to face him. I closed my eyes and tried to get the courage I needed. I opened my eyes to look up into his, full of questions, full of concern.

I looked away again, full of self-doubt. "You'll probably think it's stupid, or that I'm over-reacting." I tried to move away, but he held firm, cupping his hand on my cheek, making me look at him again.

"What did I say?" he demanded.

He really didn't know. I blinked back the tears stinging my eyes as I whispered the words that had stung my heart. "You said we'd put on enough of a show."

It took a second. I saw the wheels spinning as he replayed in his head where and when those words had been uttered and then his eyes got wide. "Hell, Grace. That's not what I meant. Jeez. No wonder you were pissed."

He pulled me close, wrapping his arms around me, and I slowly lifted mine to clasp his back, my face pressed against his chest. Thankful I didn't have to look at him as all the anger I'd had brimming at the surface seeped away.

"It was a poor choice of words, that's all." He lifted my chin to stare down at me. "I never meant to cheapen what we did."

"I know that now," I muttered as his lips caressed my forehead while he continued to hold me close. "There's more," I mumbled into his chest. In this position, being held tight against him and not having to look into his beautiful, intense, all-knowing eyes, I could speak a bit more freely, so I let the words pour out. "Last week, the entire week, was fun, and I really like spending time with you, when we're not arguing, and it scares me because I want more of what we had on Friday. But I also want, no need, to go home. Is it crazy of me to say I wish I could have both, when I know I can't?" Now I know Caleb couldn't ignore the flush that tingled my scalp down to my toes.

"I don't take relationships lightly, either," he admitted. Once again, he lifted my chin, forcing me to look in his eyes, to see how much he meant what he said. "How can I? I grew up in a town steeped in tradition of marriage and family. I've only ever been with one other woman; my first wife."

First wife. Technically, I'm his second, a fact which began to sink in. His tone, as he continued, demanded I believe what he said.

"Maybe we moved too quickly under the circumstances. I never planned on what happened between us Friday. It was unexpected, but I hope you know I am attracted to you, and I enjoyed giving you pleasure."

I closed my eyes again as another wave of heat flushed my face. Dear God, I am out of my depths. I had to change the subject. Fast.

"About Saturday night. I don't want you to think anything happened between me and Jake." That made him chuckle, and I gave him an inquisitive stare. "Why is that funny?"

"Sweetheart, I know nothing happened, other than maybe you opening the door wearing nothing but a towel?" He gave a satisfied nod at my obvious look of guilt. "Besides the fact the bed was still made, and you aren't one to make it, I know what you look like after being made love to." His voice became low and husky. "I've seen how full your lips get after being thoroughly kissed. I've seen the way your body glows when you've had an orgasm."

My breath hitched as the memories flooded. Changing the subject hadn't worked. Not one iota.

"There was none of that. Plus, your friend was in too foul of a mood when I arrived to have just left your bed."

I honestly didn't know what to say. I tilted my head away, looking out to the vast fields in the distance. I think Caleb took pity on me as he continued to hold me to his chest. "Grace, I don't regret what we did. Do you? I need to know the truth."

"No," I whispered.

"Good. Can we start over? Maybe take things a little slower?"

I nodded.

"We need to head back to town." He motioned with his head down the hill, and I saw the cruiser on the road, an officer standing beside the car. "Greg hates going outside the gates."

He stepped back and went to lead me toward the horse, and I stopped short. "That's Goliath."

"Yeah, why?"

I put my hands on my hips as I looked back and forth between man and beast. "You can't expect me to get on him. Look at him. Look at me. He's enormous. And mean."

Caleb laughed. "Goliath is not mean. He's spirited." I raised my eyebrows asking what the difference was, but he continued to smile. "You have nothing to worry about. I've got you."

"Why couldn't you have ridden Jazzy? I am so going to regret this," I mumbled as I was hoisted up so I could swing my leg around. Then Caleb mounted behind me while the horse did a few steps back and forth as we adjusted on his massive back.

"Yikes, this is high off the ground." I squeezed my eyes shut, not wanting to see the distance I could fall.

Caleb was pressed against me from his chest to his thighs, and his arms came around my waist to grab the reins. "Lean back and enjoy the ride."

I couldn't relax, though. I was stiff and awkward as the horse began his walk. Eventually, though, I got used to the slow pace, and I relaxed my shoulders a little, leaning back against Caleb's chest.

"Better," he murmured in my ear and I tried harder to relax which had the opposite effect, so he decided to change my focus by pointing out and naming trees and local flora until I was no longer concentrating on the horse, but on his knowledge of the nature in his hometown. I pretended to pay attention, but inside, I knew the only thing I would remember about the ride was how Caleb's large, strong, warm body felt around mine as the horse meandered down the path.

Aaron was waiting for us when we got back to the farm and offered to care for the horse. From the questioning look he gave, I knew he was looking to see if everything was better between us. I gave a slight smile and nod before he walked the horse into the barn and I got into the front seat of the cruiser to head back into town. I still had difficulty thinking of the apartment as home, but at least tonight Caleb and I weren't arguing any more.

When we pulled onto our street, I groaned. Waiting

outside the apartment building was none other than Head Honcho Roger, his side-kick Scott, Harry the gargantuan, and the old geezer, Bill. The only one missing from the elected officials was the silent lapdog, Jay.

Chapter Twelve

The hairs on my body rose, and I slowly sat up in my seat. Caleb put the car in park and reached over to pat my leg. "Let me do all the talking, please."

I opened my mouth to argue, then closed it again, pressing my lips together. I didn't promise, but I unsnapped the seat belt and followed his lead as we exited the car and met the men on the sidewalk.

"Gentlemen," Caleb gave a nod of greeting. "How can I help you, today?"

"You know damn well why we're here." Bill tapped his cane on the ground. His loud, wobbly voice echoed down the empty street. "Your wife has been gallivanting."

Caleb took my hand and lifted it to kiss my knuckles. "Since when has exploring been cause for the entire council to convene?"

Roger stepped forward, his finger pointed at me. "I don't believe that's what she was doing. I think she was looking to escape."

There was a reason I hadn't promised Caleb I would stay quiet. It's not in my nature. "Well, if you didn't hold your residents hostage..."

Caleb gripped my hand and side stepped to be in front of me; he might as well have told me to shut up, as he quickly spoke over me. "If you check your tracking device, you will see Grace had lunch with her best friend, which led to her roaming the herb gardens, and in turn she followed the path up. She was exploring, nothing more."

"Right," Roger sneered, "which is why you had to go rescue her."

I bit my tongue as I wanted to scream and shout at the horrid man, but Caleb's tone remained calm and friendly. "Gentlemen, you are reading far too much into this. I am supposed to be on my honeymoon but have spent the entire night at the station, dealing with—" He offered Roger a pointed look "—wayward children. When I was done, the first thing I wanted to do was be with my bride. I wasn't on a rescue mission at all."

The town's top councilman took yet another step closer, and I saw Caleb's shoulders tighten slightly, the only sign of his growing temper. "There is a reason I have a tight security on the two of you," he said in a snide reminder. "She—," he pointed at me, moving in my direction, "—is trouble and I don't trust you to follow through on your responsibilities."

Caleb stepped in front of me, blocking me from Roger and his waving finger. "Watch yourself." His voice went stone cold. "Do not go near my wife."

Every time he said that word, *wife*, something tugged inside, something I can't explain. Something I had to push to the back of my brain as I continued to watch the drama unfold or at least what I could see, since his stance shielded me from view. When I stepped to the right, trying to see around the stone wall of a man, it was like he sensed my movement and moved with me.

I stepped closer and grabbed the back of his shirt. This way, he knew where I was and I could stand in place and lean my head to peek around his massive back to see Roger's eyes narrow at the veiled threat. Harry pulled at his collar, and Scott's eyes went back and forth, waiting for an altercation to begin.

Roger stepped closer again, his nose pointed up as he attempted to stare down the imposing police chief. "Are you threatening me?" the older man sputtered.

"I am making a promise, Roger," Caleb stressed his name. "If you put so much as a single finger on Grace, I will snap it in half."

The councilman went white. I wanted to giggle as a mean thought crossed my mind. While Roger wasn't a short man by no means; however, next to Caleb, he could have been Lord Fardquaad next to the Ogre from that children's movie. For all his bravado, he knew when he'd pushed things too far. Roger wasn't one to not have the last word, though. He raised an eyebrow at me, almost mocking at the way I still peeked from behind my protector.

"I'm watching you both. I told you what will happen if you help her leave these gates." He motioned for his minions, and they loaded into the old Lincoln Continental. It wasn't until the car was down the block before I exploded.

"Holy Mary, Mother of God, you were amazing. You should have broken his finger, though. He freaking deserved it, the pompous ass." I nearly jumped in place as the adrenaline continued to pump through my body.

Caleb rolled his eyes, and I noticed his shoulder muscles relax.

"How do you maintain control? I had everything I could do to not talk. And thank you for protecting me. That was, well, great." I stood on my toes and planted a kiss on his lips.

I wasn't thinking when I did. It was not planned. But once they were there, I didn't pull back. At first his lips were tight, not expecting anything, but when they softened, I pressed in until I felt him comply.

Then it was his lips leading. He didn't touch me anywhere else. Only his mouth. Answering. Seeking. Calming me and exciting me at the same time.

When he slowly pulled away, I didn't want it to end. And if the storm in his blue eyes were any indication, neither did he. He licked his lips and stood straight, still not touching me.

A couple hours ago we'd agreed to take things slow, but the heat between us was going to make things difficult. But leave it to Caleb to keep his word. "Shall we go in?"

And I knew with a single tone, that amaze-balls kiss was all I would get tonight.

****

It was like we started over. The only intimate gestures were while we were out in public. We mostly spent time with his children, ensuring no extended periods of alone time. Except at night.

I always went to bed before he did, pretending to be asleep when he came later, much later, staying well on his side. We were roommates and nothing more.

It was for the best.

Friday, I woke extra tired, extra cranky, and with the familiar signs Mother Nature was due for her monthly visit. I checked the closet, and because they are stingy about how much they hand out, I knew I had to make a visit to the pharmacy to get tampons. That prospect made my mood even more sour.

When Caleb came out of the shower, I was stomping around the kitchen, slamming pans and muttering to myself. Most men I know would have stayed far away from me, but not him. He strolled over, grabbed a bacon slice, and leaned against the counter.

I pointed my spatula at him. "Did I say you could have bacon? No, I didn't. Don't think you can have more than your share when we sit down.

He continued to eat, obviously not threatened in the least. "What's got you worked up today?"

I moved back to my work at the stove. "I woke in a mood. Can't I have a bad day once in a while?"

Toast popped in the toaster, and he grabbed it. "Do you want butter or jam?"

Damn, I had zero patience today. "What do you think? What do I usually have?"

Caleb didn't engage. Instead, he spread jam and moved to put the kettle on for his morning cup of tea. He'd been introducing new teas to me each morning, but I was in no mood to discuss the benefits of whatever choice he made today.

I folded his pepper and onion omelet, removed the home fries from the oven where I'd kept them warm, added a couple more slices of bacon to his plate, and shoved it at him. "Here."

He grinned. "Thank you, Grace. It looks delicious."

Then he leaned down and kissed me, freezing me in my spot, with a spatula in hand. My body reacted instantly as anger disappeared and something much hotter consumed me. Before I could react, he stepped away and headed to the table as though he hadn't changed the entire dynamics of the week.

"Why?" I licked my lips. He hadn't touched me in

four days. "What was that for?"

He plopped a forkful of food in his mouth and took his time before answering. "Wanted to say thank you."

I slowly turned back to the stove and poured my eggs into the hot pan and prepared my omelet on auto pilot. When I finally came to the table, Caleb was finishing his meal. He brought his plate to the sink then returned with two cups of tea and sat across from me as casual as any other day.

I was halfway through my meal before I realized he had shifted my mood. Sneaky bastard. "Are we heading to your mom's again today?" I muttered,

"We could. It's supposed to rain later. How would you feel about taking the brood to the movies?"

I'd been here nine weeks and hadn't gone to their theater, and it's not like they had a huge selection of places to go in the tiny town. "Sure." I took a sip of tea. "What's in this?"

Caleb finished his last bite of bacon and pushed his plate away. "Hmm, I believe that particular blend has lavender."

Even novice that I am, I knew he'd chosen it for its calming effect. It wasn't going to work today. I changed the subject. "I, ah, need to go over to the pharmacy first."

Caleb raised his cup but not before I saw the slight lift of his lips. Damn him, he'd suspected. Of course, he'd grown up with sisters and had been married before. "Not a problem. We can go together."

"You don't have to," I muttered. "I am capable."

He didn't hesitate. "Am I going to get a call because you threatened bodily harm to Sean?"

I shifted uncomfortably in my chair. "Depends on

if that little nerd gives me a third-degree, but I'm not making any promises."

"We'll go together." While his tone was decisive, the sparkle in his eye made me think he was more than a little amused at my expense.

It was time to change the subject before my morning moodiness turned back to testy again. "I want to go to the store, as well. I told your mom I would cook dinner. No need for her to cook every night when we're always there."

We cleaned the kitchen together, like we had every morning, then I took my turn in the shower. It was like the mood-changing kiss never happened. Except it did. Sure, I'd figured out his motives for the kiss, and it had worked, but it didn't change the fact it had ignited the flame I'd stifled for the past week.

Not that I hadn't been physically aware of him every moment of every day, because I had. Every time he'd put his hand on my back, or held my hand, or even brushed by me in the tiny confines of the kitchen, my every nerve ending had strummed a happy song.

I was especially aware of him when he climbed into bed at night. Yes, I was excruciatingly aware he wore only his briefs—and I suspected he did so only for my benefit. Every night I concentrated on keeping my breathing slow and even, while inside I noticed how long his legs were next to mine, how broad his shoulders are, and how much room he takes up in the king-size bed. I was learning his breathing patterns, and that he doesn't snore. I'd lay on my side, my back to him, forcing myself not to roll over and curl into his warmth.

I dried my hair and looked at myself in the mirror.

My hair had grown this summer, but that wasn't the only difference. I looked older. Or maybe I felt older. It was my eyes. The brown seemed darker than I remembered. More serious. More reflective.

I was twenty. For another few weeks. Yikes. But this summer had changed me more than I had ever planned. It should have been full of fun and excitement, being away from home. Instead, I'd been handed the weight of the world. I was trapped in a town and didn't know how I was going to leave. And, I was married—sort of—to a man I was attracted to and could easily fall for if we didn't keep our distance.

"Ready, Grace?"

I closed my eyes against my reflection and breathed deep. Another day in paradise. I could do this.

When I went back into the bedroom, I saw everything back in its place. One thing I'd discovered about Caleb is that he's a neat freak. When I am in the shower, he goes into the bedroom and makes the bed, with perfect hospital corners, and folds or hangs any of my clothes I'd left on the floor. After the towel incident with Jake, I promised myself I'd get better at picking up, but mornings are not my time to think clearly. I blame it on the lack of coffee.

I slipped on my flip-flops and my sunglasses. Despite my nasty mood today, we still had a role to play in public. It seemed Caleb didn't have any issues being the doting husband, so I needed to change my focus a bit. It shouldn't be too difficult. All I needed to get into character was to remember the kiss from this morning.

Chapter Thirteen

The pharmacy was busy with two people in line ahead of me. Before long, there were three people behind me, including my former boss, the sour-faced Jackie. If this was like a normal pharmacy, people could roam the aisles, choosing their own products, but *Nooo.* The control freaks in this town had to question every person about every selection.

My foot was tapping in agitation by the time it was my turn, and I saw the pharmacist's eyes widen when he saw me. Asking Caleb to wait outside may have been a mistake.

"Morning, Sean. I need tampons." Short. To the point.

The string bean of a man motioned for me to scan my bracelet, which I did, and all my information popped up on his screen. And then the inquisition began. He stared straight at the screen, avoiding me as he spoke. "It says you are now married. Do you have your menstrual cycle tracking book with you?"

"The what?" It took me a second before I grasped what he meant. "You mean the calendar Dr. Todd gave me?"

Oh, hell, this was going to go downhill faster than an Olympics Luge run. When Caleb stepped up beside me, I knew he must have been watching through the doors waiting for my turn. He wasn't going to let me do this alone, God bless the man.

The pharmacist gulped as he continued with what must be a script he was forced to read. "The book Dr. Todd provided helps you determine when your most fertile days are and…"

I gave a pleading look to the large, controlled man beside me and allowed him to take over. "Sean, haven't you learned anything the past two months with Grace? She is not going to discuss her sex life with you, or the several patrons in line behind us. She is requesting a specific item which implies an answer to the unasked question."

Sean's Adam's apple bobbed as he looked from Caleb, back to his screen, and then to me. "But I have to fill in the screen before I can requisition the item."

"I see." Caleb maintained civility while I nearly shook. "What exactly do you need to know?"

"Um, well, I'm supposed to use the book to fill in which days and how often you logged your, um…" String Bean couldn't continue his sentence so he rushed forward. "I'm supposed to remind you as a married couple, it is your duty to preserve the future of this town by…" He slowed, barely said each word. When I looked up at Caleb's cold, dark expression, I could see why. "…providing children for the next generation. And, uh, if you are having trouble conceiving, Dr. Todd can run some tests."

The people behind us stepped back as the man beside me straightened to his full height. Now he knew how I felt when I walked into this place.

"Let's break this down so you can put in your notes. One: have you seen my wife? She is sexy as hell. So, no problems in that department."

There was no denying the thrill his words sent through me. Part of me knew it was all talk, but I couldn't help the satisfied smug. I rocked back on my heels as he continued. "Two: I already have three children, so I think we've answered the fertility question. Three: We have only been married twelve days so let's not expect miracles. Do you think you can fill in your boxes and get Grace what she asked for?"

With wide-eyes, the thin man typed quickly into the computer and disappeared behind the doors to the supply area. This time, when we left the pharmacy, it was my turn to calm Caleb.

"Mother of God, why did I not see this before I left the first time?" he murmured. "Before I brought my children back here to live? One of these days my own daughters will feel forced to answer those same questions."

I pressed my lips together at his blasphemy and put a reassuring hand on his arm. "You held it together a lot better than I would have. Maybe we got everyone in there thinking. Maybe they'll start to question things as well." I could dream, right? "Well, except for Jackie. She actually looked smug at the inquisition, but she hasn't liked me from day one."

He ran a frustrated hand over his chin. "Jackie's harmless. Ever since her son died, she's been on a crusade to have stricter regulations on prescription drugs." He stopped to look back at the pharmacy entrance, and I finally got my chance to find out about my former boss and her unapproachable personality.

"What happened to him?" For once Caleb wasn't on track with me so I continued my prompt. "Jackie's son. She told me he died outside the gates. How?"

The distraction seemed to help as Caleb took my hand as we strolled away from the clinic. "He fell off a tractor and broke his back. The town sent him for physical therapy three times a week at a nearby town's hospital facility. Joshua became addicted to the pain meds they provided. He stopped going to PT and instead used the co-pay we were sending him with to purchase stronger drugs. Until he overdosed. Jackie blames the 'low-life druggies' for his death. Then she became the biggest crusader for stricter prescription drug protocols. I guess, since then, the changes at the pharmacy have become as strict as the rest of the security in this town."

He looked down at me, his eyes full of sorrow. "I have been foolishly blind. I'm sorry, Grace. I followed orders to bring you all here without seeing the big picture."

"It's not your fault." It was different, me, reassuring this usually unflappable man. "I know you were still reeling from your wife's death. I don't blame you." The shake of his head told me he blamed himself, and there was nothing I could say or do to change it.

I looked up at the gray sky as I felt the moisture tap down on my head. "Come on. The rain is starting, and I still need to get groceries for supper. If you haven't noticed, I am a pretty darn good cook and I like to bake, too. If you tell me what you want, I'll make dessert for tonight."

The distraction worked up until we were heading toward the checkout when we were accosted by Frank. "Oh, good, you're here. You saved me a phone call. Come with me."

It was the longest and also shortest walk to the

jewelry department at the back of the store. My feet felt like lead as we followed the tiny man until he disappeared around the counter then popped up and excitedly presented two ring boxes. "Did you know the wedding band dates back almost five thousand years." The jeweler explained, as he opened both boxes and placed them on the glass counter. "It's believed to have originated with the Egyptians."

I tuned out the troll of a man as Caleb took the smaller band out of the box and lifted my finger, sliding the shiny gold band into place. I couldn't look at him. I was thankful I'd left my hair down today, as the long strands hid my face as I stared at our joined fingers. Knowing what was expected, I fumbled with the other box, as I repeated the gesture while the jeweler continued to talk incessantly on my deaf ears about wedding rings

We were both silent during the exchange, but I couldn't hide the shake of my hands. This made it all real. Living with Caleb, well, I can pass it off as us being roommates. Like living in the dorms, having guy friends crash on the floor. Except here Caleb shared the same bed.

Nothing about this unity was normal. We'd stood in front of the town in mud-soaked clothes, while the pastor proclaimed our marriage. No vows had been made. Now, we stood in a crowded warehouse of a store, exchanging rings while shoppers brushed by without a care in the world.

Caleb watched me, and I knew I was supposed to say something, do something, to keep the appearance of our farce alive while Frank stood with an expectant grin. What were supposed to do? Did he expect us to say: *With this ring, I thee wed?*

"And then there is the symbolism for the ring being round," he continued, "is to represent a love with no end."

I think that's when I may have gone white. I know that's when Caleb became very aware of my increasing trembles. He kissed my knuckles then my forehead before moving his lips to my ear. "We're in this together, Grace."

As quickly as he could, he thanked Frank and ushered me through the aisles. I pushed the carriage back to the front of the store to the registers. I knew Caleb kept looking over at me, I could see he wanted to speak, to say something but I think he knew I was beyond words. I remained quiet, but my eyes kept returning to my left hand and the new gold band circling my finger. This symbol changed things. This, more than any kiss I'd exchanged with Caleb.

The rain pounded on the ground as we exited the building, and we moved under the covered shuttle bus stop. The pounding on the roof above seemed overly loud but still not enough to drown out the one thought continuing in a loop in my head. *This is real.*

"Are you okay?"

It was a simple question but a difficult one to answer. My fingers clasped together in a twisted knot. "No, I don't think I am." We weren't alone. It wasn't the time for this discussion, and going straight to his mother's house meant Rita and Conrad and three children running around. I was glad for the reprieve.

The rain suited my mood, but it also meant being cooped up indoors with three children. The movie only took a couple hours. I spent the rest of the time in the kitchen, preparing dessert first, then helping with supper, all while maintaining the proper conversation with the rambunctious family. Working with my hands, though, I continually saw the shiny gold band with the intricate design on my finger, and while I made all the right motions throughout the day, I wasn't really present.

After dinner, Caleb kissed his children goodnight, thanked his mom for being there for them, and escorted me out, opening an umbrella for us to share as we stepped out into the humid weather. "Let's skip the music tonight. I don't think you're in the mood for dancing, am I right?"

"No, not really, but I don't want to go home, either." No, being alone with Caleb in an apartment was definitely not something I could handle.

He didn't hesitate. "Then I think this calls for milkshakes and French fries."

I looked up as we pressed close under the large umbrella and gave him a wan smile. "Okay."

At this late hour, the shuttles only run sporadically. We could have called for a special run, but it was easier and quicker to walk. We found a booth in a far corner of the diner and put in our order.

Caleb, a man of action, a man who needs to fix every problem as it arises, lifted my left hand and rubbed at the ring. "You're spooked by this. Want to talk?"

It wasn't a question so much as a request. I looked at my hand, swallowed up within his much larger one. Part of me wanted to pull it away, hide it under the table, pretend the matching gold bands didn't exist on our fingers.

The music blaring from the old-time jukebox was upbeat which was in total discourse to my contemplative mood. I struggled to find words to describe the emotional tide that had kept me unusually quiet for most of the day.

"Did you know my parents have been married for twenty-six years?" It was a strange answer to his question, but somehow I'd meander along the path of my thoughts. "They were both heavy into their careers before I came along. Mom had me at thirty-six and Sarah at forty. Even with the challenges Sarah brought into the mix, my parents still managed to build a restaurant business and keep their marriage and family a priority."

Caleb said nothing. He knew I'd eventually get around to the topic at hand. "It's not easy to work together and raise two children, one of whom has a disability. My parents have had their fair share of arguments. Dad says the secret to their marriage is communication and honesty, but most of all, always remembering to honor the vows they took on their wedding day."

I nodded to my hand still clasped in his much larger one. I worried my lip. "The wedding, if you can call it that, was surreal. We didn't exchange vows. We didn't make any promises. It was, Bam! We say you're married, so you're married. Next thing you know, you and I are, well, basically roommates."

"That about summarizes it. So what's different now?" He continued to rub at the outline of the band and the back and forth motion was actually a bit soothing.

What'd different? Nothing? Everything? "I don't

know. I can't explain it."

I stopped talking as the waitress brought the shakes. Caleb took his drink in one hand, while maintaining his hold of my left hand with his other, effectively keeping the object of our conversation in full view.

I sipped on my strawberry shake while staring down at our clasped fingers. There was a question I wanted to ask, but I never liked to bring Jill up. I knew it made Caleb sad.

"I know your first marriage was different. You were in love. You had three children together. When," I worried my lip. This was more difficult than I expected. "When did you stop wearing your ring?"

His lip twisted up in a scowl and as much as I wanted an answer, I regretted asking. "Wellington policy. Six months after the death of a spouse, if you are under the age of forty-five, you now become eligible for remarriage. The ring comes off, and when there is an opportunity, a match is made. Like my mom and Conrad. Granted my mom and dad divorced, which was a scandal, but Conrad's wife had died two years prior. He's a Wellington, my mother isn't, so the marriage was approved."

I snorted. Typical backward mentality I'd come to expect from Wellington. The waitress came back with our fries and I reveled in the taste of salt and fatty foods before I focused again at our joined hands. While Caleb had answered my question at face value, it didn't answer what I truly wanted to know, so I sucked up the courage and went for it. "How did you feel when you took your ring off?"

His fingers gave a reassuring squeeze as he spoke.

"I know where you're going with this. No, it wasn't easy, but for me the ring wasn't a symbol of marriage, it was a reminder of all the memories we shared.

"And we don't have memories together," I interrupted, if not a bit petulant at the same time.

"I didn't say that." I looked up at the huskiness in Caleb's tone. "We've made a few memories together." I felt myself blush when he lifted my hand to kiss it. My pulse quickened at the gesture and despite my confused mental state, my body had a mind of its own when it came to this man.

"By law, we are married," he continued. "Yes, this ring is a symbol for everyone to see that we are united together. Our relationship, though, that's between us. It's what we make of it. Friends? Partners? Lovers? No one knows but us. Don't let this gold band scare you, Grace. You said we didn't say vows. You're right. Not publicly. But we did make a promise together that we will figure this all out. We promised that despite how you got here, and why you're still here, we will work together to get you home to your family."

I felt the sting of tears behind my eyes, but I blinked rapidly to push them back. "You're a good man, Caleb. I'm lucky to have you on my side."

We sat together in the diner, eating our fries, and I let his words sink in, but I still couldn't help thinking our relationship, now that these rings were on our hands, was about to change. I just wasn't sure if it would be for the good.

The rain continued on Saturday, but it had become more of a drizzle. Still, it had soaked the ball fields and the game was canceled. However, rumor had spread that if the rain stopped by mid-day, there was to be a bonfire behind Logan's barn in the evening.

After several days of being cooped up, a night outside sounded like fun to me. Rita and Conrad had already promised the kids they would go bowling, so it was only Caleb and me heading out.

He grabbed a tarp to put down on the damp grass as well as a wool blanket and a five-gallon bucket. Logan's home was on the northern part of the compound and wasn't too far from the town center making it easy access for most people to walk.

The party was in full swing, and we found a spot near Aaron and Caroline to put down our tarp before we headed across the field to a barn. "What are we doing?"

Caleb grinned. "Getting water. It's customary for everyone who comes to a bonfire to bring a bucket of water. Everyone does their share for fire safety. We use it to put out the flames at the end of the night."

"Why not bring in the fire engine?"

He gave me a lopsided grin. "What fun is that? The way we do it, some of us might get a little bit wet."

I shook my head. "Basically, you're all a bunch of kids."

"Absolutely."

There had to be about a third of the town on the farm to burn the brush from the wind storm from two weeks before. I was amazed at how many people I recognized. I may not have interacted with each one over the past nine weeks, but I knew most by name.

Kurt Jr. was there with his wife, Abigail, as well as his sister, Shelby, whom I spotted hanging with Theresa and Barbara. While I did see Leland with A.J, Hope and Jake were conspicuously absent.

There was a game of tackle football where those

playing were covered in mud. Caleb and I, as well as Aaron and Caroline, sat and chatted with Annalise and Kyle, who were planning their wedding for September.

All things considered, it wasn't my favorite topic, but with the lovey-dovey newlyweds feeding them on, Annalise and Kyle were like bees to honey. I did enjoy myself though, and the night sped by.

And when it came time to douse the flames, I offered to do the honors. I grabbed the bucket by the handle, poured half the water on the fire, then turned quickly to dump the remaining onto my un-suspecting companion.

I doubled over with laughter as Caleb slowly turned, surprise evident as he looked down on his soaked to the skin shirt then back at me. "You're right, this is more fun," I sputtered.

"Is that how it's going to be?"

His slow drawl should have been fair warning, but I ignored it. "I believe you are the one who told me this was the best part of the night."

"Oh, it is. It is." There was no doubt his intention, so I turned and ran. He grabbed the bucket Aaron had brought and reached me in seconds to dump the chilly water over my head. I squealed as it ran down my neck and was distracted enough for him to tackle me to the ground.

Ever the protector, he made sure to take the brunt of the fall then rolled until he was on top, one arm around my waist, the other holding my head up from the ground. We were face to face.

"I love your laugh." I almost think his words were not meant to be said aloud, it was as though Caleb was talking to himself. For a brief moment, time stopped, and I knew he was about to kiss me. And I knew I wanted to kiss him back.

Then he grinned. "Tag, you're it." He pushed himself up and sprinted across the field. I followed, but my brain was still back on the ground trying to analyze what had happened. Or not happened. While we chased each other around the grounds, I tried to convince myself Caleb not kissing me was for the best.

There was a full-fledged water fight going on with everyone still at the bonfire. I don't know how the fire was actually put out. I saw more buckets dumped on people than on the flames, but it was out when we all finally gathered our belongings to walk home.

Caleb took the wool blanket and wrapped it around me. "Don't want you to catch a chill."

I giggled. "It's eleven at night, and I think it's still around eighty degrees. I don't think I need to worry about hypothermia." But I didn't take the blanket off as we made our way back to the apartment. Aaron and Caroline walked with us, and it was obvious by the looks and the touches and remarks they were hopelessly in love.

Caleb had his arm around my shoulder, keeping me close as he carried the tarp under his other arm. Could others tell that we didn't really know what our relationship was? Eventually, we split from our friends, but we weren't truly alone until we entered the apartment building. Suddenly, I felt shy, and I didn't know what to say or how to react around my enigmatic roommate.

I dropped the blanket on the living room floor and looked up to see dark heat in Caleb's eyes as they skimmed my body. I looked down and saw my wet clothes plastered to my skin. In the harsh light of the apartment, there wasn't much left to the imagination.

But his wet shirt didn't hide much either. Why didn't I admit that I wanted a repeat of what we had last weekend? We both stood, watching the other. No, I didn't need to say what I wanted. It was more than obvious to us both, we were on the same wavelength. I was weak. I had enjoyed our one night together way too much not to want a repeat.

"If you want, I'll take the wet clothes and get a load of laundry going," Caleb offered which immediately set my mind to seeing him with his clothes off. I was in trouble. He had promised to take things slow, and he was a man of his word. If I wanted things to progress, I needed to make the first move. And if the huskiness of his voice, or the way his eyes kept drifting to where my nipples puckered against my wet shirt was any indication, it wouldn't take much.

I pulled my shirt away from my skin, noting how Caleb's hooded eyes watched my every move. "We're both a mess from the mud and grass. Why don't we clean up together?"

I saw the visible intake of his breath. "Grace, are you…?"

"Yes." I cut him off, then took the initiative and moved in to steal a kiss. By the way he responded, I wasn't the only one who'd been holding back all week. His groan filled my mouth as his lips ground against mine. I clasped the front of his wet shirt keeping him close while his hands moved down my back.

"You're not making this easy," he gasped when he finally released my mouth. He tilted my face up. "Everything about tonight was perfect."

My breath caught as he rubbed his thumb across my lips, still tingling from his kiss. His deep sigh held both a hint of longing and regret "The way the moonlight and the glow of the fire danced across your skin. How you leaned against me, letting me wrap my arms around you. But most of all, hearing you laugh. You don't do that enough."

"Ca..."

"No." He pressed his thumb against my lip, silencing me. "As much as I want this night to end differently, I made you a promise."

I closed my eyes. Why did he have to be so good? The carefree evening had swept me away, but he continued to be strong for the both of us. His lips pressed against my forehead, and the gentle gesture had a spark of tears press against my eyelids.

"I know you're right," I whispered. "I got caught up in the fun of the night."

He pressed my head into the crook of his shoulder. "Don't get me wrong, Grace. I want you." His voice was husky and the way his hands pressed me to him, I knew he held tightly because if he didn't, he'd lose control. I knew how he felt. "If there were a way we could have it all, I wouldn't hesitate a single moment to take it."

Chapter Fourteen

We returned to work on Monday. It had been two weeks since our forced marriage. Two weeks of getting to know each other. I'm sure I can guess what the townsfolk of Wellington expected of their newly married couples during their honeymoon, but that hadn't been the case for us.

Although, after what happened Saturday, there was yet another shift in our relationship. Caleb wanted me. I wanted him. The attraction was mutual. If I'd been at college where men and woman acted on their impulses a lot more freely, Saturday would have ended with us doing a lot more than sleeping in that bed.

If I were still at college, I'd still be taking my birth control, and we would have access to condoms. Here in Wellington, sex doesn't happen until marriage and then with direct intent to procreate. The more children the better.

Roger had also laid down an edict. If I got pregnant, I would have to stay here. No Wellington child would be raised outside the security and over watch of the residents of this town.

So we stayed away from each other as much as we could. We were back to being roommates. When Caleb handed me my cup of tea in the morning, he was careful to not allow our fingers to touch. When he looked at me, I'd catch a glint in his blue eyes before they shuttered over, and he'd give me a casual smile. But I saw the tightness in his shoulders, the clench of his jaw. He was in control mode.

Every day was routine. I made breakfast. He made me tea. We went to work. Dinner was at his parents' house. His children slowly warmed to me. At night, we slept beside each other, not touching, but completely aware of each breath and every move of the other.

Living together was becoming more difficult by the day. Keeping our thoughts and our hands off each other was a slow torture. Maybe this was the whole point of the forced marriage: get them together and eventually nature will take its course.

Another Friday arrived and I sat at my desk, entering paperwork from the early eighties into the computer system. My busywork for a job created for me. I didn't mind, though.

I looked up as Caleb and Randy came out of the dispatch area together. "Hey, Chief," I called out, "I was wondering if I could leave a little early today."

He stopped and turned around to face me. "Sure. For what?"

"I need to go grocery shopping for supper. I was talking with your mom last night about it and well, she said she was going to make *real* pot pie."

He smiled, one of his warm, relaxed, smiles that twisted my insides into goo. "Yep. Mama makes great pot pie."

I raised an eyebrow. "Well, from how she described it, it is nothing like what I know. I mean, it doesn't even have a crust."

He shook his head. "Nope. It's *real* pot pie, cooked in a pot. Pennsylvania is known for it."

I shook my head. "That's what she said, so we decided we would each make our own version tonight to compare."

"Sounds great." He turned, took two steps away then stopped, slowly turning back. "Ah, you're not going to make me choose which I like better, are you?"

I hadn't thought of it before, but the question and his pained expression couldn't be ignored. Besides, Randy, Tom, and Greg were all listening and waiting. I lifted my chin and gave an innocent look. "Why, Caleb, would you choose your mom's cooking over mine?"

He closed his eyes, and I knew I had him. "Ah, Randy?" He turned to his brother in-law, "Don't you and I…"

Randy shook his head. "Don't drag me into this one. It's all you, bro."

I couldn't keep a straight face, and I doubled over in my chair with laughter. Until I looked up to see Caleb looking down at me, and his expression held something more. Yes, there was amusement, but behind his eyes, there was more than laughter, there was heat. This easy comradery had turned him on.

I sucked in my breath, as my own laughter came to a stop. His eyes drifted to my lips as my tongue slipped out to wet them, then they returned to mine, a message loud and clear passed between us. It was getting harder to avoid the sexual tension between us.

I know nothing had happened so far only because he was a man of his word, but maybe even he had his limits. There was still a room of men still watching our interaction and Caleb, of course, was the first to take control of his emotions. He took two strides back to my desk and captured my mouth in an unexpected, but toe-curling kiss. "Not to worry, wife," he exclaimed loud enough for the on-lookers. "I know whose bed I lie in at night." Then he turned to his officers. "And don't you be telling anyone I dissed our famous pot pie, either. Now get back to work."

Easier said than done. For either of us. The morning dragged. Several times I looked up, peering into the glass window into Caleb's office to find his eyes on me. While his kiss had been for show, a distraction for the officers, it had licked the embers between us into a full flame.

These casual, fun moments were rare. This town had placed a heavy burden on the both of us, and to see Caleb smile, or for me to actually laugh out loud, it hinted at the couple we could potentially be under different circumstances. And that kiss he'd planted? I ran a distracted finger over my lips. While I know he'd done it for the sake of our audience, there had been nothing casual about it. With that brief meeting of lips, I knew, without a doubt, he felt the same lustful attraction that was toying with our thin line of self-control.

Once again, I looked up into the glass window between my desk and Caleb's office to find his eyes on me. As I slowly moved my fingers from my lips, I could guess he knew were my thoughts had gone. I only wish I could read his mind as easily as he seemed to read mine.

When Tom and Greg headed out that afternoon to drive patrol through town, Caleb came out of his office and passed by me, not even giving me a glance. He went down the hallway where the cells were located. He had no residents, and the only other area on that side was the closet that Hope had broken into to get Jake's watch a few weeks ago.

Curiosity got the best of me. I went over to the counter that housed the tea and hot water and made myself a cup. I took my time, sneaking glances down the hall. The door to the closet was open.

I added sugar to my mug and stood at the counter, dunking my tea bag into the hot water. When Caleb exited, he held a small, brown, non-descript box. He closed the closet, locked it, then turned and saw me watching.

And surprise of surprises, he gave a slow, sexy smile, and I was lost. When he winked, my heart caught in my throat. What the hell was he up to? But he walked by me, box in hand, and headed into his office without a word.

The children were extra needy that night. Or maybe it seemed that way. Elena wanted to play a game; Justin was in a mood and threw a tantrum; and Shawna decided tonight was the night she wanted to potty train, so she kept asking me to go with her into the bathroom to help with her pull-ups.

It all would have seemed normal, except Caleb had a secretive smile, and for the first time in a week, he found ways to brush up against me. His hand lingered on my shoulder, and his eyes spoke volumes. When supper was served—two completely different versions of the same meal, he gave a wicked smile and memories of his kiss earlier had me hiding my face with my hair as I ate. It was like a quiet seduction and I didn't know what to make of this sudden turn of events.

When we said goodbye to his family, I was a bundle of nerves. This week had brought more rain, and it was coming down steadily as we stepped outside. Caleb put a hand on my back and rushed me out to his cruiser, opening the door quickly for me to slide in. He was around and in the driver's seat in seconds. With a quick motion, the ignition was turned on, and I got a blast of air in the face from the A/C.

"Put your seat belt on, please."

I didn't. Instead I turned to stare at him. The glow from the streetlight above shone brightly in the confines of the car. "What is with you today?"

Caleb kept both hands on the steering wheel, facing front, almost avoiding me after an afternoon of touching me at every turn. "I was thinking we should go to The Hall tonight to listen to the band. Are you interested?"

Interested? Loaded question. I was interested in knowing why he suddenly felt the need to touch me at every moment today when he hadn't in a week. I was interested to know why he had a secretive smile. I was interested to know why he'd been playing with my senses for the past several hours and now wanted to go somewhere public for the night.

"Um, sure. I haven't spent any time with Caroline lately." I leaned back. It was hard to know what to say when the man was a mixed bag of contradictions.

Then he was close, leaning over me, and I breathed in his masculine scent. The stubble on his face gave him a rough and tough aura, but the laughter in his eyes showed his softer, kinder side. He reached for the seat belt and slowly pulled it over my body, his fingers skimming across my chest to secure it in place. My pulse quickened and once again, the air around us thinned making it hard to breath. Funny how he always had that effect on me. "Have to buckle up. It's the law."

A second later he was driving as though he hadn't a care in the world, In the meantime, I hadn't recovered. A week ago, I'd practically offered myself to him, and he'd said no. Not because he didn't want me, but because he'd made a promise. What had changed? The kiss today? That had been for show. Hadn't it?

We made a quick stop back at our apartment to change for the evening, and he was back to not touching me. I gave him the bedroom to change while I grabbed clothes and headed to the bathroom for privacy. I chose a simple yellow sundress with matching sandals, scooped my hair up off my neck, and ran lip gloss across my lips.

I wanted casual, but when I looked in the mirror, my eyes sparkled and I didn't see casual, I saw expectations. "Stop. Despite his mood, you know you can't be with him." I talked to my reflection. "Your goal is to find a way to get out of this Stepford town and return home, not to give in to a moment of lust."

I pressed my hands against my face, hoping to squash the blush that tinged cheekbones. "Even if you sleep next to the man every night and have wished over and over for a repeat of what happened two weeks ago, the answer must be no. Keep your eye on the ball, Grace. Home. Family. You can do this."

I exited the room to find Caleb in the kitchen. He slowly lowered the glass of water he'd been about to drink and stared at me. "You look beautiful."

I swished the short skirt of the dress aside and looked down. My pep talk of a moment before forgotten. I felt shy and my voice was barely more than a whisper. "Um, thank you. I picked this up the other day and was waiting for church on Sunday, but, well…"

"I'm glad you didn't wait. You'll be the prettiest girl on the dance floor tonight."

I wasn't immune to his husky voice. He motioned for me to head out and again, he didn't touch me, not even a hand on my back, as we left the building.

The moment we arrived at The Hall, Caleb was waylaid by Greg, the officer on duty, so I excused myself and made a beeline to Caroline. I needed a breather from the man's intense, heated stare. Straight and True was on fire tonight with the fast and fun songs, and Caroline and I headed out to the dance floor, without the men, to gyrate to the music and work off our energy from the week.

Aaron was at the mike, singing a song about ladies loving country boys and I sang along, like everyone else on the dance floor, when I spun around and spotted Caleb across the room, watching me. I forgot the words as our eyes connected. The noise of the room faded, and in that moment it was just the two of us. I know the band still played, and that I moved in rhythm to the music, but when he looked at me, I felt like I was the only one in the room.

When the song came to an end, he strode to me in a few long steps and took me into his arms. "Dance with me." Three husky words, and I was his.

It was like the band knew to switch to a slow song. "Let's switch things up a bit now, folks. Here's some Shania Twain with *You've Got A Way*."

The young girl with the amazing voice, who I'd discovered was Aaron's youngest sister, Emalee, came forward and sang the love song with a voice years older than she was. Caleb moved me across the dance floor with slow, even steps, while his gaze never left mine.

"Caleb, I have to know—" I broke our locked gaze to look around the room, "—is all of this tonight for show?"

His eyes softened as he shook his head. "I don't give a damn what anyone in this room thinks. Right now, at this moment, I only want to enjoy having you in my arms."

"Oh." It took me another moment before I could find my voice again. "You're different today. You've been so cold the past week and now…"

"No, sweetheart," the endearment caught me off guard. "The only thing cold about me this week has been my showers."

"Oh." I didn't know how to handle that revelation. So close to how I'd been feeling, yet we'd agreed on our final destination. This, none of this, was in line with our goal.

"Do you know why I wanted to come here tonight?" He moved across the dance floor with an easy grace while I seemed to be all left feet as I tried to keep with his rhythm in the bright overhead lights of the room.

Why? I can't even think straight, never mind come up with a reasonable explanation of his sudden mysterious behavior. "No. I couldn't even begin to guess."

"It's because I love to watch you dance. Here and on the baseball field are about the only time you stop living in your head, over thinking everything. Here, you give in to the music. You smile. You relax. You really do look amazing in that dress."

If only he knew how un-relaxed I felt right now. As I tripped over my own feet, he pulled me closer. I was aware of every inch of his body against mine. How his hand at my back burned through the cotton. How his denim-clad legs brushed against my bare legs below the hem of my dress. What had I told myself earlier in front of the mirror? Whatever it was, I'd forgotten it already.

"Why do you keep looking at me like that, Caleb?" I pleaded for an answer.

He gave another of his slow, secretive smiles. "How am I looking at you?"

I knew but did I dare say the words? He spun me around to the music and I couldn't resist the magnetic pull between us. "Like you're undressing me with your eyes."

His gaze flared with an instant heat and my mouth went dry.

"Let me ask you something," Caleb lowered his head so he could speak in a low tone and still be heard with the music. "If I said that I'd found a way to pick up where we left off last week and still be able to keep my promise, would you walk out the door with me right now?"

I stumbled again, forcing us both to stop. Two frozen figures on the dance floor as other couples swirled around us.

"Um, is it even possible?" Holy crap, was it possible? Possible that tonight I would have Caleb's lips on mine? That we'd be doing more than sleeping alone while being in the same bed?

"Yes."

Chapter Fifteen

Yes?

We walked off the dance floor before the song ended and were out in the rain, heading toward the car parked a block away at the station with that single word hanging between us.

The drive back to the apartment was only a few blocks, but Caleb held my hand the entire time. A couple times he'd lift it to kiss my fingers sending swirls of heat throughout my entire body. The rain pounded down as we pulled to a stop and ran inside, laughing and swiping at our wet hair and clothes. Then the laughter stopped.

We made it just inside the entrance before he pulled me to him and kissed me. More like ravaged me. His hand tangled in my hair as he pushed me against a wall near the stairs. The past weeks had been full of restraint, but the attraction between us went further back. Before he'd brought me to orgasm with his fingers. Before we'd been forced to marry. All the way back to that day on the ball field when we'd collided and crashed to the ground. I pushed up on my toes, meeting him and giving back what he gave.

"I wish this building had an elevator," he murmured as he pulled away to grab my hand. I giggled as we sprinted up the stairs.

We brushed by another couple coming down. I

know they said hello, and Caleb responded, calling them by name, but I barely noticed them, as I was too intent on what was ahead.

Somehow, we managed to get behind closed doors of our apartment before I was back in his arms. "Sweet, sweet, Grace. Do you have any idea how difficult it has been for me to keep my hands off you? To not kiss you, because if I did, I wouldn't want to stop?"

I shook my head. "No. I thought… Actually, I didn't know what to think. You seemed to manage fine. I've spent the week going crazy because I felt like a fool, offering myself to you last week and you were too much of a gentleman to do anything about it."

"Gentleman?" He scoffed as he pressed his lips against mine again for a soul-searing kiss. "No gentleman would spend every waking hour replaying the one night I did have you naked, in our bed, writhing under me, and wondering why, in all that is merciful, I didn't take you, then and there."

"Oh." That one syllable seemed to be the only thing I was capable of saying tonight.

"I haven't felt like a gentleman in weeks," he admitted between kisses. His body pressed mine against the door, and I heard an urgency in his voice in between his touch. "And I have spent the last week, watching your every move, wanting to give you the world, but feeling selfish enough to consider any and all alternatives."

His mouth trailed down to my neck and my entire right side, from where his mouth moved all the way to my toes, tingled. I tried to maintain the conversation despite my major distraction. "Like what kind of alternatives?"

"First, I studied the calendar Dr. Todd gave you and thought maybe we could skip having sex on the days he'd marked down as your most fertile."

With the way Caleb scrambled my mind with his touch, anything he said would sounded plausible. "Um, okay. Is that what we're doing now?" I groaned as his mouth lingered a moment longer at the pulse in my throat.

He stepped back and I would have felt abandoned if he didn't take my hands in his. "No, I have something better."

It was the pride in his voice that piqued my interest. I followed him into the bedroom where he pointed toward his nightstand and the brown box he'd taken from the closet at work earlier. "Open the box, Grace."

Curious, I lifted the flaps and reached inside. There were two other boxes inside. I pulled one out and gasped. Condoms. Caleb had gotten his hands on condoms.

"Contraband," he said, giving his eyebrows a wiggle.

Someone, Jake most likely, had packed these for the summer and it, like so many other items, had been confiscated when we arrived. Now, Caleb, the police chief who'd sworn to uphold the laws and edicts of this town, had stolen items from his own station. God bless a man of desperation.

"You were right about that dress," his voice was husky. "I do want to take it off."

I liked where this was going. "Only if you promise tonight I won't be the only one undressed."

He stepped closer. "I promise. And I always keep

my promises."

Time slowed. Caleb gave me a quick kiss before heading to the window to pull the shades down. He took off his boots while I slipped my bare feet out the flimsy sandals. Caleb pulled the blankets down on the pristinely made bed before he met me in the middle of the room.

His hands moved around to my back where he slowly slid the zipper of my dress down, while my hands unbuttoned his shirt. Every move we made was slow and deliberate, building up for more. I was nearly shaking by the time I pushed the fabric from his shoulders giving me access to kiss the center of his chest. He slid my dress off and I stood in front of him in bra and panties wanting him more than I'd wanted anyone or anything in my life.

"I have been imagining this night for weeks," Caleb groaned. He reached for the strap of the bra, but I shook my head and stepped back, giving him a better view as I reached behind me and undid the clasps. I slowly dropped the scrap of material as I watched the blue of his eyes darken.

Before I knew what his intent was, he swung me up in his arms to place me in the center of the bed. He dropped his pants in a pile on the floor, and I reveled in the moment of seeing him naked. From his wide shoulders, down to his sculpted abs, down further past his narrow hips, and then to his very erect male anatomy. When I looked back up, Caleb was finishing his own perusal of my body, and our eyes did the talking. *No more waiting.*

He knelt onto the bed, and finally, finally we were skin to skin. As much as we both wanted, no needed this night, it was all about taking it slow. Savoring each touch. His fingers explored, roaming from my collarbone, down to my breasts, circling and rubbing the hardened nipples. But he didn't kiss me. Not yet.

He wasn't the only one exploring. My fingers followed a similar trail on his well-defined chest, exploring the curves and contours. I wanted to memorize his body. While there were plenty of condoms within the two boxes, I didn't really believe we would have another night like this. So I would remember the feel of him, every sound. Every word he said.

His voice was low and seductive. "Your skin is so soft, Grace."

His wasn't. His fingers were calloused, and the roughness felt good as they trailed downward where they sought entrance under my wet panties.

"Ahh," I arched upward. I already knew the magic his fingers would have on me. I wanted more. I reached down to take his fullness in my palm, eliciting a groan from him. We were both primed. As his fingers pushed inward, I had to release him to grab at the bedsheets below me. I couldn't make my body do what I wanted. No, it belonged to him. We'd waited, longer than either had wanted.

I was panting, needing more. "Caleb, please."

"I know." He pushed away from me, stood, pulling my panties down my legs. I saw him grab for a packet before he was kneeling back on the bed.

He kissed my palm and then my ring finger where there was a gold band before intertwining his fingers in mine.

That one gesture was worth more than any words.

In a single kiss, Caleb had acknowledged our marriage, and my heart filled in a way I didn't know was possible.

"Look at me," he whispered. I couldn't look away even if I'd wanted to. His blue eyes spoke to me as he slowly pushed inside. "Keep your eyes open, Grace," he pleaded. I did.

I watched him as he set a slow steady rhythm. In. Out. I saw the slight lift of his lips when my body began to quiver. I noticed when his breath became shallow as his pace quickened. But I couldn't keep my eyes open any longer when my body exploded into a thousand pieces. Then I heard his own echoing cry as my body pulsed around him, bringing him to his own release.

"Oh, Grace." Caleb's lips brushed across my cheeks as he pushed my damp hair from my face. This was a new beginning. We may have been married for a few weeks, but tonight we'd become a couple.

Chapter Sixteen

Before I had my eyes open, I felt Caleb's hand tracing a random pattern on my shoulder. The light touch was all I needed to remember what we'd done the night before, and my body instantly reacted.

I let out a low moan as I opened my eyes. He leaned on his side, looking down at me and when he saw I was awake, he immediately leaned in to take what breath I had left away.

When I could, I stretched, allowing my body to press against his. "Good morning."

"How good?" he asked with a grin, and I knew I had the upper hand as to where we went from here. I ran a fingernail down his chest, down to his stomach and stopped short of the intended mark I felt pulsing against my leg.

"How good? Hmmm?" I moved my nail back up to where I'd started before trailing down again as Caleb watched with heavy-lidded eyes. "Depends on your stamina."

"Sweetheart, did you just offer up a challenge, because I never back down." He used his knee to nudge my legs apart and shifted so I could feel his fullness between my legs. "The question is whether you can keep up with me?"

"Game on." I leaned forward and sucked on his nipple and had an instant reaction. The bed became our playground as we nipped and tugged, rolled and laughed, until the laughter turned to moans as Caleb ripped open another foil packet, and we had a repeat of the night before.

"Your kisses scramble my brain," I admitted as I collapsed on him, my legs still on either side of his hips.

"And you don't think you have a similar effect on me?" His fingers went up and down my spine. He was still fully sheathed inside me and I was loathe to break the connection, but he eventually lifted my hips and rolled me to the edge of the bed. "I don't know about you, but I could use a little sustenance."

He disposed of the condom in the trash can beside the nightstand and then strolled naked around the room, picking up the empty packets.

"You're such a neat freak." I grinned. "What would you do if I insisted you didn't make the bed today?"

He looked down at the covers. The comforter was already on the floor, and the sheet tilted at an angle across the bed where I held it against my body. He shook his head.

"Aw, come on, you can do it. Must drive you crazy that I rarely make the bed. Why bother, I'm crawling back into it later."

"Uh, uh. Too many years in the military," he admitted. "I find it fascinating how you're meticulous in the kitchen, but not so much anywhere else."

I giggled. "Blame my parents. Their kitchen is their domain. It must be spotless. The rest of the house was out of sight, out of mind, most of the time."

He shook his head in wonder before changing the

subject. "Why don't you shower first, and I'll make you breakfast."

He stood there, Full Monty, and all he could talk about was food. Not me. All I could think about was that we had a half-full box of condoms in the nightstand, and another full box available. I pushed the sheet away and strutted to him. I ran my hand down his chest then downward and slid my palm around him, feeling him pulse beneath my fingers. "Shower with me and we can cook together."

In a quick move, he pulled me up, wrapping my legs around his waist. "Doesn't hurt to save water." He grabbed another packet off the nightstand before carrying me to the bathroom.

We did manage to eat. Caleb went to his parents for part of the day, as he'd promised the kids he'd take them to the lake. I opted out. There was no way I could watch that sculpted male body in nothing more than swim trunks and not want to sneak off into the woods. With three kids in tow, I was better off staying behind to focus on a meal to serve after church the next day.

He did have supper at the apartment, though. Just the two of us. No parents. No children. Somehow we finished the meal, but we spent the rest of the night making up for the honeymoon where we'd done everything and anything but give in to temptation.

Caleb was already showered on Sunday when he kissed me awake. "Wake up. I want to go by my mom's to help get the kids ready for church."

I stretched and yawned. We hadn't slept much in the past two nights, and my body was slow to move. Besides, morning had never been my best time.

I rolled to my side to watch as he moved to the

mirror to put on a tie. "You miss being with them, don't you?"

He didn't hesitate. "Very much, but my mom is a saint. She's been a lifesaver since I've been back, taking on the bulk of raising them."

"You're a good man, Caleb Wellington."

With a few steps, he was back at the side of the bed and leaning down to capture my lips in a brief kiss. "Don't be getting all serious on me. Let's go have a good day. Come on, sleepy-head, time to get moving."

I headed to the shower, knowing the bed would be made and the apartment spotless before we left.

At church, I tried to ignore Pastor Rick and his sermon of doom and gloom and instead focused on the man beside me as well as his family. Elena sat all prim and proper between her father and grandmother, trying to be the perfect child. Justin sat between me and his father, pulling constantly at the collar of his Sunday best shirt. Shawna, typical three-year old, couldn't sit still and spent the hour crawling along the pew and wanting to be held by any adult who would take her.

Caleb was the epitome of patience with each one of them. He gave Elena's hand a squeeze and earned a smile from his princess. He unbuttoned the top button for Justin, then loosened his tie so he could also release a button, winking at his son at their unity. As for his youngest, he held and snuggled with her, bouncing her in his arms as though she weighed nothing more than a feather.

He caught me looking at him, and the smile he sent my way was full of content and happiness and my heart filled. I looked at the gold band on my finger. I was in the midst of a situation which was in a continuous, out of control spin. I'd been forced to marry Caleb, but I was the lucky one. He was kind, generous, and had found a way for us to give in to what we wanted without compromising on our goal.

I felt a slight pang of misgivings at the thought. For the past couple days, I hadn't given the end goal a moment's thought. Home. Vermont. My family. I'd been so wrapped up in Caleb and being with him, I'd completely forgotten why we'd waited so long.

Shawna reached out for me, and I took the child into my arms. "Can we go to the park, Grace?" her question overly loud in the reverent room.

"Shh." I gathered her close to whisper in her ear. "Let's get through breakfast first, then we'll see."

"I love you, Grace." The child had not mastered the art of whispering yet, and her outburst had people staring. But when she wrapped her chubby arms around my neck and squeezed, I squeezed back. I'd spent a lot of time with these kids the past weeks, and they'd wormed their way into my heart.

Crap. What was happening to me? I was losing my grasp on reality.

We were halfway through eating when I spotted Jake moving across the room heading toward one of the food tables. I stood and put my hand on Caleb's shoulder. "I want to say hi to Jake. I'll be right back."

I came up behind Jake and wrapped my arms around his stomach, but before I could say anything, he whipped around shoving me away.

"What the...?" I teetered, but he grabbed my arms and pulled me into an embrace.

"I'm sorry, Grace. I didn't realize it was you. I thought it was *her*."

"You look horrible." I reached up to his face with both hands and rubbed at the dark circles under his eyes and the stubble on his un-shaven face. "I've never seen you like this."

He closed his eyes and put his forehead down to mine. "We need to get out of here. Soon. I'm going to crack under the pressure."

"Jake, I'm sorry. I should have checked on you before this. I didn't realize how bad things have gotten for you." I placed a gentle hand on his cheek. "You should have come to me."

I heard the screech a second before my hair was pulled and I was yanked away from my friend's arms. "Get away from my man, you bitch!"

I reacted instinctively. I twisted, trying to get Hope to release my hair and in doing so, I took a wild swing, which caught her in the eye.

I heard a yell from a nearby table and a melee ensued. "Cat fight."

In seconds, people from the closest tables were standing to watch, but heaven forbid if they were to get involved. Jake stepped between us, but the blonde diva was hysterical. "Damn it, Hope, let go of her,"

"Sure, take her side. I'm your wife, and this whore is trying to take you from me," she shrieked.

She raised her arm, fist swinging in my direction, but Jake was quick to push her back far enough to be ineffective. It was all I needed to push me over the edge. She'd made this my fight, and there was no way I was going to let this go. I took two steps toward her when a steel bar went around my waist and lifted me off the ground.

"Let me down, Caleb," I yelled. "She started it."

He did put me down, but not before moving me back toward a wall. "Don't move." It was an order I knew he expected me to obey. Except now Leland had moved forward to defend his sister, and Jake was his target.

"When are you going to start treating my sister better?" he huffed before shoving at his new brother-in-law. "You're married now, you ass. You can't be kissing other women."

Jake was pissed and ready to fight. "Like hell I'm married. I don't give a damn what anyone in this town says. Hope was nothing more than a summer fling. I only came to this God-forsaken, one-horse town because of Grace. She's the one I love."

"Oh, dear God," I whispered as Hope began to wail. Jake loved me? Before I could truly process the unexpected confession, Leland's fist made contact and Jake went down. Caleb grabbed Leland by the shirtfront and pushed him back.

It was like having a replay of the day at the barn. While I had run away from the madness that day, I wasn't about to back down today. When Caleb released Leland long enough to turn to check on the downed man, I went after Hope.

To get to her, I had to zag around the police chief to the right, which distracted him enough for Jake to move to his left. Jake got back to twin one while I never made it to twin two.

Once again, I was off my feet, swinging at air as I was forcibly moved. "For the love of God, Grace, can you for once do as you're told so I can stop this thing before it goes any further?"

"But…"

Caleb stopped my argument by capturing my mouth with his. "Stay." It was all he said when he released me and I stood in silence, as he left me and went to separate the fight. Brent had moved through the rows of tables, pushing through the crowd to lend a hand while the rest of the room watched and stood off to the side.

Except for Roger. Daddy'O was spitting mad and turned his hate onto Caleb. "You need to get that girl of yours under control. You need to remind her who she is married to. I saw her. She started it by kissing my daughter's husband."

Of course Roger would blame me. "I did not kiss him." I argued, ready to jump back into the fray. Caleb turned to give me a warning look.

Jake, still being held back by one of Caleb's hands, opened his mouth to retort but was on the receiving end of one of his 'don't go there' looks as well. My friend took the hint.

In his police chief voice, he turned back to Roger. "There was a lot of physical altercations here. I can take everyone to jail and let them cool off, or we send them all home to figure out their relationships."

Roger turned a nasty glare toward Jake, and I knew where he wanted to send him.

Caleb continued to talk. "But everyone will serve the same fate. If I send one to jail, they all go."

Hope continued to wail. "Daddy! Please."

Roger's lip curled back, but he wasn't going to send either one of his children in for lock up. "Fine. They can go. But everyone needs to go to their respective homes. These kids need to resolve this situation."

"A situation you forced on them," Caleb reminded him. "It's a huge adjustment; you shouldn't expect miracles overnight."

"Don't push me," the older man hissed.

Caleb didn't heed the warning. "I'm stating the facts. Your intentions for your children was decided on long before you brought in college students." I stood only a step away as Caleb laid into Roger, but the crowded room was silent as they all watched and listened. "You can't be surprised when not everyone complies with your absurd plan."

Roger did not appreciate being taken to task in front of the town. "You listen here, you had a part in this plan, as well. The entire town agreed with me, and we all carried it out. Everything is done now,and we aren't going back on it."

Jake tried to move, but Caleb's fist was still gripping him by the shirtfront like a steel bar, but he managed to point a finger at his father-in-law. "I don't care what you say, when I don't go home in August, my father will look for me."

My parents would look for me as well, but Dr. Collings had the means and contacts to find us even if we were in a completely different state from what we'd told them. My stomach twisted in a knot, and I couldn't take time to figure it out.

Hope clung to her father's arm. "Daddy?"

Roger threw a look of pure hate toward the defiant Jake before patting his daughter on the arm. "Don't worry, baby. I'll take care of it. Let the kids go home. Straight home, all of you. Jake." He pointed a finger at him. "Actions have consequences. Despite your denial, you are married to my daughter. It's time the two of you figured out what that means."

"I'd rather go to jail," he spat, then turned to Caleb. "Can I go to jail?"

Roger turned a beady eye on me. "And you, girl, keep your hands to yourself and off other women's husbands, or I'll see to it…"

I pressed my lips together and took a determined step forward, but Caleb reached out his free arm to block my path and gave a pointed look down at Roger's raised finger."I've told you before not to threaten my wife."

The older man folded his hand into a fist, more so, I believe to keep any digits from Caleb's grasp. "You need to get your house in order. Another man just declared his love for your wife."

There was a cold edge of irony as he responded. "Tell me something I don't know. It's been obvious from day one, but I know where she is at the end of the day."

I gulped looking back and forth between Jake, who stared at me with abject longing, and Caleb who wasn't fazed by the confession and wasn't worried at all, but perhaps a bit more possessive. Only a few moments ago, I was ready to fight, now I was rooted to my spot, unable to take it all in.

Jake, the friend I had known forever, loved me. I was sleeping with Caleb, a man I'd been forced to marry. And I didn't know what I felt for either one.

Roger turned back to his children. "Leland, go home. Hope, take Jake and try to make up." He looked back at Caleb. "*She*," he nodded to me, "was part of this as well. She goes home, too, or she goes to jail."

Rita rushed to fill plates for us to take home, and I

walked beside Caleb, holding the paper plate and mulling the events. Jake loved me? Did I love him?

Of course I did, but as a friend. Right? I mean, look at all the girlfriends he'd had over the years. He was a player. Not one to settle down. Then again, I know the other side of him, the caring, compassionate side he reserves for his siblings and closest friends. Had I missed the signs? If he had followed me here, then everything that happened was inadvertently my fault. I worried my lip until I tasted blood.

What about Caleb? I sneaked a peek at the man as we climbed the stairs to our apartment. I know I had feelings for him. But what? I was madly attracted to him. The sex was a-maze-ing. Thinking of it sent butterflies skittering off in my belly.

I liked Caleb. Truly liked him. I respected him as a man, as a father to his children, as a son to his mother. He was always fair and honest. While I'd hated him at times when I first arrived, I had grown to admire him, especially over the past couple weeks. But did it matter in the end? Jake and I were leaving Wellington as soon as we could make an escape plan, and Caleb would be staying behind. My heart hurt thinking about it. I couldn't afford to allow my feelings to be any more than friends with benefits. Really good benefits.

He took our plates and put them on the counter then turned to me where I stood in the center of the living room. "Do I want to know what you are thinking about so intently?"

I shook my head. There was no way I could talk about this with him. With anyone. I was too confused to sort it out in my own brain, never mind actually discussing it. I couldn't think about it now, so I did what comes naturally, I picked a fight.

"Why didn't you punch the pompous ass in the face? I was ready and willing, but you wouldn't let me get by."

Caleb's eyebrows lifted, and I waited for him to get mad. He didn't say a word, which, as usual, pissed me off more. I stood still in the quiet apartment. Part of me was ready to pace the room with frustration, but I actually had too many contradicting thoughts happening in my head that I was rooted to my spot. So I let my mouth do the running.

"You could have laid him out flat. Both Roger and his son. Hope, too, for all I care. What the hell is wrong with that family? They all need a good thrashing, and I was more than happy to dish it out if you hadn't stopped me."

"You know why I stopped you." He took a predatory step to me and I couldn't judge his mood but I was doing a nice job working myself up.

"Who do you think you are, interfering all the damn time? I can take care of myself."

"I watched you as we came home. Your mind is whirring a mile a minute, and you don't like to think about your feelings, do you?" He took another step toward me, and my heart began to race in my chest. He was getting too close. I need space. I needed to vent. I turned to my left and headed around the loveseat, doing my best not to look at him but knowing he continued to take careful, deliberate steps in my direction.

"Feelings?" I rambled. "Aren't they obvious? I'm royally pissed. At Roger for being completely unreasonable. And at you for not letting me fight my own battles." I whipped around to find he was only a step away.

"You didn't know about Jake's feelings for you, did you?" I quickly looked away, stepping back as he continued. My heart did a rapid pitter-patter in my chest. He had to stop talking. He had to stop being so reasonable. "But I also did not imagine what happened between us this weekend, either."

I shifted as the back of my legs met the edge of the chair. I still couldn't look up. His words were too close to the bulls eye. I bolted again, this time heading to turn on a lamp, keeping myself busy and away from Caleb, but he followed me, like a panther hunting his prey.

"I've come to know a lot about you, Grace, and I know you get extra feisty when you don't want to talk about something."

I gulped. "Then maybe you should take the hint." Despite the words, there was no heat behind it. It sounded more like a whine.

"I'm not afraid, Grace." Caleb now stood toe to toe, and I closed my eyes when his hand gently tipped my chin up. "I care for you."

My heart raced double time as I felt the twinge of tears forming at the huskiness of his words. Don't go there. Please don't go there. Jake just declared his love. I'm too confused to think.

"And I think you care for me, as well, don't you?" Damn it all to hell. He wouldn't stop talking. "Look at me, sweetheart."

I licked my lips, trying to salvage some moisture in my dry mouth. I slowly lifted my lids, and the first thing I saw was Caleb's smile. It was like a sucker punch to the heart, opening it to the feelings I was trying to deny.

"Why can't you be the type to argue back?" I whispered, and I spotted the flash of humor in his blue eyes.

"Talk to me, Grace."

I licked my lips again and his eyes darkened with heat and every fiber of my body responded in kind. I shook my head that I wouldn't say anything, but the words I didn't know were there escaped. "What we have scares me. I am undeniably attracted to you."

He waited, and I continued to stare in his blue eyes and at his mouth, only inches away from mine, as he continued to hold my face up to him. If I didn't breathe, I would start to cry and I didn't want to cry again in front of Caleb. "I don't want to think about what this all means. Us. Being together. I can't think future, because I still want to go home." The tears I tried to hold back escaped. "All I do know is I want to be here with you, and I can't think beyond one day at a time."

"Then let's do one day at a time. Together." Caleb brushed a droplet away with his thumb, and I leaned my face into his palm. "I made a promise to you, and the more I get to know you, the more I want to make it come true, no matter what the consequences."

When his lips pressed against mine, I knew he was a man of his word. I felt his longing, but I also knew he held back, waiting for me to respond. Waiting for me to make a decision.

It was easy. While I was here in Wellington, there was no other person I wanted to be with. Caleb got me. He understood me on another level that no one else did. Maybe Jake did, but it had taken years of friendship to understand. I think Caleb had figured me out within days of knowing me.

I lifted up on my toes, deepening the kiss. We emerged from the bedroom several hours later to pick at the food we'd brought back from the fellowship meal.

As I pushed my nearly empty plate aside, I glanced over at Caleb, wearing nothing more than a pair of gym shorts he'd grabbed before leaving the bedroom while I wore a tee that barely covered my panties. He was watching me as I polished off the brownie his mom had put onto the plate.

At his intent stare, I asked, "What?"

"You amaze me." He shook his head. "Some days you forget to eat and others it is like you have been starving in a desert for weeks."

I giggled. "Can you blame me right now? I mean, a week ago you were saying you would take it slow with me, and now you can't keep your hands off. I'm famished here."

Caleb cocked his head to the side. "So you're saying I don't keep my promises?"

I narrowed my eyes, trying to assess where this was going. "No," I hedged, choosing my words wisely. "Maybe you're not sure what the definition of slow is."

He stood and moved to stand before me and I looked up from my chair. "Well, if we are going to quibble."

"Quibble?" I laughed.

"Yes, quibble." He brushed brownie pieces from my shirt then took my hands to have me stand. "Then maybe you don't know how to listen."

"My ears are perfectly fine." I grinned at him.

"Ah, yes, but when I told you to stay put earlier, you jumped back into the fight."

"Oh, that," I admitted. "Nope, I heard you fine."

He raised his eyebrows. "So you admit you don't like to take orders."

"Guilty."

"Then how about we try an experiment. I will attempt to take things slow with you, and you will have to follow directions." Caleb followed his suggestion with a long, deep kiss which had me rocking up on my toes and sending my brain on hiatus. If he continued to do this, I would agree to anything.

"Sure," I murmured against his lips. "We can try. Can't make promises."

"Let's start now," his hand squeezed my ass and pulled me against him. "In the bedroom."

"Ooh. Doesn't that defeat the experiment?" I already felt lost when he walked away from me, leaving me to follow in his wake.

He tossed the blanket off the already disheveled bed as he spoke. "Not in the least. All I promised was to take things slow with you. And I will. Right now. You have the hard part, dear. You need to follow my orders."

I groaned as I saw the intent in his eyes. "What do you have in mind?"

He pointed to my shirt. "Take your shirt off then lie face down on the bed."

What was he up to? I had no idea what he had in mind, but after our afternoon in bed together, I was game for another round. I tossed the tee on the floor then scrambled across the bed to lie with my cheek on the pillow. Caleb straddled me and leaned over to push my hair away from my neck. "Now, I am going to kiss every inch of your body and your job is to lie still."

That sounded easy enough and fun. "Okay."

I closed my eyes, and he leaned down to kiss the base of my skull then rained tiny kisses along the edge of my hairline. By the time he'd reached under my ear, my body was already sensitive. He worked down my arm to my fingers then sucked each digit into his mouth. I groaned. Then he moved back up my arm across my shoulder blades and down to work his magic on the other side.

The air conditioner hummed in the background, sending its cool air over my body, heated by Caleb's touch. The combination had my skin tingling, and I realized this experiment wasn't exactly fun. No, it was becoming a slow torture of sensation and need. I was learning something about myself though. I didn't want slow. I wanted to jump in, with everything I had. I knew what Caleb had to offer, and I was ready. "Okay, you've made your point. You know how to take it slow." I wanted to touch him, and I turned to tell him so, but he placed a hand in the center of my back.

"Uh, uh. I didn't tell you to move, and I'm not done."

I had no choice, with his body pinning me down, to lie complacent as his mouth continued down my spine, but Caleb's hands now ran lightly, up and down, swirling around, making random patterns and my entire back was alive with nerve endings.

What he was doing to me was incredibly erotic and almost hypnotic. I was relaxing, but at the same time my entire body was alive. It wasn't as though I wasn't enjoying this, I was, but being told not to move made me want to move all the more.

His hand moved between my legs to cup me. I felt the warmth of his palm, and I pressed down against it while he continued to work his mouth against my buttocks. When he pushed my panties aside to slide two fingers inside me, I bucked.

I felt his smile against my skin as he gave an amused chuckle. "Stay still."

"I can't. I want more." I know I begged, but I didn't care. I had no idea how long he had been working his way down my body, bringing it to life, but what his fingers did to me now, I was near the edge of no return.

I panted as I opened my legs for him, giving him permission for better access. Instead, he left me hanging. Wanting.

His fingers now moved across my thighs as his mouth continue its path downward.

"Caleb?" I twisted. I needed to see. Needed to complete what he'd started.

"If you turn around now, we have to start from the beginning," he stated. "I believe I am keeping my part of the bargain."

I pouted as I grabbed a fistful of sheet and pushed my face into the bed to let out an exasperated scream. "You're not playing fair. I concede."

He ran his tongue down the arch of my foot, and I turned my face into the pillow. "I love when you make that little 'meep' sound when you try to stop from making noise." How could his voice be so controlled when I was about to lose my mind? It was so unfair. "Now you can turn over,"

Finally. I did as instructed, but then I went to sit up, to pull him to me from where he now stood at the edge of the bed he shook his head, denying me my need to touch him. Dear God in Heaven the man was blessed with beauty. From his chiseled jaw, a chest that was expertly carved, to his erection standing tall and firm.

My mouth went dry. "Now, Caleb. Please."

He shook his head. "I haven't kissed you all over yet. You need to be patient so lay back down."

I flung my hands over my head, whimpering. "I'm not good with patience. I like instant gratification."

He lifted my left leg, pressing his lips to the side of my foot. "Too bad. You're the one who said I didn't know the definition of slow. You cast the challenge."

I flopped back against the pillow and moaned as he continued his ever so long onslaught on my traitorous body. Up one leg until he reached the apex between, still covered by a scrap of fabric. After what he'd done with his fingers earlier, I was ready for more. Instead, he placed one hot, open-mouthed kiss there before moving on to my other leg.

I let out a frustrated groan, and I felt his smile against my thigh. Animal. Like he'd done on my back, his fingers also moved along my body, keeping every inch of me waiting in anticipation. My nipples were puckered and waiting when he finally took one into his mouth. A kiss, then a suck, then a kiss again before moving to its twin. My body was so feverish by now that where he didn't touch me I felt almost chilled.

When he finally made it to my lips, I pressed back hard, letting him know I was completely frustrated with want and need. He pulled back too soon then flopped onto his back beside me. "Now, Miss Patience, it's your turn to do me."

I rolled to one side to stare at him. Did he seriously think I could take that amount of time to kiss him as completely? Like hell.

"Fine." I huffed. "Close your eyes."

With a satisfied grin plastered on his face, Caleb did as he was told. I stood long enough to push my panties aside, then slid his shorts down. "Keep them closed." I ordered.

I ripped open a packet and slid the condom over his penis. Caleb's eyes opened as I swung my leg over to straddle him and promptly sheathed him. He grabbed me at the hips and laughed out loud as he bucked up. "You didn't follow orders again."

I arched back and pushed my hair away from my face. "On the contrary, you said it was my turn to do you. This is me doing you."

Chapter Seventeen

I groaned when the alarm went off Monday morning. I hadn't slept much since Friday night, courtesy of one insatiable and delectable man and a huge supply of condoms.

"Rise and shine, Grace."

I groaned again, pulling the covers over my head. "I hate mornings," I mumbled. "How can you be so chipper this early without coffee?"

Caleb rolled to his side and pulled the blankets to join me underneath. "You don't need coffee." His husky voice gave me fair warning a moment before his hand skimmed across my belly, and his knee pushed my leg aside. "What you need is to get your blood flowing."

I stretched, allowing my body to slide against his. Skin to skin, and every nerve ending snapped awake. I pressed my lips against his warm, inviting chest as his calloused fingers set my nipples erect and waiting. "Is that so? I suppose I could be tempted."

"Mmm. Good." He captured my lips, and I moved into his embrace, wanting, needing more of him, as though we hadn't spent the last two days exploring every inch of each other. "So why don't you get dressed, and we'll go for a run."

"Uh, huh." Then his words sunk in. "Wait? What?"

Caleb gave a husky laugh, and my insides

quivered. "You agreed we should get our blood flowing to start the day. A five mile run will do that."

I flopped back onto the bed and stared up at him, not sure if he was serious. "I thought you meant..." He lifted his eyebrows, waiting for me to say the words. "Hell, no, Caleb. I hate mornings, but I hate running more. You're on your own."

Then he cast the line. "Afraid you can't keep up?"

I pushed up on my elbows at the challenge and saw that his eyes drifted downward to where my breasts jutted out. Let him look. He'd had his opportunity this morning, and he decided on another form of physical exercise. "Keep up? With you, old man? Bring it."

"Old man?" His hand moved toward my protruding nipple that had caught his attention, but I swatted it away.

"Sure, aren't you, like, forty?" I deliberately added ten years to his age.

He snorted. "You'll pay for that. Come on, slow-poke."

It was only after we hit the pavement that I found out Caleb had set the alarm for five, and I remembered again why I hated the man when I first arrived. Sadist.

I was panting when we finished our run, which was far short of five miles. I know he had slowed his pace for me, but when we reached the apartment building again, I stopped, my hands to my knees as I stared at the staircase. "Why can't there be elevators in this place?"

He laughed as he ran in place, waiting for me to catch my breath. "Need me to carry you?"

I shook my head, envisioning him throwing me over his shoulder in a fireman's hold, as he sprinted up the stairs. While part of me knew it would be sexy as hell, I wouldn't give him the satisfaction. Instead, I bolted up the stairs with him hot on my heels.

"I call shower first," I ordered as we entered our apartment, and I pulled my sweaty shirt over my head and dropped it on the living room floor. My bra, shorts, and panties left a trail to the bathroom where I finally turned to see Caleb standing with his back to the door, watching every move I made.

I closed the door with a single thought: would he choose to pick up the clothes, or join me?

The water was steaming hot when he finally stepped in behind me, pressing his front against my back as he leaned down to press a hot kiss to my neck as his hands circled around me, to press me back against him. "Do you know what you do to me?" He ground the words out in a husky voice. "Your saucy smile; that engaging laugh? I'm a goner every time."

I froze under the pelting water. What was he doing? Sure, he'd admitted he wanted me, but that was just physical. These words were more—I felt a tightening in my gut—emotional. I had to stop him.

I twisted in his arms to face him, the water sloshing over us, the steam nothing compared to the heat between us. I put fingers to his mouth, silently asking him to stop talking. He kissed the pads of my fingers before sucking one digit into his mouth. I attempted to curb the desire spiraling through my body but Caleb wasn't done talking. "I want you, Grace. Every moment of every day. I can't get enough of you."

Shit, shit, shit. Was it wrong of me to want him this much, too? Even if I knew I couldn't let my heart get involved? I was going home. Had to go home. This was only a day-by-day affair. Sex with Caleb? Hell yeah. But what he was saying?

No. It was just words. I would ignore the intensity in his eyes. I would pretend his tone didn't hold a new level of depth. I pushed the sudden wayward emotions aside and instead focused on the here and now.

I watched as water trailed down his chest, to his abdomen, to the curve at the top of his thigh. My eyes were drawn to his erection, already sheathed in a condom—so that's what had taken him so long to join me—and I reached out, placing my hand around it before I looked back up into Caleb's hypnotizing gaze. One slight nod on my part and his hands were at my backside, lifting me up. I captured his mouth at the same time he plunged into me. It was fast and hot and exhausting all at the same time and when we were done, my insatiable lover helped me wash my hair as I no longer had any energy.

"Do you think my boss would mind if I went to work late today?"

Said boss wrapped his arms around me and I stared at him through the mirror, only now starting to lose the steam on its glass surface. "Yes, I do believe he would mind because he would miss watching you discreetly from his office, where he spends most of his time mentally undressing you."

I elbowed him. "Why, I can't work under those conditions. That's sexual harassment."

"Not if he doesn't act on it in any way."

I placed my hands on top of his around my waist. "No? But now I know what you'll be thinking."

"Darling," he drawled, causing my insides to flutter, "now you know how I have felt for the past several weeks. When I've left the office to go on patrol, it was because I needed space to get myself back to sanity."

My eyes widened as I saw the truth in his eyes. "I really do that to you?"

"After this weekend, do you have any doubts?" He took my towel and dropped it to the floor. "Your body," he ran his hands over my breasts, then downward to dip a finger inside me, still wet from the sex and shower, but then back up, "is amazing and responsive to my every touch." His eyes met mine in the mirror and didn't leave as he spoke. "But it has always been your eyes and smile that have twisted my insides to the point where I don't know whether I am coming or going around you."

I gulped, mentally arguing with myself. It's about the sex, Grace. All about the sex.

"From the day we met," Caleb continued, "I knew there was something special about you. A part of you that I wanted to get to know better." His hands continued their slow, tender exploration of my body that we watched together in the reflection of the mirror, but it was his words that seduced me. "The more we interacted, the more intrigued I became. But now." He nipped at my neck and my legs became jelly. "Now that I have gotten to know you—*You*! Who you are, what makes you tick, what makes you happy—I can't get enough."

"Caleb." I wasn't sure what I wanted to say. His hands and words had me under his spell. "Remember our first baseball game, when we crashed."

"Oh, I remember every moment."

And I saw it. The same look we'd shared that day

now reflected back at us. His hands had been on me that day, moving down my body to make sure I was okay. Now, his hands were on me again, this time on my bare, shower-pink skin. Seeing us through the mirror, watching his hands on my body, skimming across my abdomen was a new experience for me. I lifted my gaze upward to Caleb's and caught my breath. It was as though he could see into my soul.

"After you knew I wasn't hurt, I saw your look," I admitted. "And for the rest of the week, I tried to see you, but for the first time since I arrived, I couldn't find you."

"No. I avoided you." His fingers circled my hardened nipples sending shock waves through my body. "Because I knew then I was in trouble. You were off limits."

Watching him touch me and seeing my body react made me a bit weak in the knees. I pushed back against him, leaning my head back against his shoulder. "I'm not off limits now."

"No, no you're not," he whispered. "But I am definitely in more trouble now than I ever realized."

Before I could ask what he meant, he scooped me into his arms and carried me to the bedroom. We made it to work at precisely eight o'clock, but only because we didn't eat breakfast.

Whenever I glanced up from my desk, I saw him watching me through the window of his office and when he'd give me his slow, sexy grin, I knew what he was thinking, so I would quickly turn my back and begin typing. I had to redo several of the pages when I realized my fingers had been on the wrong keys of the keyboard, and I hadn't noticed despite my intense forward stare to the screen.

So began a new routine. Caleb loved his morning run. He was happy to get back into that on a regular basis. I hated it but joined him anyway. We'd pick up breakfast and tea at the diner as we continued to linger a bit in the shower.

Dinners were still at Rita's house as Caleb spent every moment he could with his children, but we didn't stay long into the evening.

No, the nights were reserved for us. We barely made it behind closed doors of the apartment before we stripped each other down.

Work was a killer. We didn't touch each other at all. We barely spoke. But our eyes spoke volumes.

The next weekend, we spent dealing with three sick children after Rita came down with the stomach bug. We never left her house from Friday afternoon until late Sunday. I was so caught up in my own domestic life that once again I didn't call or check in on Jake.

Monday morning, I arrived late to work after we'd had yet another vigorous workout. Our morning run wasn't any shorter mile-wise, but we'd picked up our pace in order to have our second round of aerobic exercise which started in the shower and ended up with us back under the sheets. Caleb showered again first and hurried out while I took a little extra time to catch my breath. We were taking this day-by-day seriously. Each day could be our last together, and we were sure to take advantage of every opportunity, if the dwindling box of condoms was any indication.

While I turned on my computer at work, Caleb placed a steaming cup of tea on my desk as he spoke into his cell phone—a luxury item he was currently not allowed to bring home at night due to my restrictions. Also, each call made on any cell in Wellington was logged and flagged in dispatch. Any number with an outside exchange would be immediately disconnected. The Nazi's.

"Is she still running a fever? No? She wants some daddy time? Of course. Give her a big hug from me and tell her I will come by shortly."

I put down my mug, recognizing the blend he'd introduced me to which seemed to do best for me in the mornings. It still wasn't the jolt I was used to from my overload of caffeine filled java, but it did help some to get me energized.

"Which one?" I asked.

"Elena. I'm going to head over there for a bit. Check in on her." His oldest had been the last of the kids to fall ill, but when we'd left yesterday, Rita was back up and running and had taken the helm once again with caring for her grandchildren.

I nodded as he checked in with Brent before heading out. Before he could exit, Roger strode in, and Caleb stopped him at the door.

"What can I do for you, Roger?" Funny how I could now tell the subtle differences in his tone. While at first, he sounded pleasant and welcoming, I recognized the steel underneath meant he was anything but happy to see the visitor.

The councilman brushed past. "I'm here to see the girl."

Caleb shut the door, and I knew he wouldn't leave me alone with my arch-nemesis. "The girl has a name, Roger." He stressed the man's name. "Why do you need to see Grace?"

I spun my chair around to face them as the town's manager made a direct route to my desk. He took out a folded paper from his shirt pocket and handed it to me with a satisfied look on his face. "This is for you. It's a copy of a letter I sent out this morning."

Curious, I unfolded the single page and read the typed letter.

Hi, Mom and Dad: You won't believe the incredible time I've had this summer. Jake and I love it so much we are now married and settling into our new lives here. I know it all sounds crazy and impulsive, but it's hard to understand unless you're actually in our shoes. Don't worry about college. I am transferring my credits to a local university, and the town is going to pay for the rest of my education. I miss you all. I will write again soon. Love, Grace

Caleb tore the page from my shaking hands. He read it quickly before crumpling the paper and tossing into the trash can. "You can't send this," his voice boomed.

Roger snorted. "I already have. One for Jake's family as well." He gave a smug grin. "I will not have him running out on my daughter and that means making sure his family doesn't come looking for him."

He gave a pointed look at the hand Caleb had resting on my shoulder. "It benefits you, too. I hear the two of you have been getting along quite well."

The fingers tightening in my shoulders told me Caleb barely had his anger under control. "You've made your point, now get the hell out of my station."

The older man wiped his hands, as though he was done with us, and sauntered out. The shaking was nearly uncontrollable now as I gasped for breath.

"Grace." Caleb turned my chair to face him, and he squatted down to my level. "Sweetheart. Breathe. Please."

I couldn't though. Despite everything which had transpired this summer, despite the original plan for our escape, I'd still had the ace card of my parents looking for me when I didn't come home at the end of the summer.

Brent brought over a glass of water and placed it on my desk then stepped back as Caleb ran his hands up and down my arms.

"I can't... He can't... I'm never going home, am I?" The sobs finally hit, and I lunged into his arms. I'm not sure how long we sat there, but when I finally stopped, I felt completely wrung out. Caleb sat with his back against the desk, his legs straight out with me across his lap. He reached up behind him and brought the glass of water down for me.

I took a sip and set the glass down on the floor. We continued to sit there until I glanced up at the clock. "Your daughter is waiting for you."

Caleb ran his hands soothingly up and down my arms. "My mom is there. You need me right now."

My body was numb, almost like the days immediately after the forced marriage. It was as though all my emotions had been physically wrung out of me. "I think I want to go back to bed. Can I take a sick day?"

He pressed my head into his shoulder, wet from my tears. "Of course, but no hiding out for days, okay?" He kissed my cheek. "I'll take you home and get you settled."

I pushed away and wiped my face with my palms. I

was a bit lightheaded from the crying, but what I wanted was to be alone. "I'm okay. I'll walk. Besides, your mom's house is the other way."

"I don't want you walking." I heard the concern in his voice, and I wasn't up for the arguing. But then Brent spoke up.

"I can drive her, Chief. I'll make sure she gets home."

I pushed to my feet, only to see Randy had come from his office down the hall and had joined Brent over by the hot water, both drinking tea. Both having watched my meltdown.

Caleb stood. He took my face in his hands and forced me to look up at him. "What do you want, Grace?"

He was asking. Not telling. He'd already let me know what he preferred, but now he asked and my lower lip trembled. "I promise, I only need to sleep right now. Brent can drive. Elena's been waiting long enough."

He kissed my forehead before he nodded to his officer. Within minutes, I was sitting in the front of a squad car being driven the few blocks back to the apartment. When we arrived, I exited the car, but Brent was out on the sidewalk by the time I stood.

"You don't need to come up," I mumbled.

"Yes, I do." He made sure I was in the apartment, but before he closed the door, he gave me a long look. "Grace, I need to ask you something. Were you ever here of your own free will?"

I nearly choked at the lump in my throat. "Don't you know?" He stood, silent. Waiting. Damn, did he take lessons from his chief? "If you mean, did I get onto the bus back in Vermont willingly? Yeah, I did. But this?" I pointed to the wristband everyone in town wore. "I may as well be shackled to a wall with the amount of freedom I'm allowed. I didn't sign on for this, or to get married. Or to never go home to my family again."

Brent gave a slight nod and closed the door. But I saw it. I saw the questions he had. He was a police officer outside of the Wellington gates. Maybe, just maybe, his question meant he was beginning to open his eyes to what was happening in his home town.

Chapter Eighteen

I slept. When I woke, it was after two, and there was a pop can and sandwich on the nightstand. Caleb had come to check on me. He was a good man.

I took a bite of the turkey and cheese before carrying the plate and drink to the kitchen table. While our plan to wait a few weeks until the town council calmed down and lowered security had sounded reasonable when we'd made it, it was time to speed things up.

The security in place was still a definite issue. While my relationship with Caleb had become more than the farce we'd wanted to project, it was Jake and Hope's warfare that I believed warranted the security ratings to remain on high alert.

I went to the phone on the wall and picked it up, praying Connie wouldn't answer. I couldn't deal with her chattiness now.

She didn't and after calling the furniture factory and finding out Jake wasn't there, I threw on the first set of clothes I could find and went to his apartment on the ground level.

He answered my knock, and when the door swung open, it was like looking at a different man than who'd arrived on the bus almost three months ago. Gone was the county club attire and the perfectly styled hair. Gone was the charming smile and flirtatious attitude.

His hair stood on end, and his face was pale. He wore only a pair of track shorts, giving me a view of his very perfect, lean, well-defined body. He'd said he loved me. But today, I knew I loved him only as a friend. One who was in desperate need. His blue eyes were gray and lifeless. If this had not been a dry town, Jake Collings would most likely be hitting the bars and probably would have been too drunk to stand.

"Are you alone?" I asked.

He pushed the door open wider and since the woman in question wasn't glued to his side, or curious to see who'd knocked, I had my answer, but I was not venturing inside.

"Put on some clothes and come to my place. That's an order." When he hesitated, I turned him around and pushed him back inside. "Do it. Now."

He came back a moment later, the only thing different was the tee-shirt he'd pulled on. He didn't even bother with shoes as he closed the door behind and followed me up the stairs. I motioned for him to take a seat at the kitchen table. "I take it Roger came by your work today."

"You, too?" He nodded dejectedly. "Sorry, Grace. I don't think he even thought about our parents looking for us until I said something last week."

"Can't know for sure, but I guess it's time to start coming up with ideas. This is what I've noticed about this place." I grabbed a pen and paper and began to scribble as I talked.

Caleb came in shortly after five while Jake and I sat, heads together, over our notes.

"Hi, Grace. Jake." I knew he was surprised, but he wasn't about to show it in front of a visitor.

I gave a wan smile. The day truly had worn me out. "Hi. Thank you for the sandwich. And for checking on me earlier."

He came over and I lifted my face for a kiss, which he gave, albeit brief as he looked over my shoulder. "What are you two doing?"

I hesitated. He knew we planned to leave, but after our time together, it didn't make it an easy conversation. "We're making a list of exit strategies." I pointed to the paper. "I know both the police station and the hospital have machines to disengage the trackers and I know that unless they are taken off properly, an alert will go out. Also, we are compiling a list of vehicles which leave Wellington on a regular basis, so maybe we can hide on one of those until we are outside the gates."

If I hadn't seen the darkening of his eyes, I would never have known he stuffed his emotion back. Instead, what he did do, was nod and say, in a much too calm voice, "I can probably help add to your list." Then he pulled out a chair and asked to see the paper.

"How is Elena?" I needed to change the topic, despite Caleb taking the pen.

"She started throwing up again around one. My sister took the two younger kids for the night so Mom can give Elena undivided attention."

I wrangled my fingers together at the almost forced conversation, while Jake sat next to me, quiet, almost sulking at no longer having my attention. "Do you need to go back?"

Caleb nodded. "Later. We can pick up a pizza then I'll head over to check on her." He slid the paper back to me. "Here, I've included some of the delivery trucks which come in to town."

Jake looked at the addition. "Since when do trucks come here? I've never seen them."

Caleb sat back. "There is a warehouse on the north side of town, about a mile in from the gates. Most deliveries here are delivered to the warehouse then separated out and delivered by our own vehicles into the center of town. Even if I could get you onto one of those trucks, I am still locked out of the security access until further notice and without the trackers disabled, even getting you out to the north section of town without setting everyone on alert is going to be difficult."

I tapped the pen against my lips as I gave it more thought. "If I need to have an x-ray, they would take off the tracker."

"Not an option." My head bounced up at the dark, menacing tone. "Anything which involves you being hurt in any way is not on the table. End of discussion."

I sucked in my breath as I met his gaze. Dear God, he was serious. I gave a slow nod to acknowledge I'd heard him then crossed the hospital off the list.

Jake pushed back from the table. "As much as I'd like to stay and work on this more, I've got to go deal with the ball and chain." He leaned down and kissed the top of my head, and a part of me wondered if he did it to deliberately taunt the other man. "Thanks for coming for me today."

That, I knew, was deliberate. I reached up and squeezed his hand. "Be good to you, okay?"

I watched as he strode across the room and left the apartment before I turned to Caleb, not quite sure what kind of mood he was in. I fiddled. I closed the notebook. Slid the pen over the cover. Pushed it to the side of the table. Then, only then, did I reach across the table to take his hand. "Thank you. Tonight wasn't easy."

He didn't look at me, but instead he nodded toward the notebook. "It was inevitable. I suppose we should have started this list a while ago."

He stood and went to the kitchen counter, avoiding me. So unlike him, the man who likes to face things head on, the man who has forced me to talk about my issues immediately.

With a heavy heart, I stood to follow him. "Are you mad at me?"

I moved up behind him and wrapped my arms around his waist, leaning my head on his back. I felt his sigh, more than I heard it. "Talk to me, Caleb. If the tables were turned, you would make me spill the beans."

He gave a resigned sigh. "I was surprised to see Jake here, that's all."

"Really? I mean, considering the letters?" I moved to stand in front of him, my arms still around his waist, and looked up to see his hooded stare. "Oh my God. You're jealous."

"No. Of course not." He denied but I saw the flash of something more in his eyes. "I just thought maybe we had something together, but you turned to him first."

He was jealous. Holy shit. I couldn't help but grin and his eyes narrowed when he saw it. "What's so funny?"

"You are jealous." I nudged his shoulders with my fist before lunging in to hug him again. "Jeez, Caleb, after the last couple weeks together, I would think you'd know I don't take what we have lightly." I felt his arms tighten around me, and I hoped it meant he was coming around. "I thought about calling you to let you know I was awake, to thank you for the sandwich and checking on me, but I figured you had your hands full with Elena. Then I thought if I had reacted like I did about the letter, I should go check on Jake. He was in a bad way and needed a friend."

Caleb ran a stroking hand down my hair and I knew we would be fine again. At least I hoped we would. Except for the fact I was actively looking for a way to escape Wellington, which meant leaving him, too. Writing the list with Jake, I was on point and hadn't wavered. Once he came home and started to help, I'd felt a stab of pain in my chest. I knew what it meant, but I pushed it aside.

Scarlet O'Hara was becoming my muse. Think about it tomorrow. But tomorrow was coming. Time to change the subject.

"Should we go to your mom's and check on Elena? I could make chicken soup. Your mom's pantry is better stocked than ours, anyway."

"Probably not a bad idea." His sad eyes looked down at me. "Are you up for it?"

Yes, we definitely needed a distraction. I was almost grateful Elena was sick. "I like your children, and I'm not afraid of a little stomach bug."

With Rebecca and Randy keeping the younger two for the night, Elena got a lot of attention, and she loved it. When we finally went to leave, Elena gave me a hug.

It tugged at my heart. She was finally warming up to me, and I was planning on leaving. This was not going to be fair to the kids.

I noticed Caleb standing outside the kitchen door and went to join him, but realized Randy was with him. Their low tones implied a private conversation. I honestly was going to leave them alone, but once I caught a few words through the screen, I took a step closer.

"You're the one who brought me here," Randy argued. "You're the one who insisted there was no place safer than Wellington to raise your children. Now, being here, I couldn't agree more."

"I'm not asking for me. I'm asking for Grace."

"Right," Randy's voice was tight. "Like you're going to let her walk away when it's obvious the two of you are thick as thieves. And what about your kids? They adore her."

"I know." Caleb sounded tired. "They've really come around to having her as part of the family, but don't you see, Grace didn't want to be married. She has a family of her own to go home to. She's not a runaway needing a place to fit in."

Randy grabbed Caleb's arm, giving it a shake. "After what you've been through, losing Jill, the way she died, you'd really let another wife go back out where there is danger everywhere? Rip another mother away from those kids?" He released Caleb and threw his hands up, frustration evident in his hushed tones. "Plus, you said Roger will ban you from town if you help her escape. Are you really willing to take that chance of never seeing your kids again? No, I won't help. I can't be a part of that."

I moved away. Caleb was still trying to find a way to help me leave. Despite the fact we were settling in as a couple. If I had met him under different circumstance—Who the hell am I kidding? There were no other circumstances where we would have met. No other circumstances where we would have been forced together as quickly as we had. No other circumstances where I would be wearing a gold band matching his. Sure, the sex was great. Sure, we got along most of the time now. Randy had a point, though. If Caleb helped me, the consequences of his actions were losing his children. Was I that selfish that I would force him to choose? But what choice did I have? Wellington was not where I belonged.

****

On Tuesday the sun shone bright in the sky and it was in complete opposition to my mood. Tom was the officer on duty, and he was never as fun to have around as Brent. Besides, once I'd discovered Tom was Roger's nephew, I always felt he watched and reported back to his uncle and the council.

Randy breezed through the station on his way to his computer room, but he refused to look at either me or Caleb. Neither of them knew I'd heard their conversation, but I had a feeling the rift between the two men was only going to get bigger, and I would be the catalyst.

Then there was Caleb. As usual, he kept things strictly professional while at work, but it was last night that bothered me. The sex had been different. Maybe it was all on me, but I don't think so. There was almost a sad desperation in the way he touched me. I couldn't blame him, though. It was time for me to go home. Our day-by-day had to eventually come to an end.

Despite that, I needed him. I didn't want what we

had to end badly. I wanted to take every opportunity I had to be with him and to enjoy that time.

Caleb got called back to work while we had dinner, and he didn't get home until after I'd fallen asleep. I vowed the next day I would make it a night to remember.

It was almost four on Wednesday when I went into his office. He'd spent most of the day patrolling through town, and he'd come back to the station only an hour before.

He looked up as I entered, but I went around to the back of his chair and put my hands on his shoulders to give a massage. "Your muscles are tight."

At first, I thought he was going to tell me to stop because we were at work, but he didn't. Instead he let his head roll forward as I worked the traps on his shoulders. "That feels great."

"I was thinking I would skip dinner at your mom's tonight." I kept my voice casual as I felt the muscles tighten at my words. "Before you say anything," I leaned down to whisper in his ear, "it's because I want to prepare a dessert just for you."

Caleb tried to spin his chair around, but I stood firm, blocking it. "Come home early, and I'll be waiting."

"Grace?" There was a question in his voice, but he couldn't hide the huskiness as he tilted his head back to look up at me. "What are you up to?"

I leaned over to kiss his forehead. "I do believe my work day ends at four, so I'm going to go shopping now. See you later, husband."

The word was out before I realized it. Not once in the four weeks we'd been married had I acknowledged our marital status. Caleb had. He'd referred to me as his wife more than once.

He was out of his chair and standing before I knew what was happening and, despite being at work, his hand cupped my head back as he pressed his lips to mine in a fierce possession.

"Go," he mumbled. "Do whatever you have planned." He captured my lip between his teeth, the raw hunger evident. "And I'll be home early."

I'd set out to seduce Caleb and instead I walked away hot and aching. It's a good thing the people in Wellington couldn't read my mind, because with how that man made me feel, my thoughts were far from pure.

I wanted to rush through my shopping, but it seemed like everyone I'd met and made friends with had all decided to hit the store at the same time. And damn, they all liked to chit-chat.

It took me a full hour before I walked back to the apartment, my hands loaded with bags. First things first, I headed to the shower, shaving and rubbing the new honeysuckle lotion over my body. I dried my hair and twisted it up in a messy bun. A hint of blush and lip gloss for make-up. I added earrings, just a little something sparkly to dangle from my lobes. Then I donned the barely-there red lace bra and panty set I'd found. While this town appeared modest on the surface with the clothing they provided, they were all about spicing things up in the bedroom.

I looked at myself in the bathroom mirror. There was no doubt my intention for the evening. Caleb said he'd be home early. There was one more item in the bag. I grabbed the apron that had a huge grilling fork and spatula on the front, slipped it over my head, tied the strings behind my back and headed to the kitchen.

I'd never cooked nearly nude before. I was getting turned on with the mere thought of what Caleb would think or do when he came home to find me this way.

I made cheesecake filled cupcakes. I'd discovered the recipe several years ago when Sarah was having a particularly challenging time. She loved cheesecakes, I loved chocolate, and this recipe combined the two. It became one of our favorites.

Caleb did come home early, but everything was ready. I'd set the table. Tablecloth. Cloth napkins. Lit candles. But I don't know if he saw them. His eyes went straight to me as he closed the door.

"What are you wearing under that apron?" His voice was thick.

I looked down. The apron was wide enough to cover where it needed, leaving only the red straps of the bra as the only evidence there was anything more than skin beneath.

I stayed behind the counter as he sauntered across the room. "Have a seat. Dessert will be ready in a moment."

He hesitated, glancing at the table then back at me. I knew what he was thinking. "No." I insisted. "You need to sit."

He did, but his heated eyes never left me as I worked on the finishing touches. "How was dinner?" I asked, trying to maintain a casual tone, but failing miserably. Between my near nudity and Caleb looking like he wanted to leap over the counter, I was far from unaffected.

"Is this how we're playing it tonight?" his voice

drawled. I had to use everything in my power to continue with what I was doing. I dabbed on a spoonful of whipped cream frosting to the top of each cupcake. It was the best I'd ever made.

I untied the apron and slipped the top over my head, dropping it to the floor as I took the plates from the counter sauntered to the table in my barely-there panty set. Caleb's eyes were hooded as I came toward him, but I saw how his fingers twitched as he fought to maintain control.

Playing seductress was new for me, but I was enjoying toying with him. I gently placed the plates on the table before sitting across from him. "Eat your dessert," I ordered though my voice cracked, betraying my own emotions.

"Which one?" He raked his eyes down my scantily clad body, and I couldn't take my eyes off him. Who was seducing who?

"First one, then…" I left the rest hanging as he slowly lifted his fork. I don't know what he thought of the dessert. He didn't speak. I have no idea if it was even edible, as I only took a couple bites.

'To hell with this." He pushed his plate away. "Come here."

I was a moth to a flame. I was standing in front of him before I knew I could move. His hands grasped my hips so he could lift me up. I wrapped my legs around his waist as I sat on his lap. "Kiss me," he ordered.

When I came up for air, he moved his lips downward to suck on a nipple under the red lace. "This is so incredibly hot," he mumbled. "If the condoms weren't in the other room, I would do you right here on the table."

His mouth moved to my other breast as I struggled with the buttons on his shirt. "Then what are we waiting for?" I asked.

He grasped my ass, holding me against him as he stood. "Dear, God, woman, what you do to me." His lips captured mine as he strode across the room toward the bedroom. There was a noise, but it didn't register with me until he halted and his mouth moved from mine. "Go away," he growled. But the noise came again and I realized someone was at the door.

"Caleb, it's me. Brent."

Chapter Nineteen

Closing his eyes in defeat, Caleb slowly let me down to the floor. "Go. I'll be there in a moment."

I nodded and closed the bedroom door before I heard him open the door to the entry hall.

"I need to talk with you," Brent's serious tone had me pressing my ear closer. "Is Grace here?

I was thankful the apartment was so small as I could hear the response easily. "In the other room. Do we need to go to the station?"

"No, this concerns her. Is she available?"

I looked down at what I wore and scrambled to the bureau. I quickly put on shorts and a shirt sporting my college logo and opened the door as Caleb motioned the unexpected visitor toward the chair in the living room. He was more of a host than I'd have been. Hell, with the way my body was zinging, I'd have told Brent to zip it and I'd call back later, but my husband—Yikes, I still can't take that in—continued the niceties. "Have a seat. Would you like something to drink?"

"No. I'm not staying long." He didn't sit, instead he turned his gaze at me. "Monday, when Roger came to the station, as well as the scene at our fellowship meal the week before, got me thinking. This whole summer program thing, it isn't what it was proposed to be, is it?"

He looked at his chief for confirmation. With

Caleb's shirt half un-buttoned and my hair falling from its bun, I'm sure Brent was aware of what he'd interrupted, but he didn't say anything. Caleb wrapped an arm around my waist, pulling me closer.

"No. Bringing in runaways from off the street wasn't good enough for Roger's children, and as he refused to allow the twins to attend college off-site, the only way he could bring in eligible candidates was to come up with a plan to bring in college-aged suitors who might be malleable to the town's ideology."

"I see." Brent nodded. "For the most part, though, it worked. Nine of the eleven don't appear in any hurry to leave at the end of the summer."

Caleb shrugged. "Eight, at least. After spending a night in the hospital, Penny might be looking to leave. The others all have broken families. For them, Wellington is pretty much Nirvana. Grace and Jake, however, both have loving families at home expecting them to return."

"So after all is said and done," Brent summarized, "Roger's kids happened to choose the two who had no intention of staying, and he retaliated by fabricating a cause for a forced marriage?"

I nodded, remaining silent, which is unusual for me, but I was still reeling from what had been interrupted to this sudden topic of conversation.

"That's what I gathered," Brent stated. "Okay. I will help you leave, if it's what you want."

A flash of hope filled me while at the same time pain pierced my heart. "You will?"

He looked at me with a determined expression. "I'm a police officer. I took an oath, and holding people against their will is against the law." He looked back and forth between me and Caleb. "I've never questioned how Wellington has been run, with all its advanced security, but the last couple days I've tried to look at this town as an outsider. Even making an outside call from this town is nearly impossible. I noticed that you're not even taking a phone home with you at night."

Caleb nodded. "Roger had security upgraded on both me and Grace once we were married. My cell phone at work will only allow incoming calls, and any attempt to go through the switchboard for an outside line will automatically be shut down and the members of the council will be notified."

I bit my lip. I hadn't even known the extent of what had been ordered.

Brent nodded, as though he'd already figured it out. "I spoke with my wife about this, and while the ramifications scare her, she agrees it's the right thing to do. So, if you want me to get an outside agency to come into Wellington, I'll do it. Working outside the town gives me more freedom to make those calls."

Caleb looked at me. "What do you want to do?"

"Seriously? You want me to decide?" I wiped away a tear that had escaped as I tried to reason out the question. "So what happens if you do something like that? Do they arrest an entire town because they were blindly led to believe this is all normal? Do they arrest Roger and the rest of the town council, for what? Kidnapping?" I looked up at the man I'd been forced to marry. "Would they arrest you because you followed orders and brought us here and provided the upgraded security?"

Oh, dear God that was a strong possibility, and his

stone-wall face meant he knew it. I gulped. "What's going to happen to the two of you," I nodded to him and Brent, "for helping us leave? What is Roger going to do? He's already threatened to ban you from town and from seeing your kids? He might do the same to Brent if he helps."

Caleb tilted my chin up. "Listen to me, this is about you. About getting you home where you belong. You're right. I did help get you here and keep you inside these gates, but I won't be a part of it any longer."

I licked my lips. He didn't answer my question. What kind of ramifications would the town council slam on these two officers for their part in our escape?

"I don't trust Roger," I whispered. "He'll make your lives miserable for helping me; for helping his precious Hope's husband to escape."

His fingers tightened slightly on my chin, almost as though to punctuate his words. "Don't you worry about me, sweetheart. I can handle him."

I pressed against his chest and knew he could. Knew Roger no longer held any power over Caleb. I pushed away to look at Brent. "What about you? You have a family to consider, as well."

He nodded. "I have a duty to uphold, whatever the cost."

I looked back and forth between the two men. Both officers of the law. Both willing to step in the line of fire in a town steeped in strong beliefs fostered by fear.

I worried my lip as another thought crossed my mind. "Do you think he'll try this again next year? Another work program?"

Both men shook their heads. "Won't happen. We won't allow it." Caleb assured me.

I believed them. "Thank you, both of you. If you believe you can do this without bringing in an outside police force than, yes. Let's do it."

Brent nodded. "Be ready. It will be on a day when I have duty outside of Wellington. This weekend will be too soon, but my guess is sometime next week."

Caleb reached out a hand, and Brent took it. The two men stood in silent communication. This was still risky. The GPS trackers were still on high alert and getting to the gates of the city would be a challenge, even with help from Brent.

And though Caleb hadn't mentioned his discussion with Randy, I knew the person who had the ability to lower the security levels wasn't on board to help.

The mood from earlier was lost. As the door shut behind our visitor, I was at a loss for words. Brent had offered a solution to get me home, and my husband was on board. This was what I wanted. Wasn't it?

Caleb kissed my forehead. When had he moved back across the room to me? I was going home, but I'd fallen in lo…

Oh, dear God, no. I can't go there. I can't say the word. No. He's just a man I've enjoyed a few weeks with over the summer. That's all. He can't be anything more than that. But I stared up at him as my stomach clenched. Our day-by-day was coming to an end. Very soon.

"Sweetheart, don't cry."

I didn't know that I was. Caleb swept me in his arms and carried me to the bedroom and pulled me close. I curled into his chest and let silent tears fall.

I'm going to miss this. I'm going to miss him.

I clutched his shirt as his hand stroked my head

until I drifted to sleep.

****

I barely ate the dinner Rita made Thursday night. Caleb noticed, which didn't surprise me, but I noticed he didn't eat much either. The last several weeks with him have been great. I actually enjoy being married to him, and that's not something I ever thought I'd feel.

We stayed at his parents until after the kids were tucked into bed before heading back to our apartment where I couldn't sit still. There were no televisions to pretend to watch. My mind was too occupied to sit long enough to read, like Caleb was doing—or not. His eyes followed me around the room. I'd already baked cinnamon rolls with the kids after supper, so I didn't want to be in the kitchen.

"Why don't you put the radio on and come sit with me," he suggested. It wasn't a bad idea so I fiddled with the stations, but I couldn't find one with music which suited my mood. After five minutes of fiddling, I shut it off and began my pacing again.

I needed a distraction. I needed Caleb. I practically stomped across the room to lean down and forced my lips against his. I knocked the book out of his hands and straddled his lap.

When we came up for air, he put his hands on my face, holding it back so he could look at me. "Don't try to figure me out, Caleb. I need you right now, so let's do this, okay?"

After yet another few seconds, he capitulated. The couch, though, was not made to be comfortable. He stood, and I kept my legs around his waist as he carried me to the bedroom. I tried to move things along. I wanted fast and hard. I needed to forget some things. I needed to remember others. I needed this moment.

But he took his sweet time, damn him. When I wanted to rip our clothes off, he held my hands together and instead kissed me wherever my skin was exposed. When I wanted our mouths to come together, he moved his to my neck, melting me slowly instead of the fuse of fire I craved. When I let out a grunt of frustration, he kissed the tears from my cheeks.

My tears were flowing when we finally came together. I was going to miss this man more than I wanted to admit. My feelings for him—No. I still refused to admit it. If I did, it would make leaving so, so much harder.

I eventually curled into him as his hand stroked my back under the sheet he'd pulled over us. "Thank you." It was a whisper. "I needed this tonight."

He kissed my forehead. "I think we both did." For being as close as we were, we were both a million miles away.

My hand pressed against his chest as I settled my head into his shoulder. "Thank you for agreeing to help us leave. I know there will be fallout."

Caleb turned onto his side and gave me a long kiss. "I would do anything for you, Grace."

My heart did a quick leap at his words. We'd never taken time to shut off the bedroom lights, and I saw the intensity in his blue eyes. I nodded.

He ran a hand down my disheveled hair as he spoke softly. "I never planned on marrying again after Jill. And while our relationship is a little unorthodox, I don't regret a moment of it."

"I don't, either," I admitted. "This wasn't exactly the summer I'd imagined."

I saw the regret in his eyes. "I'm sorry."

I gulped. "Don't. Please." I reached up to trace along his firm jawline, reveling in the softness of the scruff of facial hair. "I'm glad it was you."

His lips curled up in a hint of a smile. "Ditto. I think I fell for you the first day here, when you got off the bus and couldn't have coffee."

"When I told you no?"

He gave a half chuckle. "I found you entertaining and challenging. Your antics over those first couple weeks kept me on my toes. Police work here is monotonous at best. You are anything but. Like you said early in the summer, you're as mercurial as the moon."

I curled my hand to give a gentle thump to his torso. "Glad I amuse you."

He grinned. "You did. But you got under my skin, too. I discovered quickly, while I wanted to keep you here, I also wanted to protect you. I hated knowing you were so sad all the time."

I felt an overwhelming need to reassure him. "It wasn't all the time. You guys play baseball. I do love baseball."

I knew it was coming. I sensed it. I saw it in the way he looked at me. While my heart leaped in joy, my brain went into total panic.

"Grace, you know I…"

"No!" I pushed him away and sat up. "Don't. Don't say it." I scrambled from the bed, grabbing clothes to put on. "You can't say it. I'm leaving. Next week maybe. You can't do this to me."

I didn't even bother with a bra as I pulled a tee over my head and turned to look at him. Caleb sat up, watching me as I rushed around the room. His hair was mussed from our lovemaking. The sheet was at his waist, leaving his chest bare. I never grew tired of looking at him.

"Let's go for a walk," I demanded. I didn't really want to go for a walk, but the room felt too small. Hell, the entire apartment was closing in on me.

"Grace, let's…"

I cut him off again with a hand up. "Please, Caleb?" I practically strangled on the words. "Please, can we get some air?"

With a nod, he swung his legs off the bed and stood to get dressed. I watched. My breath caught in my throat as he walked naked around the room to gather his clothes. Damn, he was perfection. And he felt the same way I felt about him.

Those feelings which I couldn't say or hear right now.

Chapter Twenty

The outside temperature outside had dropped to a comfortable mid-seventies. The heat wave we'd had brought lots of humidity, but at this time of night it felt good to be outside.

"Where are we going?" Caleb asked as he walked beside me.

"I don't know." I turned left, heading toward the center of town. The streets were empty, and the street lights glowed brightly under the starry night. "The stars are brighter here than at home." It was a stupid thing to say, but I needed a different topic. "Maybe because it's flatter. More open. In Vermont, all we have is mountains and trees. Lots of trees. I like hiking the woods with you. It reminds me of home."

"Uh, huh."

The best thing with Caleb, he knows when to be quiet. Okay, maybe not the best thing, but in this case, it's near the top of the list. "Even though we're in the center of town, it still seems bigger, like there is nothing to block the moon or stars at night."

We walked another block, and he walked silently beside me, his hand grasping my much smaller one.

"Do you know the first thing I am going to do after I get home?" I rambled as we continued to zig zag through the empty streets.

"Have an extra-large, dark roast coffee?"

My mouth twisted up at his sardonic comment. "Ha. Well, maybe. No, I'm taking my sister to the movies. Sarah loves the movies. She dumps a box of M&Ms over her buttered popcorn and eats them combined."

"You miss her." I gave a single nod and skipped ahead a few steps. "Are we going to discuss what happened at home?" Caleb's long legs kept him in step with me, despite my trying to move ahead.

"No." I rushed forward again.

"I find it adorable how you run away from any talk of feelings," he called out and I finally stopped to turn back to him.

"Well, I find it annoying how you always say what's on your mind." I put my hands on my hips as I confronted him. "A macho guy like you isn't supposed to talk about feelings. You're supposed to just…just…grunt, then roll over and go to sleep."

I saw his mouth twitch, and I knew he was amused again at my expense. "Grunt, huh?"

"The first time I saw you I thought you were completely stoic. Emotionless. A stone wall. Then I got to know you and realized I was completely wrong. You're more of a big softy. Can't you go back to being the stone wall?"

Caleb pulled me to him. "I'm not all soft," he murmured. "There's at least one part of me that is still hard."

I snorted and punched his shoulder. "Again?"

"With you? Always." He kissed me, and I kissed back. Everything I wanted to say and couldn't I put into the kiss. I clung to him as my body trembled.

"Oh, sweetheart." His lips brushed away the tears

on my cheeks. "I'm dying, seeing you like this. You don't have to go, you know."

My heart jumped. Part of me wanted to stay. I could adapt. Eventually. I put my forehead against his chest as his hand stroked my hair. "I can't stay."

I heard his sigh. "I know."

The flash of headlights illuminated the street, and Caleb tensed as he straightened and turned, waiting for the cruiser to come to a halt. He held me to his side as Brent rolled the window down.

"Hey, Chief."

"What's up, Brent." Caleb's voice was casual and controlled. I will never understand how he can switch his emotions so quickly.

"It's Roger. I guess his tracker is pinging, and he sent me to find out what you two are doing."

I felt the tightening of his hand pressing against my waist. "I'm taking a stroll with my wife." My heart did a zippity-do-da at the endearment. "If that controlling son of a—" He caught himself, barely. "If he doesn't like it, tell him to shut the damn tracker off."

The officer pulled out his phone and dialed, and we listened onto his side of the conversation. "Roger. They're out for a walk. Yes, I know it's late. I'm not telling the police chief he has a curfew. No, sir. It's, Caleb, sir, he's not going anywhere. Since when is taking a midnight walk through our town an issue? My suggestion, sir, is to shut it off for the night."

Brent put down his phone. "This might work to your advantage, Caleb."

"How so?"

The officer nodded to me. "If you keep going out every night, maybe Roger will turn the tracker off on his own, and it will be clear sailing when it's time to move."

I hitched in a breath. Caleb reached out to shake Brent's hand. He was right. Those were the cards we needed to play. Being the loving couple was no longer an act, but getting past the tracking alerts? Brent had a point.

I was suddenly tired. I didn't know what I wanted anymore. Home was calling me. It was so close. Only days away. But the closer to Vermont I got, the further away from my husband I'd be.

Friday night Caleb had duty at The Hall. For once I was in no mood for dancing, so I sat with Caroline at a corner table, talking over the music. She glowed as she watched her husband up on the stage. While I was happy for her, I wished I could confide what was happening in my life, but I couldn't tell anyone, even her, about our plans for escape.

"Have you seen Jake this week?" I asked her and was surprised at her nod.

"He's not doing well, Grace." She sighed. "He came by last night, needing a place to hide for a few hours."

"I've been a lousy friend." I took a sip of my soda, ah, pop. "Caleb and I are getting along so well, I keep forgetting that Jake isn't so lucky."

Caroline slid the cross at her neck back and forth on its chain, a sign she was bothered by something. "He said that if he ever gets away, he is swearing off relationships."

While normally that wouldn't sound like our hometown Romeo, at this point I could understand.

"He said between what happened here with the

deceitful Hope and the crazy antics of his last girlfriend, he is going to be a monk until he meets the right woman."

I scoffed. "While I get he's unhappy, I can't see him being a monk or actually committing to one woman."

"He's loved you for a long time, Grace," Caroline stated matter-of-factly, and my heart sank that I'd been oblivious. "Now that you are off the market, and well, I guess he is, too, he doesn't know what to do."

Little did she know, but Jake would be heading home soon, and his little wifey would not be coming along. He'd recover and meet someone new.

"I don't know who was harder on him," Caroline was still talking as I took another sip of my drink. "Hope, who connived him into marrying him, or Leila, who tried to get pregnant by poking holes in his condoms."

I slowly put the can down. "She did? When? I never heard about that."

"Her roommate told Jake about it the morning we left. She called to warn him that Leila was on her way to Bennington to seduce him, not knowing he was heading out of town. I guess she'd poked holes in every third condom, a sort of Russian roulette to trap him into marriage, except he broke up with her before they had sex again."

I looked across the room to Caleb who stood by the door in uniform. He took his job seriously. He said if he sat with me tonight, he'd be distracted, so he stood guard. What would he do if he'd heard this conversation?

We'd already finished the first box of condoms.

The box that had already been opened. The box I could only assume had been tampered with by Jake's obsessive ex-girlfriend.

Where was I in my cycle? I had to be close but surely not close enough. We'd opened the second box only a few days ago, but that would mean anything after that first box should be okay. Right?

But what if I was already pregnant?

I excused myself and headed to the restroom, knowing a certain, very observant, officer watched me cross the room. I couldn't look at him, though. Eagle Eyes would know in a flash something was wrong.

I pressed my hands against the counter and stared at my reflection. Despite the heat in the building, I had gone pale.

Pregnant? The odds were—hell, what did I know of odds? Unless I looked at a calendar, I couldn't be sure when I was due for my monthly visit, and with the way Caleb and I can't keep our hands off each other, if Leila had truly played Russian roulette, the odds were not in my favor.

I was days away from going home to Vermont, but if Caleb knew there was even a remote possibility that he may be a father, would he let me leave?

Shelby came in, and I gave her a quick smile and said hello. I needed to get back before Caleb began to worry and search me out.

We were last to leave because the officer on duty always ensured everyone was dispersed before closing. The streets were empty as he ushered me toward his cruiser. "You and Caroline talked a lot tonight."

I heard the underlying question. "Mmm. She's worried about Jake. He came to see her last night. It was hard not telling her we'd be leaving within the week, so I kept her talking about him and how he's doing."

Maybe it was only the passing shadows of the streetlight, but I thought I spotted a hint of sadness in his eyes. Caleb reached over to take my hand. "I'm sure he'll bounce back to his old self once he's home."

With that, he led me to the bedroom. Once we were inside, I didn't stop him. We were on the second box of condoms. At this point, we were safe. I had to believe that because I didn't want to miss out on a single moment with this man.

Chapter Twenty-One

Saturday, we played baseball and I was ferocious. I played second like the World Series was at stake. I swung at the ball, and it hit so hard it cracked the bat. I tossed aside the broken shards and ran to first base like there was no tomorrow. But once I was stopped, Caleb, playing first base, leaned in to me. "Easy, sweetheart. You're going to wear yourself out, and I have plans for us later."

I blushed, and my mood lightened.

His plans weren't exactly what I thought he meant. He'd arranged for an evening horseback ride. It was my first time back to Jackson's farm since the incident with Leland. The day that had changed everything.

But once we arrived, I never gave it another thought. I was with Caleb, Aaron, and Caroline, and the mood was light and fun. We meandered through the trails with high-powered flashlights to show the way. It meant an evening out of the apartment, out of the town limits. Roger's security would be pinging again, but if he looked, he'd see we were not alone. Another win on our books.

Sunday we were almost late for church. We had every intention of going to Rita's to help with the kids as we usually do on Sunday mornings, but when I came out of the bedroom wearing a sundress, Caleb's eyes had narrowed.

"You can't wear that."

I looked down at the simple print then back at him. "Why? I bought it so I would have something nice to wear to church?" But he had crossed the room, and my heart flipped a bit at the desire dancing in his eyes.

"You can't wear that to church because when I see you in that dress, I remember taking it off."

To which he did again.

When we finally left the apartment, with only minutes to spare, I wore my white capris that I hadn't worn since my first day in town.

As I knelt for prayer, I looked around me. The old church was beautiful in its simplicity. Sun shone through the stained-glass windows onto the parishioners bowing their reverent heads. The cream-colored walls were a contrast to the dark stained pew benches. The organ music filled the building as voices joined together singing Halleluiah. The children sat between Caleb and me, but when he sent a look my way, I felt a connection with him.

He sat beside me as we ate. As per usual, we sat at a table in the enclosed room connecting the church with The Hall, the glass doors open to allow a breeze to counteract the summer heat. The children sat, one on either side of us and Shawna on Caleb's lap. Rita and Conrad sat across from us and conversation flowed easy. I was enjoying myself.

"Quite the game yesterday, Grace." I looked up to see Barbara join us. "You seemed very focused."

I gave a sheepish grin. "Not enough to win, though. The blue team is brutal."

"You'll get them next week," she reassured.

I nodded as she left but knew next week wouldn't

happen, at least with me on the team. I caught Caleb's glance but quickly looked down at my food, hoping he wouldn't see the wish that there would be another game.

"Grace, I was wondering if I could ask a favor." This time I saw Caleb's sister, Rose, leaning down to talk. "It's Kerri's birthday in a couple weeks, and she has been raving about your baking skills. Would you bake her a cake? She'd love it."

I cast another quick, nervous glance at Caleb. *Shit, what do I do?* I silently screamed the question to him. *I won't be here.* His answer was a gentle squeeze of my leg under the table. I got the silent message: *Fake it until you make it.*

I turned back to his sister. "Of course. I can't believe your daughter will be sixteen. It's an exciting age."

The meal seemed to continue that way, with people coming up and talking to me. I finally fit in. After three months, when my time here was ending, I realized I had friends. I blinked my eyes rapidly, in an attempt to quell the sudden spark of tears.

It was the same when we took the kids to the park. Sheila was there with her brood. I snuggled little Christian in my arms and breathed in the scent of baby powder. He was adorable as he cooed and hiccuped. The little bundle didn't freak me out as much now as when I'd held him at the hospital back in June. Now, a part of me wanted this, a tiny piece of me and Caleb to hold and snuggle; to raise along with his brother and sisters.

I'd make a good mother. I looked over at Elena chasing Shawna around the playground, and she caught me looking her way and smiled. Even she had come around to having me here. I looked at her father and saw he was watching me. He gave a nod, and I wondered what he was thinking. Had his thoughts gone the way mine had of a little one of our own?

Could that already be a possibility?

No. Don't go down that road again. I gave Christian another cuddle and handed him back to his mom. I pulled my shades back over my eyes as I crossed the playground. Caleb had followed Justin down to the climbing bars. The boy sat underneath the rounded contraption, playing with his cars in the dirt.

Caleb smiled and pulled me close for a kiss. "You're beautiful," he stated and I felt my insides glow. "You'd make a good mother."

Damn, it was like he could read my thoughts.

"And don't think I can't tell what you are thinking just because you have those gorgeous brown eyes hidden behind these dark sunglasses."

I lifted my chin. "Oh, really? What am I thinking?"

Caleb glanced over his shoulder. "Justin, stay off the bars, they're too wet from the rain last night. Play with your cars." He turned back to me. "That the job of making babies is a lot of fun, too."

I punched his arm. "No, that's what *you* are thinking."

He wiggled his eyebrows. "Why, so it is." But I saw him frown as he turned quickly. "Justin, I said no."

But it was too late. The young boy slipped from the bars and fell, landing with a loud thud on the inside of the structure.

Caleb was by his side before the child could even begin to wail. I took one look at the boy's crooked arm and rushed away to throw up in a bush.

I took the girls home while Caleb spent the rest of the day at the hospital with his son. Rita and Conrad were doting grandparents when the little boy came home with a cast.

Caleb came straight to my side. "How are you doing?"

I shrugged. "I'm glad you have a strong stomach, because I was useless out there."

He tapped my nose with his finger. "We all have our weaknesses. I've seen Marines drop at the sight of a needle. Don't be so hard on yourself."

When we got back to the apartment, he took my hand. "Let's wash this day away." It wasn't long before Caleb was stretching an arm outside the shower curtain to open the drawer on the vanity and reached for a packet. It wasn't until we were toweling off when I spotted the box of condoms inside.

"Where did this come from?" I knew the newest box was in his nightstand drawer.

Caleb was busy brushing his teeth. He spit out the toothpaste before he spoke. "That's the first box. Since we seem to have as much sex in the shower as we do in the bedroom, I moved it in here."

"Oh." I grabbed a comb and pulled it roughly through my hair as the implications became evident. "When we opened the other box, I assumed this one was finished."

Caleb dropped the towel from his waist and pulled me to him by grabbing my towel and letting it go so that we were skin to skin. I looked at our reflection in the mirror as he stood against me. My nipples reacted instantly as his hand slid up my belly to cup my breast.

It didn't matter we'd run the water cold a few minutes before, one touch and I was all nerve endings.

"Not quite," his voice was husky. "I have to thank Jake for buying the Costco-sized boxes and the first box was still over half full."

At one point, I was very thankful, too, but then Caleb didn't know about Jake's psycho ex-girlfriend. He didn't know these condoms had been tampered with.

"I have an idea," Caleb said as his callused thumb brushed across the pink peak. I dropped the comb into the sink as I watched in the mirror while his large, tanned hand moved across my paler skin. As his mouth moved to my ear his deep voice turned my insides to mush. "Let's see if we can finish off both boxes before you have to leave."

"There has to be about fifty of them left." I scoffed, but when he swung me up onto the counter and grabbed another packet, ripping it open with his teeth, I pushed the lingering thoughts away. "Okay, forty-nine."

I lay awake long after Caleb slept. He was curled around me, his arm around my waist, his breath steady and strong at my neck.

Normally, I slept with layers, even in the summer with the air conditioner blasting, I would huddle under the blankets with a night shirt and sleep pants on.

No longer. This large man was a human furnace wrapped around me. Clothes would only get in the way as we tended to make love going to sleep and again when we woke. We couldn't get enough of each other. I slowly rubbed at the hairs on his arm as my thoughts raced.

Maybe I should get rid of what was left of the

condoms in the bathroom. If I took some out of the box in the bedroom, maybe he wouldn't notice? Or should I look at each package and see if I can tell which one's Layla had poked?

Or was it like closing the barn door after the horse had escaped? How many of those had we already used? And when was I due for my period? I couldn't remember, my time here had started to blend together, and I hadn't been tracking my cycle.

My other option was to stop having sex in the shower and use only the condoms in the bedroom. Caleb shifted. I pressed his hand more firmly against my belly, scoffing at the idea.

Right. If things went according to Brent's plans, I could be leaving sometime in the next week. My time with Caleb was limited. I wasn't going to deny myself the pleasure of rubbing the bar of soap over his chiseled abs or allowing him to lather shampoo in my hair. How could I resist him when he used his calloused pad of his thumb to bring me to the brink every time before lifting me up to wrap my legs around him so he could find his own release?

I squeezed my legs together, as memories of us together sent heat pooling in that direction. I should sleep. There hadn't been a morning yet, where one time hadn't led to a second before heading to work. Slow and sensual in bed. Fast and furious in the shower.

But sleep eluded me. Instead, my thoughts, not a rested body, had me hot and ready as my man stretched in the early hours. It was me, turning to him, me stroking his penis, me ripping the packet open and straddling him. Me, wanting to delay the inevitable, when I would wake alone in my own bed in Vermont.

Later as Caleb reached for the foil packet when he stepped into the hot water of the shower behind me, I ignored the pesky voice in my head and met him groan for groan, thrust for thrust and when we were done, I closed my eyes and sent a silent prayer to the God I didn't know if I believed in, asking him to forgive me.

Chapter Twenty-Two

I was starving by the time we stopped at the diner. Instead of my usual fruit and yogurt, everything on the menu appealed to me. I settled on a bacon, egg, and cheese on an English muffin, a banana, and the tea Caleb insisted I drink. My husband shook his head at my appetite but kept his mouth shut when I sent him a glare warning him not to comment.

Brent and Greg were both on duty, and I didn't think anything of it when Brent disappeared into the chief's office shortly after we arrived. When lunch time approached, Caleb informed Greg that he was taking me out to lunch for a change, instead of eating in the station.

That was unusual, and my heart began to race. But when he drove us back to our apartment, instead of heading across to the diner, I had to ask, "What are we doing?"

He gave me a heavy-lidded stare as he put the car into park. "I need you."

It was the look of desperation in his eyes that had my hands shaking as we climbed the stairs of the building. I felt the difference in his kiss. His hands were slow and determined as they lifted my shirt over my head. I closed my eyes as he pulled my hair out of its hair tie.

I helped him out of his clothes, waiting as he sat to

unlace his work boots, pulling them off so I could slide his jeans down his legs. He joined me on the bed and lay there looking at me, not touching for what seemed an eternity, and then finally he crushed me to him in a long kiss.

His mouth moved downward to my neck, my clavicle, my shoulder. His hands clasped mine, pulling them to lay on either side of my head. "Caleb, please, what's wrong?"

"Shh. Let me do this. Let me have this time." His lips moved down my chest, bypassing my breasts where my nipples were puckered, waiting. Instead he moved to my stomach and brushed across my abdomen.

I sucked in my breath? Did he know? Had someone told him about the condoms? Did he know I wondered if I were already pregnant?

If he did, he didn't say. He moved back up, finally taking a nipple into his mouth. My body was his. It was always ready for him, but this slow onslaught in the middle of the day was unexpected. His facial hair scratching along my sensitive skin as I moved myself into position. I spread my legs, wrapping them around him. I lifted my hips, telling him without words I was ready for him. His full erection was pressed against my thigh. I wanted to touch him. I wanted to reach for the drawer in the nightstand. But he hadn't released my hands.

His tongue circled my areola, and it hardened to a peak. His mouth captured it, sucking it and my back arched. "Caleb, you're killing me."

I felt his smile against my chest. "Well, I can't have that." He released my hands, stretching to reach a condom, but as he did his erection, already full and pulsing slid deliciously close to my center. All I had to do was shift my thigh ever so slightly and it was there, pressed at my entrance.

Caleb's breath hitched. He froze. His penis pulsed. I was wet and ready. "Grace." His voice was tight, and I could tell control was barely on his radar. "You don't know how much I want to come inside you."

He shifted slightly, and I felt his tip push past my pubic hair. "Part of me, Grace, says I can do this. Part of me says, just one thrust then cover up." I groaned at the thought, and my body reacted on its own, my hips lifted, but he moved away and I heard pain in his voice. "No. We can't. Not now. Not today."

He leaned down and kissed a tear from my face, one I hadn't realized had escaped. "I could never stop with one thrust with you, sweetheart." He finally grabbed a packet, and he kept his eyes steady on mine as he used his teeth to open it. "Help me," he whispered. I took it from him and reached between us to sheath him. With my hands already filled with him, I guided him back.

"Keep your eyes open," he ordered and then pushed forward until he couldn't go any further and he stopped. "Feel me inside you, Grace."

"I do." But it wasn't just being full of him. He kept his eyes open, and the intimacy was beyond anything I'd ever experienced. My body quivered in response when I watched his eyes dilate. He slid slowly out then back in and I forgot to breathe.

Then his hand was between us, his finger rubbing me, rotating while he kept his pace slow. "I am ready to come, Grace. It's not going to take much, but before I do, I want to watch you fall apart first."

"Caleb."

In. Out. His finger moved between us, making circles while he continued a steady rhythm. In. Out. I couldn't keep up with what he was doing to me, but it was getting harder to keep my eyes open. I gripped the soft cotton sheets. My heels pressed down on the firm mattress. My hips gyrated. Then when I didn't think I could see any more stars, Caleb grasped my hips and thrust forward with a cry of his own.

He collapsed on me, still holding my thighs at his waist. "Never enough," he mumbled into my neck.

My legs were shaking when he finally rolled away. He discarded the condom then pulled me to him, wrapping us with the sheet. We lay like that for a while, content to bask in the afterglow. Our lunch hour was heading toward two when he let out a sigh.

"Brent came to see me this morning." I stiffened against him, finally understanding our nooner; knowing what was coming next.

"When?" It came out almost as a cry.

He rolled me onto my back, to look down on me. He brushed a hair from my face, and while he tried to keep his face impassive, I saw resignation in his eyes.

"Wednesday." I was still reeling from our first work hooky to comprehend at first. "Wednesday?" Then it hit me. "That's only two days away." And my birthday. I'd hoped to at least have that with Caleb.

His hand folded over mine. "I know. Day by day, right?" Right. I nodded. That's what we'd agreed on. "We have to continue on as though nothing has changed."

I heard his voice, but a part of me had shut down. Two days. That wasn't enough time.

"Talk to me, Grace," he pleaded. He still leaned on his elbow, looking down at me. I pressed my cheek into his hand. I was going to miss this.

A nasty part of me wondered if Caleb knew how much I liked sex with him, and that was why he waited until after to tell me. Then I caught myself. No. I saw the naked need in his eyes when he'd brought me home.

The news had affected him, as well. "I'm going to miss—" I choked. Should I say how much I would miss him? That would give him too much power over me.

I scoffed. Who was I kidding? This man owned me, body and soul. The feelings I had went beyond a forced marriage, went beyond the gold band on my finger. It even went far beyond the amazing sex we shared. Somewhere along the line, I'd discovered Caleb Wellington was a man of honor. A man I respected. He had a gentle and warm heart. He was a protector of those he loved.

He'd brought me to Wellington under false pretenses. He'd kept me from leaving under strict orders. Despite everything we'd been through, in the end, he had captured my heart.

"Don't cry," he begged, but I couldn't stop the tears from escaping.

He brushed the tear with a padded thumb, and I once again turned my cheek into his palm. This time, I thrust my tongue out, taking the salty teardrop into my mouth. I heard Caleb's breath hitch.

He gave a long sigh. "We need to go back to work at some point."

"Always the voice of reason." I sighed. "I'd rather hide out here."

His kiss was long, and I thought for sure he was

going to agree, but he eventually pulled back. "Come. There are things I need to do to put things in motion."

For Wednesday. For me to leave. He didn't say the words exactly, but it hung in the air as we dressed and headed back to reality.

One of the things he needed to do was let Jake in on the plans. He dropped me off at the station then left immediately to the other side of town to the furniture factory.

I wish I could have seen Jake's face, or heard what was said, but by the time I left work two hours later, my friend had managed to prepare a backpack, and it was hidden away from Hope in our apartment.

I figured I should do the same. Caleb was off doing police work—a few teenagers had decided to hike up White Pine Ridge, and it was getting late in the day. Brent was patrolling outside the gate, and Caleb was taking Goliath up the path to usher the kids back into town.

He was going to be gone a while, so I roamed the apartment to find what I felt was most essential to pack. I threw a few clothes in the bag, but not my favorite baseball hat. I wanted Caleb to have it. I did pack some of the different teas he'd introduced me to, though. While I could probably buy them back home, I wanted the ones he'd chosen.

When he got home, Caleb looked like he wanted to do nothing more than head straight to the bedroom. Or maybe that was my thoughts, but he had other ideas.

"We need to keep Roger's security pinging. I know it's late, but how about we go hit a few balls down at the field?"

We tossed the ball back and forth under the

cloudless sky. The stadium lights came on at dusk giving us more time out on the field. This was where it had all changed for me. My love of baseball had given me my first sense of belonging in Wellington. And here had been where I'd first recognized my attraction to the town's police chief.

While we weren't really outside the inner-blocks of the town, it wasn't long before a cruiser came by, its headlights lighting the field. As Brent had been on duty today, I'm sure he made the call to the town manager, again, informing him what we were doing.

Despite our afternoon spent in bed, it didn't curtail our nightly routine. Caleb tried to keep the mood light, teasing me about baseball, saying I hit like a girl. I knew what he was doing. I played along. But we both knew it was a distraction.

Tuesday came faster than I'd hoped. I wondered if we would have a repeat of our lunch date the day before, but duty called and the police chief was called out around eleven because Jimmy was dared to drive the fire engine, and not having a clue how to drive anything, the large vehicle was much more than he could handle and he crashed it into a light pole. That took the entire day.

Of course, we were expected at Rita's for dinner which was the usual raucous affair. Justin had filled up on extra sugary sweets at a friend's house and was full of excess energy, causing Elena to snap at him like a mother hen. Shawna forgot she wasn't wearing pullups anymore and had to be changed. When the kids were finally tucked in, I expected us to go back to the apartment to crash. But Caleb drove away and didn't stop until we parked at the path to the lake.

It was after nine, and we were definitely not within the inner town limits. Roger was going to freak. As I didn't really care, I happily made the trek through the wooded path.

I sat on a blanket with Caleb as my backrest. We watched fireflies as the pale moon cast shadows around us. There was nothing but quiet, which we welcomed after the hectic night with the children.

"This has always been my favorite place here." I leaned my head back against him. His arms wrapped around me like a blanket in the cooling night air.

"I know. Mine, too. It's not going to be the same without you, sweetheart." I gulped at the wistfulness in his voice. It was good to know I was not the only one struggling with the upcoming event so I kept talking.

"I remember the first time we came here, on the horses, and had the picnic. I couldn't stop staring at you." In the near dark and over a month of being married to Caleb, I still found it embarrassing to confess how much I'd ogled him. "You didn't have a shirt on, and I was quite impressed with all these muscles of yours."

"Is that a fact?" He nuzzled my neck, and I was thankful for having put my hair back in a braid as it gave him better access. "Because I remember the day as well, with you in your little black and white bikini. I had to stand waist deep in the water to hide what seeing you did to me, especially as Leland had claimed you as his and my role was nothing more than to keep you in line."

"Truly?"

His mouth began a journey from my shoulder up to my ear, sending shivers throughout my body. "Truly.

Want to go for a swim?"

"Mmmm." His hands slid under my shirt and worked their way up to my breasts. "I didn't bring a suit."

"We don't need one. Besides, I'm looking to make a new memory of this place with you." He bit my earlobe sending shivers down my body. "And we're going to end up without clothes in a few minutes anyway."

He slipped away from me standing as I hesitated to look around. 'We can't. What if someone sees us?"

"No one is here. It's just the two of us," the deep timbre of his laughter echoed around us. He'd said before that he rarely heard my laughter. Same was true for him. We were both too serious. When he held out his hand, I took it and stood beside him.

I looked around the deserted field once more before I slipped my shirt over my head then released my bra. I shimmied out of my shorts and panties as Caleb's eyes followed my every move. The laughter disappeared and instead I saw desire, dark and deep, in his eyes.

"Dear God, help me." His voice broke with huskiness and with a few fluid moves, his clothes joined mine on the ground. "I want tonight to last and the only way I can stretch this out is if we get into the lake now."

The heat of the day had dissipated, but the water retained its warmth, doing nothing to cool either of our growing needs. Once we were in far enough, I dove under and came up for air several lengths away, but Caleb was right there with me.

I glided over to him, letting my body skim across

his before pushing away again, and the next several minutes became a dance. We swam under in the dark depths only to reach out and run our fingers across each other's body, wherever they would find.

It didn't take long before we were no longer swimming away. Our hands and mouths focused on exploring every inch of the other until finally Caleb wrapped my legs around his waist and walked out of the lake back to the blanket. He let me go only long enough to find the foil packet he'd had the forethought to put into his pants pocket and then he was back.

His body covered mine, I wanted to remember everything about this moment. The way our wet bodies slid together; how the cooling air puckered my nipples. How the crickets sang a nightly tune that seemed to set the pace of our breathing as we began a slow, rhythmic motion which shut my brain off and I forgot everything else but us as one.

When I came down from whatever star I'd been flying on, my heart continued to race. "This is definitely one memory I will forever keep close."

"You are amazing," Caleb continued to lean over me, stroking my hair and face as he slowly slid out of me. "I don't want this night to end. God, you are beautiful. You have no idea what you do to me."

"Make time stop. Please, Caleb, I need one more night." I tried to look away as the reality of tonight sunk in. This was it. Tomorrow night I would be on the other side of the gates.

"Don't, Grace," I heard the tightness in his voice. "Don't disappear into your head. Don't think about tomorrow. Be here with me, right now."

I gave a gentle smile. "I think even after tomorrow,

I'll still be here with you."

Caleb rested his hand on my heart. "That means more than you will ever know. Come, let me hold you for a while."

Eventually we dressed and headed back to his cruiser, using a flashlight through the wooded pathway. A second cruiser was parked beside it, and Caleb squeezed my hand before heading over to see the officer.

"Evening, Tom."

"Hi, Chief." The officer's voice was sheepish, and I knew he was out here due to orders from Roger. "Sorry about this."

Caleb leaned a hand on the cruiser as he spoke through the open window. "Not your fault. Do you need to check in?"

"Nah, about thirty minutes ago he said he was shutting everything down for the night, but and I quote, 'I trust you'll do the right thing and ensure they arrive home.' I took it to mean I had to wait the duration."

"Sorry to keep you from your family. We'll go straight home." Caleb shook hands with the officer and motioned for me to get into his car as Tom drove his cruiser down the main road to town.

When the doors were closed, I ran my tongue over my lips. "Do you think he walked out to the lake to check on us?"

"No. The tracker would have showed exactly where we were. No need." While I heard the words, I noticed the slight hesitation before he put the car into drive, and I wondered if he believed his own words.

Chapter Twenty-Three

"Happy birthday, Grace."

I smiled at officers Tom and Greg as they handed over a large cupcake with a single candle in it. "Aww, thank you, guys. This is so sweet of you."

I gave them each a peck on the cheek, and Greg's face turned beet red as he mumbled. "We like having you around. You're a breath of fresh air."

"What you like," Caleb interjected, "is she doesn't have any problem telling me where to get off."

Tom laughed. "It is refreshing, Chief."

I settled at my desk before joining Caleb over by the water carafe to get my morning cup of tea. "What kind do you have in store for me today?"

"Today is a simple blend of decaffeinated black tea with ginger, vanilla, cardamom, and star anise. It's both a pick-me-up to boost your energy in the morning but also provides calming effects as well."

I gave it a smell and was impressed. "Any sugar?"

He tapped me on the nose with a finger. "You are a heathen. It doesn't need it, but for you, yes, I added sugar."

I grinned before taking a sip. "Mmm. Not bad." He shook his head before heading off to the back area to check in with dispatch.

At lunch time, when both Tom and Greg headed over to the diner, Caleb disappeared from his office for a few minutes. When he returned, he held the bag containing everyone's cell phones. "Which ones belong to you and Jake?"

I sorted through until I found the two cells and watches, shoving them into my pocket while the chief put the bag back under lock and key in the closet.

"Bring them into my office. Let's see if we can give them a quick charge for tonight."

It was an odd feeling, sneaking around in a police station, hiding the phones as they charged. I prayed neither officer would have a reason to enter the chief's office when they returned.

At around two, Caleb and Tom were dispatched for a disturbance of the peace. I didn't think too much about it until they returned with Jake in handcuffs.

"Oh, Jake." I wanted to rush over to him, but a shake of Caleb's head warned me to wait. It wasn't until Tom had locked the prisoner behind bars did I get a chance to speak with him.

"What did you do now?" I admonished as I pressed against the cell door.

His hands reached through where the food tray goes, and I clasped them. Instead of the remorse I expected to see, my friend had a grin on his face, and he gave me a wink.

"Just having another bad day with the ball and chain, and my mood kinda spilled over at work." When he began to whisper, I realized those first words weren't for my benefit, but for whoever might be within earshot. His next words were for me. "It's all part of the plan."

I looked around and didn't see Tom anywhere nearby. "The plan?"

He nodded. "The only way Caleb was going to be able to keep Hope far enough away tonight was if I was here."

It clicked into place. "I was wondering how we were going to get to you."

I heard a door and peeked around the corner and spotted Tom coming. I raised my voice. "I don't know what to tell you, Jake, but you seriously need to get a hold on your temper. This isn't good for you."

Tom reached my side, tapping my shoulder as he nodded for me to head back to my desk. "Let him stew for a while, Grace. He doesn't deserve visitors now." He looked at the man behind bars. "Be prepared, you'll probably need to fix the hole in the wall tomorrow."

I looked back and forth between the two men. Jake shrugged and gave a sheepish look before I headed back to my desk as Tom instructed.

Hope came into the station around four to plead for her husband to be released so he could come home. The chief held firm. "Sorry, Hope. There was property damage which means a night in jail. No exceptions."

The leggy blonde didn't look like the diva seductress she'd been at the beginning of the summer. With her hair hanging straight and red under her eyes from crying, she looked barely old enough to be out of her teens, never mind married. She threw her hands up in defeat before turning to her husband behind bars. "You are such a disappointment. When are you going to grow up?"

But at five, after Tom and Greg left, Caleb strolled to the cell. "Come on, prisoner, you're coming with me." He opened the door and placed cuffs on Jake's wrists. "I never leave anyone here alone, but I'm not about to miss the birthday meal my mom made for Grace, so you get to come along."

"Are the cuffs, necessary?" I asked.

The chief nodded. "We need to make it look real. At least until we get to the house. What if Roger is outside?"

It made sense, and Jake was a willing participant. Anything to keep him away from his clinging wife and closer to escape.

The children greeted me the moment we entered. Even Elena gave me a huge hug which would make leaving tonight harder. Caleb's three sisters were all there, with their husbands, and I noticed Randy looking at Jake, minus the cuffs, more than once. Caleb would put the right spin on it, and I kept my mouth shut.

The meatloaf was divine. The vegetables were cooked to perfection. The cake, which the kids had helped decorate, was moist and delicious. And when the children gave me the cards they'd made, I couldn't help the tears.

Caleb handed me a box, and I slowly unwrapped it. Inside was a gold locket and I felt a fresh set of tears starting as I opened the clasp to see on one side a photo of the three kids and on the other, a picture Rita had taken of me and Caleb.

"I, ah, excuse me a moment." I rushed from the room and closed myself inside the bathroom. "Shit. Shit. Shit." I sat on the closed lid of the commode and pressed the heels of my hands to my eyes.

There was a soft knock on the door. "Grace? I'm coming in." And without waiting the door opened and Caleb was in the tiny room with me. He knelt on the floor. "You okay?"

"No. I didn't think this would be so hard." I wiped my face with my hands. "They all sneaked into my heart."

He took my face between his large hands. "Look at you, admitting to your emotions. You've come a long way."

"Shut up." But I did laugh a little. "They're good kids, Caleb. I can't even say goodbye to them."

"Shhh. We're doing the right thing. You need to be with your family."

Family. Huh. Funny how in a few short weeks Caleb and his children had become a part of mine. Sure, I was going home tonight, but my heart was staying right here.

I took a deep breath and forced the emotions aside. "I'm okay. Let's go back. I want to spend tonight with them, having fun." At bedtime, I tucked each child in and gave them an extra big hug and kiss.

Once all the other adults had left, we escorted the handcuffed prisoner back to the station and into the cell. Caleb laid out a deck of cards to pass the time just as Roger and Scott strolled into the station, with Scott folding an umbrella. The rain had arrived. It suited my mood.

"Can I help you, gentlemen?" Gone was the fun, loving husband, Caleb, he was back to being the police chief.

"Saw the lights on, thought I'd check in, see how my son-in-law is behaving." Roger brushed a few raindrops from his sleeve.

I bit my cheek at the outright lie. The man was tracking our every move. There was no doubt he knew his daughter's husband had been with us for dinner. Our going out every night, causing the security to ping hadn't worked. The controlling town manager still watched us like a hawk.

The chief's response was easy and nonchalant. "Everything is status-quo."

The older man turned a deliberate stare at me. "Shouldn't you all be home at this time?"

Caleb didn't blink an eye. "You know I never leave anyone alone in the station. If I have someone in the cell, I stay the night."

Roger sent another look my way, and I knew he was waiting for an explanation of my presence this late at night, but while the older man refused to ask the question, my husband used his silence, or what I call his Jedi mind tricks, on Roger. I have to give it to the town manager, I would be blubbering by now asking the questions. Instead, he pressed his lips together in anger.

Scott was oblivious. "What time are you going home?" he asked me.

"What's it to you?" Nope, I still don't have my husband's restraint.

Caleb took over, ever so calm. "It's Grace's birthday. We are enjoying a bit more time together before I send her home. We might leave here around eleven-thirty or so."

I sucked in my breath with his choice of words. Holy shit. He'd managed to tell the truth as something else altogether. I need to take lessons from him instead of becoming instantly defensive and sarcastic.

Roger gave a grunt. "Let's go, Scott." As they left, the minion, Scott, turned back. "Ah, happy birthday, Grace."

"Thanks." I wasn't sure what else to say as the men

left the station.

"That was great, Caleb," Jake called out from his cell. "You put those two scumbags in their place. I hate him. I hope the fleas of a thousand camels infest his armpits."

Caleb picked up his cards as though nothing had happened, but my heart was still racing. "How do you stay so calm?"

"Training. Ready to play?"

Training? Police training? Military training? Growing up around these assholes? Whatever it was, I did know him enough to see how, despite looking cool, there was still a hint of tension in his shoulders and his eyes no longer held his casual warmth.

"Can I come out now?" my friend called from down the hall.

"We're going to continue to play this straight, Jake," the chief answered. "You're behind bars until we leave."

Which wasn't long, or not long enough for someone who wanted to stretch out the last hours. Before I knew it, Jake was once again put into the back of the cruiser, this time without handcuffs, while I sat in the front as we drove back to the apartment where Caleb shut the engine off.

"We'll sit here for a few minutes. If Roger is still awake, he'll see we are here as expected. He'll know I'd walk you upstairs and when the car starts again, it won't be unexpected."

"Do you think he's still up? Will he see us heading out of town?" I was twisting the ends of my hair as I looked at Caleb in the dark car as rain pelted the windows.

He put a reassuring hand on my thigh. "More than likely he is already asleep. This is an added precaution. Don't worry."

I put my hand on his, and he turned his over to clasp mine. We sat in silence as the minutes ticked slowly by. With a final squeeze of my hand, Caleb released it to start the car and put it into drive.

Within minutes we drove past the station and kept moving. Past the clinic. Past the streets on the east side of town until the houses became scarce. Beyond the wipers swiping at the rain, I spotted the corn fields and remembered our first attempt at escape which hadn't ended well.

This time, though, we had the police chief on our side, and we had another officer waiting for us on the opposite side of the gates.

We were almost at the town border when Caleb's phone rang. We all knew who it was before he answered, putting it on speaker. "Yes?"

I could hear Roger's booming voice. "What the hell are you doing, Caleb?"

"My job, of course." His tone held a hint of reproach, as though he was tired of his boss questioning his every action. "I had a report of a possible dead animal on the road. Going to check it out."

Roger's beeping phone was obviously keeping him awake, and he wasn't happy about it. "Can't it wait until morning?"

While Caleb's voice seemed relaxed, his white knuckles on the steering wheel revealed his tension. "Why? No need to wait. I'm not going to put off the duties of my job, just because you don't trust me. I'm going to do what I've always done. If it keeps you up at night, it's not my problem."

Another mutter came over the line before the phone disconnected. I pressed my hands under my legs on the seat. If I didn't, I'd be twisting my fingers into knots on my lap. "Do you think it worked?"

Even in the dark, I saw the shake of his head. "Once he looks closely, he'll see I am not alone in the car. Within a couple minutes, he'll have called Tom to see what we are up to. By the time he arrives, though, you'll be with Brent."

Jake was antsy in the backseat, twisting and turning to see if we were being followed yet, but we made it to the gates before anything happened.

Caleb used a remote, and the gates slid open and a cruiser from another town was waiting on the other side. Brent got out to meet us.

Jake jumped from the cruiser the moment Caleb opened the door. "I can't believe this is happening. Thanks, guys." Jake pumped Caleb's hand then went to do the same with Brent. "I honestly thought we'd never get home."

Caleb popped the trunk, and I followed him to the back to get our backpacks. The rain was steady and cool on my face, plastering my hair to my face.

"How are you doing, sweetheart?" he asked and the only thing I could do was shrug.

"It was raining the night we arrived." Leave it to me to avoid what I really wanted to say. He pulled me into his arms, and I pressed my cheek against his chest as the rain pummeled us. "Thank you."

He lifted my face, brushed away the raindrops then leaned down for a kiss full of sadness from both of us. "If you need anything at any time, you call me."

I nodded, but a part of me knew this goodbye was going to be permanent.

He gripped my arms and almost shook me with his intensity. "I'm serious, Grace. I have money in an account outside of town, so anything at any time. "

I didn't know what to make at this sudden revelation. He lived in a town that didn't exchange money, how was that even possible? "What? How?"

I caught the wry smile, in the glare from the car taillights. "From Jill's death. Her life insurance. Her wrongful death settlement. I had it all deposited into my checking account to save for the kids. When I moved back, I didn't tell anyone about it."

Whether he realized it or not, he'd provided himself and his kids a way to leave before he'd even come back. For a brief second, I almost asked him to come with me, but I knew it was impossible. "No, that money is for the kids, not me. I'll be fine."

I didn't know if my heart would be fine or not, but somehow I would manage.

He brushed his thumb over my lips and then said the words I craved—and yet wanted to avoid—hearing. "I love you, Grace."

The lump in my chest finally exploded and the tears started. "Damn you, Caleb. You weren't supposed to say it."

"I won't apologize for my feelings." He leaned in to place a gentle kiss on my forehead. "You need to go home, and I will do anything to get you there because I love you."

My lip was now trembling. I loved him, too, but I couldn't say the words. "I—I—"

He brushed the tears and rain from my face and

pushed my wet hair back to stare down at me in the rear lights of the car. "Shhh. You don't have to say anything. I already know."

I was sure he did. I held up my left hand. "May I keep the ring?"

He took it and kissed the digit with the gold band. "Always. It belongs to you."

Brent stepped around the car to interrupt. "Caleb? We have to move. Roger knows it's me meeting you. He's calling. It won't be long before he has someone hitting the button to secure the gate."

Caleb nodded and grabbed both backpacks and walked me to the other cruiser where Jake was already in the front seat. Brent pulled a device from the glove box and used it to release the bracelets. I heard the alarm go off on Caleb's phone. As police chief, he was being alerted about our bracelets being removed.

Free. Oh, dear God, could this really be happening?

Brent handed the trackers to the chief. "Good luck. If Roger didn't call Tom and Greg first, their phone alarms will have them moving fast." The officer placed a hand on Caleb's arm. "My captain knows what we are doing. I had to tell him why I needed to leave city limits. If anything goes south, the word goes viral."

Viral. An outside entity coming into Wellington. What would that mean for Caleb? I rubbed my wrist, bare of the tracking device, while Brent opened the rear door for me.

I opened my mouth to say goodbye, but the words couldn't form. Caleb understood. He nodded and motioned for me to get into the car. "Go. It's now or never. You have to leave." I heard the sirens in the distance. They were coming. There was a rumble, and the gates began their slide closed. Caleb stepped back into town limits just in time for the gate to latch.

Brent closed the car door. I stared at my husband, my protector, my lover, through the rain as long as I could while we drove away. I had to bite my lip to keep it from trembling.

He'd risked everything for me. He and this officer whisking us a way. While Jake and I were free, what would that mean for these two who'd helped us escape? There was a chance they'd lose everything.

And me? I put a hand on my stomach. I'd lost my appetite around the time Justin had broken his arm. It was also the day before Brent said we were leaving. I could pretend it was all nerves, or I could acknowledge we had been using condoms that had been tampered with. There was a very strong possibility that I was pregnant, and I hadn't told Caleb.

If he found out I'd left knowing there was even a possibility that I carried his child, he'd hate me, but I hoped, more than anything, I was pregnant, because while I couldn't stay in Wellington, at least I would have a part of the man I loved with me.

Chapter Twenty-Four

The radio offered a forecast of heavy snow throughout the day when I wandered into the kitchen of my parents' restaurant at nine. Christmas was only days away, and this type of weather was welcome in the ski country of Vermont.

Since the restaurant didn't open for another couple hours, it was only my parents at this early hour, doing prep work for the day.

"Morning, sweetie," my dad said as I went straight to the mugs to help myself to a morning cup of tea. Since being home, I no longer drank coffee. Even the smell of my once favorite beverage made me nauseous.

"Hi," I said around a yawn.

"You slept in late." My mom walked over and kissed my forehead. "Did you get any rest?"

"Not really." I put a hand on my slightly protruding belly. "This one thinks two a.m. is play time. I can only hope it's not going to be normal practice once he or she is born."

My dad chuckled. "Don't expect miracles. It took us forever to get you to sleep the night. Your sister, though, was a different story. All she did was sleep."

I rolled my eyes but gave a warm laugh. "Yeah, I know. She was an angel. Speaking of which." I nodded toward the back window. "Snow has already started. Want me to pick her up from school at two?"

My mom shrugged. "Let's see how the day plays out. Holiday weeks are hit or miss with customers. Let's see how busy we are. This place could be busy. We might need your help here."

I dunked my herbal tea bag in the hot water, letting it steep. I added sugar and smiled to myself. Caleb would be proud that I was staying away from the caffeine in the black teas, but he'd have rolled his eyes at how I still needed to add the sweetener.

"Jake called for you," my mother said, and I sighed. I knew what was coming. "His divorce is final. He wanted to know if you want his lawyer to work on papers for you."

I placed a hand on the locket at my neck. "We've had this conversation before. I have no intention of filing for a divorce."

I gave my mom credit, today she didn't bang any pans. "I really wish you would talk about what happened at that place. Maybe if you did, I would understand. But, no. You come home, married and pregnant, and all you'll say is 'it's complicated'."

"But it is, Mom." I looked to my father for help. He wrapped the dough he'd made in Saran wrap, placed it in the fridge, then washed his hands before moving onto his next task in the kitchen.

He finally saw my stare and came to my rescue. "I need to see who is working today. Would you grab the duty roster from the office for me and then can you check all the salt and peppers on the table for us after you've had your tea?"

I blew on the hot liquid. "I can multi-task." I headed down the hall to the office. It was good to be back home, despite my mother's exasperation. I'd gone back to college at the end of August determined to finish my senior year in one semester, but I wasn't able to fit in all my final credits.

I nearly doubled my workload though. My body was physically exhausted, but it kept my brain from thinking too much about Caleb. And Jake had been by my side the whole time.

Jake had been the one I turned to when my hormones went into overdrive and I needed to cry. He cheered me on when I was so tired I didn't think I could study for exams. And, he had offered more than once to marry me and help raise my baby.

I placed my hands over my stomach again. Caleb's baby.

Despite all of it, I didn't love Jake. Not the way he loved me, and it wouldn't be fair to him. He would be heading back to Burlington at the end of Christmas break to finish his degree, but I was staying home. I still had two more classes to complete, but I could do them online and I would make sure they were done before the baby arrived in April.

Before I grabbed the duty roster from the desk, I spotted my backpack in the corner. I pulled out a worn folder and opened it. My birthday cards from Caleb's family. I ran my hands over the handmade drawings from the kids before putting things away. It did me no good to live in the past.

Once I delivered the duty roster to my dad, I escaped my mother's loud sighs by heading out into the restaurant area. A Christmas tree stood by the entrance, and I turned on the lights. All the tables had tablecloths reflecting the holiday season along with ornaments hanging from each light fixture. Before the first patron arrived, we'd turn on the music.

Every season we changed the décor, but Christmas is my favorite. I sipped my tea as I moved from table to table, filling the salt and pepper where necessary. I then went to wrap the utensils in the red napkins. I was only half done when I heard a knock on the front door.

I looked at the clock and gave a huge sigh. "Can't people read? We don't open until eleven." Despite my muttering, my parents had taught me to provide good customer service. I saw a family outside, bundled up in their hats and coats as I unlocked the door. "I'm sorry, but we're not open yet."

The smallest of the children rushed at me and grabbed me around the knees. "Grace."

She was bundled up, and I couldn't see her face, but I knew that voice. I looked from the small head at my legs and turned my gaze upward, to the man in the bomber jacket, and my heart caught in my throat.

"We were hoping you'd make an exception."

I heard him, his voice as familiar to me as my own. I saw him, but I didn't believe my own eyes. "Caleb?"

Elena and Justin both moved in to give me hugs, and I squeezed them to me as I continued to look up at the man I'd thought I'd never see again.

He nodded to the door behind me. "Do you think we can come in?" I melted at his smile. "It's cold out here, and you're not dressed to be outside."

Then reality hit me. My eyes were not deceiving me. "Oh, ah, of course. Come in. Oh, dear God, please come in." Instead I rushed outside onto the snowy sidewalk and into his arms. "You're here. You're really here."

His arms wrapped around me, and his mouth met

mine in a kiss saying more than words. Homecoming. Damn, I'd missed him. I didn't want the kiss to end. When he pulled away slightly, I pressed further against him.

"Daddy, are you two going to kiss all day, or can we go inside where it's warm?"

I laughed. Elena always spoke her mind. "Inside. Definitely, going inside. But I can't promise there won't be more kissing."

As Caleb released me, I saw his eyes narrow as my body slid away from his. He knew my body as well as I knew his and being pressed this close I caught the sudden suck of breath in as his glance went down and back up as realization dawned.

But the kids were already going through the door, and I saw my mother coming from the kitchen. The moment of reckoning would have to wait.

My mother, ever the professional, stopped to greet everyone. "Hello, can I help you?"

I still had Caleb's hand in mine and my mom looked at the two of us and I saw when she figured it out. "Alan," she yelled. "You might want to come out here."

Caleb moved forward, hand outstretched. "Mrs. Adams. Mr. Adams. It's a pleasure to meet you. I'm Caleb Wellington."

I finished what was left unsaid. "This is my husband." I motioned to his kids. "And I'd like you to meet Elena, Justin, and Shawna."

My parents did a quick, silent communication with their eyes, and I knew they had a hundred and one questions they wanted answered. But I waylaid them. "Would you take the kids into the kitchen so Caleb and

I can have a few moments together?"

"Of course," my father was quick to respond.

My mother went into mom mode and whisked the children into the other room, taking their coats and asking what they liked for breakfast.

"How did—" I started.

"Why didn't—" he began.

Caleb moved first. Within a single stride he was standing in front of me, his hand on my belly. "Why didn't you call me when you found out?" I heard a mix of emotions in his voice, hurt, wonder, maybe betrayal? It was hard to tell. My focus was on his large hand pressed against my belly.

I swallowed the lump in my throat. Best if I didn't tell him I'd suspected the possibility before I left. "How could I tell you? Damn it, Caleb, don't you think I wanted to? But how? Every call is monitored. I didn't think you'd be able to leave Wellington, or want to, and if Roger found out there was a Wellington child outside the gates?" I threw my hands up. "You couldn't leave. I can't go back. And I didn't want you worrying."

"I've worried every day, anyway." The baby reacted to Caleb's large hand pressing on my belly by giving a little kick, and I saw his fierce look soften. "If you'd called, I would have been here."

"How?" I still couldn't believe he was here. "How were you even able to leave Wellington to come here?"

He finally moved his hand from his baby inside me to pull me back against him. "I've missed you." He kissed my temple then moved down to capture my lips, and I felt his longing. He groaned when he finally released me, but only my lips. He pulled me back against him.

I shook my head. "How are you here? How is it possible? How did you escape with your kids?"

He stroked my face, and I leaned into his palm as he spoke. "There's a lot to tell, but the abbreviated version is that when you left, it set a major coup in motion."

That caught my interest. "What do you mean?"

He stroked my hair while I breathed in his scent. He still wore his bomber jacket, but it was unzipped, so I pressed my cheek against his flannel shirt, listening to his heartbeat under my ear.

"It was a wake-up call. Brent and I were both vocal about why we helped you. My mom finally realized maybe she shouldn't have listened completely to my father all those years ago, and she finally contacted her parents. Well, her mom. Her father passed away a long time ago, and she never knew.

"Then Penny wanted to go home, and when Roger tried to coerce her into staying, a few other people began to see the hold he and the council had on everyone. Roger was ousted from his position. Security measures were lowered, and more people are venturing outside the town's limits."

"What about the bracelets?" Part of me wanted to check his wrist to see if his was still in place, but that would mean moving from his embrace.

"Still wearing. Remember, it's how everyone pays. Tracking is still in place, too. People feel secure with it, especially as they venture away from town. Things aren't going to change overnight, but at least they are making some progress."

"I'm glad. And it gave you the opportunity to come to me." I stared up and wanted to drown in his sea-blue eyes. "I've missed you. All of you."

Caleb's lips captured mine in another quick kiss. I understood. We'd been separated for almost five months. We had a lot of time to catch up on.

He stared down at me, as though he were taking everything in. He brushed a hand down my cheek then it moved down to tap the locket at my neck. Then he took my left hand in his, bringing it up. Checking. I still wore his ring and relief crossed his strong features.

"I thought for sure Jake would have swooped in."

I squeezed his hand. "He's a friend. A good one. But that's all."

Caleb nodded. "When his divorce papers arrived, it was the talk of the town."

He turned his eyes away for a moment and I knew what he was going to say. "You were waiting for your own set to arrive?" At his nod I continued, "I won't lie to you. Jake has asked me, more than once, to marry him." I pulled away to pace, nervous. "And the thought of raising this child alone, well, it scares me. But—"

Caleb went to speak, but I held up my finger. "But, what we had in Wellington," he continued to wait, silent, and I struggled, as usual. "What we had was a bit unorthodox, but it turned into something—more. Something—"

When Caleb raised his eyebrow, I knew he wasn't going to help. He'd declared his love for me when I left. It was my turn. Instead I returned to my task of wrapping utensils in napkins as I changed the subject.

"I kept the drawings the kids made me on my mirror in my dorm. They're in a folder in my backpack now."

"You went back to school? I'm glad." I knew he

smiled by his tone.

"Would you believe I haven't had a single cup of coffee since coming home?"

"No?" He chuckled, and the sound sent warmth and comfort through to my heart. "Good girl." There was a slight hesitation, and then his voice went low. He was beside me again in two strides and once again his hand went to my abdomen. "Especially now."

I'd had people put their hands on my baby belly before, but it had never felt so intimate. This was Caleb.

"How are you feeling? Do you have morning sickness? Is the baby healthy?"

I placed my hand over his and pulled back to look at him. His expression said so much. To think at one time, I thought he was nothing more than an emotional drone. A stone wall. I'd been so wrong.

"We're fine, Caleb," I reassured. "I had a little nausea at the beginning, but not bad, but mostly this child doesn't like to sleep at night, so my body clock is all out of whack."

"Jill had the same problem with Justin. Maybe you're having a boy?"

I grinned. "Who knows? But maybe we can find out together. I have an appointment next Wednesday for an ultrasound." I held my breath. He hadn't mentioned how long he was staying. Christmas was three days away. I didn't think he'd be leaving before the holiday, but what about after? He said people were venturing outside Wellington, but the trackers were still in use. I looked down at his arm, but his jacket hid his wrist. Did he still wear the bracelet? Did he still feel Wellington was the safest place to raise his family?

"I wouldn't miss it for the world." His answer gave

me some hope a moment before he gave me yet another deep kiss searing me all the way down to my toes. Memories swamped me of kisses and where they all eventually led us.

I moaned when he pulled away. "Oh, dear heavens, I forgot how easy we fit together."

"I know how you feel," was his answering groan. "However, we probably need to rescue your parents from my children."

"Mmm hmm. They do have a restaurant to run." I agreed. "Where are you staying? Did you just arrive?"

"No, we got in late last night," he said. "As much as I wanted to come straight here, the kids needed sleep. It's a long drive from Pennsylvania."

I turned to lead him to the kitchen. "Are you at one of the hotels on Main Street?"

"No," he again reached for my hand and ran a finger along the wedding band, stopping me from leaving the main restaurant. "I hope you don't mind, but I went under the assumption—as I never received divorce papers—that you and me—" It was my turn to raise my eyebrows as Caleb struggled for words, something new.

"That we would want a bit of privacy. I rented a house on the outskirts of town. Would I be wrong in assuming my wife would join us?"

Wife. Oh, how that word sounded so right. My heart did a somersault. And a house rental? That had to mean he was staying. "No, you're not wrong. It won't take long for me to pack."

On Christmas morning, we headed back to my parents' home where we had a huge breakfast before opening gifts. In three days, my mom had managed to leave the restaurant long enough to shop for her brood of new grandchildren. I'd actually left Caleb's side long enough to do the same, but it wasn't the store-bought gift that I was anxious for him to see.

He unwrapped the box I gave him and pulled out a purple journal. When he opened the first page I saw his eyes widen. "Grace? What is this?"

"I wrote to you every day."

August 10th.

Dear Caleb: As I ride the bus home to Vermont, I have a lot of time to think. You told me you love me. You said it more than once, but I am a selfish woman. I couldn't say the words. Not because I didn't want to, but because if I did, then I knew in my heart that I would stay in Wellington with you. You know why I need to leave and you did so much to make sure I got home. I wish I could tell you how difficult this really is for me, knowing I will most likely never see you again.

I love you, Caleb. While I was attracted to you very early in the summer, I'm not sure when, but I did fall in love with you. Behind your rough and stern exterior, underneath that calm façade, you are a warm, loving man, loyal to your family and determined to do what is right, no matter the consequence. How could I not fall for a man with such depth?

You once told me that the ring on my finger was a promise that you would help get me home. As always, you kept your promise, but please know this ring means so much more. It is a reminder of the moments we shared together. Our memories. With this ring, I now promise that you are my husband forever. I will write in this journal to share my every day with you even though we are apart. I love you, Caleb.

He lifted tear-filled eyes to me, and I moved from my seat to sit on his lap. "I do, you know," I admitted as I gave him a chaste kiss. The kids were now playing with their toys, and my sister and parents kept them occupied.

"Say the words, Grace. I want to hear them."

I laughed at the insistence in his tone. "I love you, Caleb. I was too afraid to say the words before. I love you. Thank you for coming for me."

"Good." He lifted me from his lap and placed me in the seat he'd occupied. "Now it's my turn to give you a present.

He handed me a little box, and I slowly unwrapped it. Inside was a custom-made ring with tiny diamonds in the shape of a half-moon.

"Oh, my goodness." I gasped as Caleb got down on one knee.

"You once told me that your moods wax and wane like the moon. Do you remember what I told you?"

I nodded. "Something about poets write more about the moon than the sun?"

"Yes, and that the moon is a powerful entity. Much like its effect on the tides, you have cast a spell on me. When you left, it was as though the night was less bright; the stars didn't shine as bright."

He slipped the ring onto my finger, sliding it against the gold band that never left my hand. "Marry me, again, Grace," he asked. "This time, with your family around us. This time, with their blessing. This time, because you want to be married to me."

I wiped the tears from my eyes. "I'm crying again, damn it. See what you do to me?"

"We'll blame it on the hormones." He grinned.

"I'm still waiting."

I giggled. "Yes, yes, yes. I will marry you again, and again, and again."

A word about the author...

Gina Leuci started reading romance at the age of thirteen and never stopped. She met her soul mate on a blind date and married him—not once, but twice: they eloped then had a church wedding giving them two anniversaries. They live in Southern New Hampshire with their son, who makes them laugh every day, and two dogs who vie for control as queen of the residence.